THE UNCOMMON
AP CLUB

HEIDI FEDORE

CONTENTS

AUTHOR'S NOTE

As a former Advanced Placement Language and Composition teacher, this novel is a nod to all the high school scholars out there who challenge their capabilities without burning out from overdoing it. This current-day story is a mash-up of four classic novels: William Golding's *Lord of the Flies*, Jane Austen's *Emma* and *Pride and Prejudice*, and E.M. Forster's *Passage to India*.

My first teaching job, in the 1990s, was in a district that opened enrollment in advanced placement classes. Our high school increased enrollment in AP Lang and Comp from 18 students when teacher permission was required to over 90 students. While there were pros and cons with this model, such as tracking so many students, I'm still honored that I got to witness the number of students who sought to challenge themselves when invited into AP classes. To learn more about tracking students, visit https://fedorewriter.com.

Lastly, there's a brief reference to suicidal ideation. Mental health practitioners advise that talking about suicide may help a person view their circumstances differently and encourage them to seek help. If you or someone close to you is feeling suicidal, please call, text, or chat 988 to speak with a trained crisis counselor offering support.

CHAPTER 1

ALONZO HERNANDEZ

An ocean wave of stress rolls in,
Forcing me to think about my future.
A receding wave pulls me back
To Now with its everyday fears.
The waves of our todays
and tomorrows crash
Over my friends and me. Awash.
Stealing our breath.
Clutching at our confidence.
Dousing our aspirations.

    This poem from my journal pretty much summarizes what's happening right now. Last February, I asked Papá, "May I register for AP Lang?" He asked what it was, then said, "You know what? I don't need to know." I should've used the full name: Language and Composition.

I asked if I could start planning for college, especially since I'm going to be a senior in the fall. He said, "No."

This morning, as Papá and I sit at the kitchen table eating breakfast, I ask the same question, different year. "May I sign up for AP Literature?" This time I use the full name rather than AP Lit so he won't get frustrated with not knowing what it is.

"I can't talk about something that won't happen for another... what... seven months? I'm focused on today, Alonzo." Papá pushes back his chair, which screeches on the floor.

I wipe my hand down my face, inhale through my nose.

With his back to me, he steps to the sink, pours the remnants of his coffee down the drain, and rinses his cup.

I get that he can't talk right now. He's busy; owns a business. But, right now, I need to register for classes. Ones that challenge me. College-bound classes. What if I sign up for the wrong course and set a path I can't reverse?

Like I wrote in my journal, I'm drowning in stress.

I'm learning about persuasive essays in Miss Halden's English class, and I'd planned to state the opposite side to him, like, *"I see your point, Papá. Having me work at your store strengthens your business."* Miss Halden said this is how you get someone to listen to the other side. I was ready to tell him that going to college strengthens our family. That we ultimately want the same thing. But he thinks college is a waste of time and money.

"What guarantee do you have?" he asks. He thinks I can earn a good living at his auto-parts store. Papá leans his hand on the table next to my cereal bowl. "Alonzo. You talk about college. But what for? To study what?"

"I don't know. Lots of kids figure it out once they get there."

"I gotta go to work." He leaves the kitchen with a whoosh, like he sucked all the air out of the room. All I hear now is the vibration of the fridge motor and someone's car engine roaring in the distance. Am I capable of handling AP Lit and subsequently college? If I fail, I'll prove Papá right. If I succeed, I'll prove Papá wrong, which is worse. As much as we disagree, Papá is my anchor. My family is my lifeline. I push away my doubts as I scoop up the last spoonful of my cereal.

Should I register for AP Lit and not tell him? Forge his signature on my registration form?

I'm tempted.

CHAPTER 2

MISS HEATHER HALDEN

It's my prep period and I hear a knock on my classroom door, which interrupts me from grading Alonzo Hernandez's essay. From my desk, I peer through the small window in my door and see that it's Mr. Mark Johnson. He's a thirty-year-old single teacher that could be a perfect match for me since I'm twenty-six and am an English teacher too. I open my door, and my stomach immediately warms at the sight of his chocolate-brown eyes.

The Life of Frederick Douglass is ten inches from my face. I recoil from the nearness of it and my hopes of being asked on a date deflate. Mr. Johnson is stabbing the air with his dog-eared, worn copy, punctuating phrases. "I saw your students walking in the hallway with this book. Those juniors will never fully understand the nuances and language in this memoir."

My hand clenches the side of my door, and I resist the temptation to slam the door in his face. "Mr. Johnson, these books aren't designated solely for AP Lang and Comp. We have at least a hundred of them, so I took the liberty of checking them out to my students."

"My students pride themselves on reading high-level material. What will they think when they see regular juniors with this book?" He stabs the book at me again.

Regular students? As opposed to irregular?

I place my hand on his book and lower it away from my face. "First of all, don't use your book as a communication prop."

"Sorry."

He's not sorry, but at least he holds the memoir at his side.

"Secondly, I stand by my decision to teach *Frederick Douglass*." I start to close my door. "Now, if you'll excuse me, I have papers to grade. I'm sure you do too."

I'm back at my desk and can't focus on grading essays. I puff out a frustrated breath from my nostrils, stand up, and march toward the main office.

Unbelievable! "Those juniors," I mutter with gritted teeth. Little does Mr. Johnson know that my students have been writing literary analyses and studying faulty logic, the same as his advanced juniors. *Post hoc, ergo propter hoc*, Mr. Johnson. Just because a few students squander the privilege of an education doesn't mean they all do.

I arrive at the main office and ask to speak with Principal Pency. His secretary, Margaret Guilder, peeks over a wraparound counter. "Let's hope he's in a better mood than earlier," she says, then lowers her voice. "He suspended three students."

I'm always curious why students are suspended. Privacy laws keep my teacher colleagues and me from knowing the reasons. For details, we rely on overhearing students' conversations and sharing intel among ourselves. I'm quite sure Mrs. Guilder wants to tell me but can't.

She says, "He happens to be in his office. Head on in there, dear."

Attempting to contain my nervous energy and anger with Mr. Mark Johnson, I sit in a swivel chair opposite Mr. Pency's desk stacked with askew papers, rumpled folders, and a teacup with a chamomile tea tag hanging off the rim. I plant my feet firmly on the floor, so I won't rotate the chair, and begin my pitch. "I predict that at least a dozen students would come to school on Tuesdays and Thursdays, from six to seven, to prepare for the AP Lang and Comp exam." I take a breath and continue. "Some students are interested in challenging themselves but don't have the time or energy to take a rigorous class like AP Lang. The AP Club would allow interested, talented students to dabble in AP." What I don't tell him is that Mr. Mark Johnson stopped by my classroom moments ago and I have something to prove. My students don't know it yet, but they have something to prove too. I want to shift the horses on the merry-go-round called education. Give students a chance to reach for the brass ring.

"I'd like to propose a PTA grant that will pay for the AP Club students to take the exam in May." I haven't thought this through but what I'm saying seems plausible enough. Studying after school will supplement what they're learning in class. It'll show my students that there is no separation between the AP elite and them.

Mr. Pency steeples his pointer fingers and taps them on his lips.

I wait, and the longer I wait, the more my palms sweat. Is this risky? Absolutely. If my students and I fail, our humiliation will be unpleasantly public. Teachers are given access to AP scores, so they can assess students' strengths and areas for growth. Mr. Johnson will know I was a fool to believe my students were capable of advanced-level coursework. Worse yet, he'll keep thinking my juniors aren't accomplished scholars. That they're *"regular."*

But he's wrong.

Finally, Mr. Pency heaves an enormous sigh and theatrically crosses his arms. "Okay."

So, here I sit, attempting to craft a flyer that will invite the kind of student I'm seeking. I need to finish this before the bell rings for class.

What if you could earn college credit
with just an exam?
What if you haven't thought about
applying for college?
Start thinking.
Join Miss Halden and like-minded juniors
on Tuesdays and Thursdays
6-7 p.m.
in room 203
Our first session is next Tuesday.

I don't want the club members to consist of advanced placement students whose parents force them to attend. I don't want *my* club to help Mr. Johnson's students succeed so he can take the credit for their success. I'm looking for recruits who haven't imagined a maximum score of five, or any score, on the Lang and Comp exam. Students who are intelligent and hardworking but perhaps haven't dreamt of or been given the chance to strive beyond their current goals.

CHAPTER 3

ADELE QUESTIN

Finally! A club I really want to join. Sure, I'm in Photography Club and Pep Club but they're for applying to colleges, for seeming as if I actually want to socialize, which my school counselor said I needed. If I gaze at another famous photo and analyze it for its contrast and composition, I'll seriously gouge my eyes out. If I stick another plastic pom-pom in my ponytail, wear a tutu and stand in the bleachers with other screaming fans at a basketball game, I'll tear my hair out. Sometimes I feel like I'm faking everything just to get into college. Maybe once I'm in college, I'll figure out what I actually like.

"Analyzing literature and essays?" I say to my one true friend, Alonzo. "Writing literary analyses in my spare time? That's more my cup of oolong."

"Oolong?" Alonzo's giving me the side-eye.

"Just go with it." I turn away from the flyer and we walk from Miss Halden's third-period junior English class.

"Of course you're joining the AP Club," Alonzo says as we tromp down the crowded stairs and wedge past four oafish guys clogging the landing. "You should've registered for AP Lang and Comp with Mr. Johnson. You had the grades and test scores for it."

Alonzo has so much faith in me. "I'd heard Mr. Johnson is tough, and I seriously didn't want to ruin my 4.0." I tuck my shoulder-length hair behind my ear, a nervous habit I'm trying to quit. "I'm happy to be in English with you and Miss Halden." I pause. "Alonzo? Why aren't you in AP Lang?"

He shakes his head. "It's complicated."

I guess that subject's closed. We're heading to lunch, so we're taking our time walking through the hallways. We eat at school daily, which isn't so bad. The commons has floor-to-ceiling windows and round tables. Great for chatting with friends, though it's usually just me and Alonzo sitting at the table.

After school, Alonzo walks from school to his job at a nearby car wash, about three blocks away. I know this because one time when I took my car through the car wash, I saw him detailing a car in a stall and pulled over to chat. It was an awkward interaction, like I was interrupting him or... I don't know.

We step into the crowded commons, and I scan the faces of people I don't know and don't want to know. Like I said, high school is a hurdle to college. Not that guys are clamoring to ask me out, but everyone assumes Alonzo is my boyfriend, which is fine by me. With his dark, wavy hair and hazel eyes, he's cute enough for me to be proud to be seen with him but not so cute that he looks like he's out of my league. I'm invisible but not geeky. Some might say my look leans toward goth because I have dark hair like Uma Thurman in *Pulp Fiction* and wear dark eyeliner. And, yes, I'm an aficionado of '90s movies. It's my thing. Anyway, I'm somewhere in the middle socially, taller than average, and not goth.

"You should totally join the AP Club too!" I say to Alonzo. "You read the same books as me and you're so insightful."

"I don't have time," Alonzo says, and his lips press together.

"Course you do." I stop walking for emphasis. "Talk to Miss Halden. Arrange it in your schedule. It's a club, so you don't have to attend every session. And I can grab extra handouts. Take good notes when you're not there. Deal?"

"I'm sure my dad won't let me join the club," Alonzo says, crossing his arms and widening his stance.

Is Alonzo angry with me right now? I can't tell but I need to convince him to attend. "Explain to your dad this is important." I tuck my hair behind my ear, realize that I've done it again, and drop my hand.

"It's not that simple."

"All I'm saying is you should go." I can tell I'm worming into his brain. He'll end up going.

We're standing in the lunch line, surrounded by a blur of students. It's like we occupy our own space. A space where we don't have to answer to anyone else's norms. Alonzo and I have each other's backs. He gets me, understands my vocabulary, and doesn't judge me for being a bit on the edgy side. I have his back, and I can be seriously persuasive. At the beginning of the school year, in US History, our classmates chose debate topics. Jax Lourde, a big-deal basketball player, chose whether Title IX has achieved equity for females in sports. My hand shot up as I volunteered to debate him.

At one point during the debate, I challenged Jax. "You've probably told one of your teammates he throws like a girl. Let's take our best female basketball player and set up a free-throw competition between her and you. Then, we'll see who throws like a girl." Some of our social studies students applauded and called out that Jax missed free throws all the time. And some gasped, like I said something I shouldn't have. I say it like I see it. Then, after school, Alonzo told me he was impressed that I didn't back down against a guy like Jax.

There are topics that Alonzo and I never touch, such as where we live. I don't describe my family's five-bedroom, four-bathroom house, which makes no sense for a family of three. The last time we used a guest room was when Obama was president. I don't tell him we have a housekeeper who prepares dinner every weeknight.

I'm pretty sure our lives are very different. Those differences are what I like most about Alonzo. He keeps me in line, tells me I'm being bougie when I need to hear it. In my neighborhood, everyone seems the same, living by the same boring, social rules, saying "Good morning" to each other when we don't mean it. Being Alonzo's friend keeps me grounded and worldly at the same time.

We find a table, and he picks up a plastic fork to start eating and I open my lunch bag.

"No note from your mom?" Alonzo asks.

I can't tell if he's being sarcastic. I don't tell him our housekeeper makes my lunch for me. "Actually, a note from my mom sounds pretty great," I say, gazing toward my sandwich. I don't tell him that I see our housekeeper more than my mom these days and swallow the lonely lump that clogs my throat.

Alonzo pulls a frayed, folded note from his wallet. "This is a note from my papá—my dad. He gave it to me the first day of school. Said, 'This should last you the whole year.'" Alonzo doesn't open the note and read it to me. Instead, he carefully slides it back into his wallet.

Both my parents work, so Maria, our housekeeper, is always there when I get home in the afternoon, if I'm not attending an insipid club meeting. After school, when I walk in the door, I'll hear Maria singing in Spanish, which I love. I wish she would keep singing but she stops when she hears me climb the stairs to my bedroom. I know she has work to do but I'm always eager to set my backpack in my bedroom, put on slippers, and head to where she is to tell her about my day and ask her to quiz me on my Spanish.

I take another bite of my sandwich, which is roast beef, lettuce, and mustard on a ciabatta, and Alonzo and I silently eat for a moment, people watching and deep in our own thoughts.

Alonzo wipes his hands on a napkin, pulls his leather-bound journal from his backpack, and places it carefully on our lunch table. I notice a couple of boys sitting a few feet from us at another table. He flips to a page marked with a silky red ribbon and smooths out his neatly combed hair. "I wrote this poem. I researched Cesar Chavez and when I searched for his last name, the *boxer*, Julio Chávez, came up before a civil rights activist. Can you believe that? Cesar comes before Julio—C before J. What does that say about society's values, ya know?"

I should agree with Alonzo, but I don't know much about Cesar Chavez. I'm not as passionate for social justice as he is, but I am interested. I make a mental note to look up Chavez to learn more and listen as Alonzo reads his poem:

Taking Ghandi and King's advice,
demanding higher wages more than twice.
Fighting a war so far away and
fighting a war in the US of A.

Alonzo's voice is sharp as a knife yet quietly calm, like a peaceful protest. I glance toward the guys sitting nearby hoping they haven't heard Alonzo. I still get glares from the entire basketball team for debating Jax in US History and that was five months ago. We don't need more shade directed toward us.

"I'm curious. What is meant by fighting a war far away?"

"Chavez served in the US military." Alonzo bores his hazel eyes into mine. "In a segregated regiment." His stare lingers a little longer than is comfortable for both of us, and I finally look away. It's times like these that make me afraid I'll say something ignorant and lose him as a friend. My only real friend.

"Five minutes before class," I say. I'm grateful for chewing and not risking saying something that'll push us further apart. We pack up, and I remind Alonzo to figure out his schedule so we can attend the AP Club together. "I'll be mad at you if I have to go alone."

CHAPTER 4

ALONZO HERNANDEZ

As I enter the kitchen, I replay what I said to Adele about Papá not letting me attend the advanced placement club. Maybe if I talk to Mama first, it'll help convince Papá. Maybe if I get Papá to agree to the AP Club, I'll get him to agree to an AP class.

I slip on an apron to help Mama prepare tamales and burritos she sells in some of the neighborhoods. These burritos and tamales supplement her housecleaning income and are also a source of pride for her.

"Mama, I want to join an advanced placement club after school starting next week. In May, I could take the Language and Composition exam and possibly earn college credit." I pause to give her time to ask questions, which she doesn't. "I'll need to cut back a little on my hours at the Sudsy Auto."

She looks up from her task and I watch skepticism swipe across her face. She weakly smiles, wipes her hands on her apron, and lightly presses her hands on my cheeks. "*Mi amado hijo.* I'll ask your father, and we'll see."

My hope shifts into doubt in two seconds. Why bother? Papá's mind is made up and nobody will change that, not even Mama. I don't tell her that my friend Adele will go ballistic if I can't attend. The opposing pressures of family versus friends and college squeeze my chest.

As I spread the masa onto the corn husks and pass the husk to Mama so she can tuck the remaining ingredients into it, I know I'm going to have to lie to my parents about this too. I already forged Papá's signature on my registration form. Just like registering for AP Lit for next year, I want to attend AP Club more than being honest with my parents. Sometimes, I picture turning eighteen, moving out, and making my own decisions about my future. If I did that, though, I would risk going against my parents. I glance toward Mama as I spread masa onto another corn husk. Papá, Mama, and my brother are most important. Having to choose between my family and going to college is like King Solomon threatening to tear the baby in half.

If I don't attend the AP Club, then I fall behind my classmates. I need to keep up. So, I start making plans to tell my boss I need Tuesdays and Thursdays off and to ask if I can work extra hours on the weekend. I also make plans to ask Miss Halden if I can stay at school to make it look like I'm going to work right after school. Doubts clamber for space in my stomach. I hope Mama doesn't see the lies in my averted eyes when I lean in to kiss her on her cheek and tell her, "*Buenas noches.*"

I'm lying in bed feeling the crush of deceit, my future, and my family. Having to share a room with my younger brother, Bennie, who is asleep by 8:30, means it's lights out for me too even when I'm not tired. At least I can read under my covers thanks to my *tía*, who gave me a reading light that attaches to my books.

Books are my escape and I'm reading *Great Expectations.* Pip wants to improve himself, be rich, and have the pretty girl. Unlike Pip wanting an inheritance, I'm going to earn my way. Be successful on my own. I work at the Sudsy Auto car wash, and my manager schedules me as many hours as he can and gives me time off when I need it for school. Adele saw me at the car wash one time, and I realized she just doesn't get what it means to work. *Really* work. She wanted to talk to me. My manager pays me to do a job, not stand around. A few times, she's made comments about poor people getting handouts and I know she doesn't mean to be ignorant. She doesn't realize the irony that she gets handouts from her parents all the time instead of earning her own spending money with a part-time job.

When I graduate, working at Papá's auto-parts store is a decent offer, except I've never cared about carburetors or catalytic converters. I care about Cather and Capote and all the authors I haven't read yet.

Papá's note to me, which I keep with me every day in my wallet, includes Dr. King's advice to "do your job well." I like that Papá tells us to honor the Hernandez name every day, but he wants me to be a different Hernandez than I want to be.

I don't know how to get him to listen.

I meet Adele near the junior parking lot fifteen minutes before the first period bell rings.

We walk up the gentle curve of the sidewalk toward the back entrance. "Pretty soon, we'll know who the National Merit Scholar qualifiers are!" Adele's blue eyes sparkle with excitement.

"I hope we both get it." I mean this.

When I took the PSAT in October, it made college feel real. I didn't tell my parents about the exam, which wasn't exactly a lie. To make myself feel better, I thought about Cesar Chavez and how he stood for better conditions for migrant workers. I'm standing up for better conditions for myself.

Last December, Miss Halden asked me to stay after class. At the time, I was earning a *B* minus, and I thought she was going to scold me for not *"living up to my potential."* Instead, she was beaming. "Your PSAT scores are off the charts!" I didn't get why it was such a big deal. She said, "You're a likely candidate to be a National Merit Scholar!"

I researched this and now know it means scholarships and college invitations. Whenever I think about college, my brain is like, *Yes, I can. No, I can't.* Back and forth like that. I'm amazed by the surge of a PSAT score, like the wave that's heading into shore, like it's pushing me. Telling me anything is possible. Then, I think about the pull of family, like the wave that's receding. I don't know. Maybe family is what keeps us afloat. And not being able to share my happiness about my PSAT score with them feels like I'm drifting further and further away from them.

Today, it's an unusually warm February day, so Adele and I sit on a concrete bench near the back entrance waiting for the five-minute bell to ring.

Adele asks, "Are you joining the AP club?"

She's the most impatient person I know, and she pressures me even when it's obviously annoying. I ignore the flip-flop in my stomach and fake a smile. "I think I can make it work." Saying this out loud makes lying to my parents real.

Adele squeals and two students standing nearby glare at us. "You are *so* going to earn a five on the AP exam. I just know it," she says as we head into the building.

"Let's not get ahead of ourselves." I laugh and swat her on the arm. I don't tell her I'm risking getting caught in a lie every Tuesday and Thursday.

As we walk up to Miss Halden's room, I see a few cheerleaders standing nearby. One cheerleader—I'm pretty sure her name is Emma—is looking at the AP Club flyer. The club could be an interesting mix of students. A cheerleader doesn't seem like the kind of student who would join, though she'd probably say the same about me. Lying to my parents almost seems worth it to see who shows up for the club.

Miss Halden is telling us about the AP Club, and Emma, who sits next to me, asks, "Could you repeat the question, Miss Halden?"

"I didn't ask you a question," Miss Halden says. "I said, 'I hope you've seen the flyers hung around the school, including you, Emma.'"

"I haven't seen them," Emma says.

Why is Miss Halden focusing on Emma? And why did Emma just lie? A wave of relief washes over me. All teenagers lie. Maybe what I'm doing is normal and not as bad as I think.

After her AP Club announcement, Miss Halden passes back our timed free-writes on Frederick Douglass's quotation: "*I prefer to be true to myself, even at the hazard of incurring the ridicule of others, rather than to be false, and to incur my own abhorrence.*" That quotation was what I needed this week.

I lift my essay off my desk and see that it's another *A*. Every *A* is proof that lying is the right thing. Emma's essay rests on her desk face down. She curls up the corner to peek at her grade, which is also an *A*.

During class, many of us take turns reading Douglass's memoir. Some students are nervous reading aloud, but I volunteer every time. Hearing Frederick Douglass's words churning inside my head is like he's speaking directly to me.

At the end of class, we pack up our memoirs and binders. I overhear a conversation between Emma and another girl.

The other girl says, "I got a *C* on my essay. What'd you get?"

"About the same," Emma says.

Again, with the lies.

The girl asks, "Are you joining the AP Club?"

Emma asks, "Are you?"

"No way."

I guess I'll see on Tuesday who shows up.

CHAPTER 5

JAX LOURDE

It's Monday, at 6:30 in the morning, and I'm in the principal's office, concealing my yawn. I'm sitting between my parents who split two years ago. Dad's knee is bouncing faster than I can dribble a ball and Mom's face is Chicago Bulls red. Dad just told Mom to shut up and let him handle this. Mom wants me to be "held accountable for breaking a rule." Her words. Dad wants me to play basketball and get a full-ride college scholarship.

"There must be exceptions to the rules," Dad says to Mr. Pency. "The basketball team could win the state championship this year. You want to get in the way of that?"

Last Tuesday, Raleigh, Nick, and I were caught with a dab pen in Raleigh's car in the parking lot during lunch, and our campus narc, Joey—Mr. Buccio, if we're talking to him—came out from behind a

Ford Taurus parked next to us. How did we miss his obnoxious after-shave? It lingers in the hallways and always tips us off when he's nearby.

It was as if he'd been waiting for us to start dabbin'. For the record? Technically, I didn't dab. But Joey hates all athletes and I'm no exception. He's not the brightest bulb on the Christmas tree, but he's smart enough to have memorized all our cars and class schedules and stalks us like Dog the Bounty Hunter. I guess his stalker skills paid off. I suppose Joey—Mr. Buccio's—hatred is justified because my friends and I have broken a few rules in our high school career, which stacks the odds against us.

"Isn't that what teenagers are s'posed to do? Break rules?" I'd said this to Raleigh and Nick just before we climbed into Raleigh's car. I wonder if Joey heard me.

When my dad learned about a suspension, he immediately called Mr. Pency and threatened to get a lawyer. Mr. Pency agreed to meet with my parents and me to discuss "possible disciplinary actions." Dad's words.

My suspension was put on hold, which is unusual. I guess it was because Joey didn't see me dab, and I was just in Raleigh's car. Dad was out of town last week, so here we are in the principal's office—the last place I want to be, especially wedged between my parents.

Inspired by Dad's presence, I chime in. "I hope no one gets the wrong idea. I didn't smoke pot but... was with people who did." God, I'm throwing Raleigh and Nick under the bus to save my butt. "I'm an athlete. But my friends," I say, trying to backpedal on my comment about Nick and Raleigh, "sometimes... rarely just need to escape." I cock my head at a pitiful angle hoping to help my bros.

"Don't we all need to escape, Mr. Lourde. Don't we all." Mr. Pency sighs as his steepled fingers push his lower lip into a frown.

I picture Mr. Pency smoking pot to relax and bow my head to hide my smirk. I feel Dad's hand on my knee as he continues. "My son has never been disciplined for smoking pot or dapping—whatever you kids call it."

"It's dabbing, Dad."

"Whatever. Besides, Mr. Pency, as we discussed over the phone last Tuesday, your campus supervisor, Mr. Buccio, has no proof that my son participated in—what'd you call it—dabbing?"

I nod.

"He was sitting in the car! Surely you don't have rules against sitting in a car!"

Dad might be taking this too far. Athletes aren't supposed to be around any alcohol or drugs, so there are rules.

"My son didn't dab! Isn't there some leniency?"

Last Tuesday, I should've thought to challenge the lack of evidence. Nick was holding the dab pen. Not me. Not Raleigh, either.

Mr. Pency's unibrow scrunches. He looks toward the ceiling, and I know he's picturing my discipline file. It's as thick as my bicep. My dad doesn't know all I've done: several harassment infractions, including breaking someone's glasses. What can I say? I'm an assertive guy. Mom usually gets the phone calls from Mr. Pency. She made me wash her car every other Saturday for two months to cover the cost of repairing the freshman's glasses.

Feeling my basketball goals slipping away, I jump in. "Is there something I could do instead of being suspended? Community service, maybe?"

Mr. Pency's eyebrows twitch as he considers my proposal. Then, he places a hand on his mouse to wake up his computer.

My parents and I watch him, sitting silently.

"I see that you have a *D* in AP Lang and Comp, Mr. Lourde." Mr. Pency turns to Mom and asks, "Are you able to get Jax to school on Tuesday and Thursday evenings for AP Club sessions?"

"Of course!" Mom says a little too eagerly. She turns to Dad. "He's with you every other week. Are you able to make sure Jax gets to these sessions?"

"We'll make it work. Jax has his own car. He can manage," Dad says, slapping his hands against his knees with the finality of a judge's gavel.

What's this AP Club that my parents have agreed to and how will I explain it to my friends and teammates? AP Club sounds like something geeks join. And *sessions*, like more than one?

Dad continues. "So this means my son can attend basketball practice and be eligible to play in games?"

Mr. Pency gets up from his desk, hinting that the meeting's over, and pats Dad's shoulder as if they're old college buddies. "Your son will play in Friday's game provided he attends the AP Club starting tomorrow and brings his AP Lang grade up to a *C*. We'll see how that goes and then decide from there."

Bring my grade up to a *C* in Lang and Comp by Friday? Doubtful.

As we leave Mr. Pency's office, I have a vague recollection... a flyer in the hallway with Miss Halden's name. I better take a closer look.

At the beginning of lunch, I sit in my car, open my laptop, and get on the school's Wi-Fi. I see Joey approaching.

"Seriously!" I yell inside my car; then open my car window and holler, "Joey! I'm on my laptop. Just my laptop. Come see for yourself." I can't believe I'm provoking him. Maybe Dad's appeal makes me cocky. Maybe I'm just really stupid.

Joey approaches my open window and peers inside. "It's Mr. Buccio. Got it? Mr. Buccio. Not Joey." I can tell he's sniffing for something. He's not gonna smell anything, other than my sweaty basketball clothes I forgot to take in the house last night. I turn my laptop screen so he can see I'm checking my grades.

"Okay," Joey—Mr. Buccio—says, and he backs away, kind of bow-legged, like he's at the O.K. Corral, still gazing into my car looking for trouble.

I open my school email and write a message to Mr. Johnson, though I don't know why I bother. Mr. Johnson is a strict, no-late-work dictator. At least email is better than facing him.

I return to the commons to look for Raleigh and Nick. I'm pretty sure they're still salty. Who can blame them? I talked them into parking on campus to dab so we wouldn't be late to fourth period. Nick had the dab pen in his glove box. We all got caught up in the moment.

Both Raleigh and Nick had their three-day suspensions. Nick answered a bunch of drug and alcohol questions and then went to some kind of Saturday classes. At least Raleigh wasn't kicked off the team, though he didn't get to play in last Friday's game. Athletes can't compete if we miss school and practice. Then, there's me. I didn't get a suspension. I still don't know how Mr. Pency convinced Coach Greenlief to let me play but I'm pretty sure my dad had something to do with it. We almost lost the game, but thanks to my three-pointers and free throws, we pulled out in front by one point.

I see Raleigh and Nick in the far corner of the commons just as the fourth-period bell rings and decide not to catch up to them, afraid to find out we're not friends anymore. I'll let them cool off for a few days.

CHAPTER 6

MISS HEATHER HALDEN

It's Monday after school, and I'm sitting at my desk planning tomorrow's AP session, which will start with an online quiz game. This way, I'll see what the club members already know. I'll have them write a thirty-minute essay, answering the prompt: *What would your best friend tell me about you?*

The session needs to be fun enough to convince the club members that giving an extra hour twice weekly is worth it and rigorous enough to separate the wheat from the chaff.

My mind wanders to what my friends would say. They'd say I have a good heart for kids, but this might not be enough. Not much is keeping me at this high school. It's already uncomfortable with Mr. Johnson's unfounded elitism that crushes my soul. Sometimes I imagine transferring to the high school across town, but I love this old school building with its brick exterior, regal entrance with original beveled glass, and location close to home. This AP Club might be the incentive to stay. It might be the defining reason to leave.

I shift my focus back to the AP Club and finding quotations that'll provoke a reaction and critical thinking. There's Mr. Fielding, a voice of reason, in *A Passage to India*.

"It was, in a new form, the old, old trouble that eats the heart out of every civilization: snobbery, the desire for possessions, creditable appendages."

Students will appreciate its present-day relevance to the high school caste system. I sigh. Slightly more than a century later and not much has changed. I wonder if present-day "possessions and creditable appendages" would include walking through hallways holding hands with a hot boyfriend or girlfriend for status. Or "snobbery" would include Mr. Johnson's exclusivity.

I'm nervous no one will show up, which is the worst-case scenario. No one shows up and... what? This isn't life or death. So, I'm embarrassed for a few days. Who cares?

The trouble is, I care too much.

CHAPTER 7

JAX LOURDE

At practice after school, Raleigh's first since his suspension, he and a few other players aren't passing the ball to me or are throwing it so hard my foot trips over the other. Then, I'm throwing the ball back as hard as I can. Coach is yelling at us to look like a team, but we just can't pull it together. I've got Mr. Pency on my butt to get my grades up; Coach yelling at me. Don't even get me started on what my dad expects of me.

After practice, we head to the locker room, and we're segregated into two groups: mine and Raleigh's. Raleigh and his disciples glance over at me, and I try to ignore their shade. Raleigh hoists his sports bag and backpack over his shoulders and leaves the locker room without a word.

The following morning, I get to school with a minute to spare, sprint to my first-period math class, and slide into my chair as the bell rings. I turn around to wave to Raleigh. He nods, his mouth a straight line. No wave. No smile.

Isolation curls around me like creeping tendrils. I swear all eyes are on me. Maybe on Raleigh too, watching how we react to each other. I need to win my best friend back. My teammates back. But, how?

I take out my spiral notebook and pencil and copy an equation from the board. Algebra II is kickin' my butt, and I can't stay after school for help from Mr. Hunter. I have AP Club and then a home game tonight at seven thirty. I need a little downtime.

After the bell rings, I ask Mr. Hunter if I could get help during lunch. He hesitates and asks, "How come you're not working with Raleigh to get on top of this stuff? You two usually help each other out."

He knows the answer. I mean, I'm pretty sure everyone knows I didn't serve a suspension. What I don't know is how people feel about it.

I shrug. "I think it's because my dad appealed my suspension."

"Ah," is all Mr. Hunter says, nodding with eyebrows raised.

Mr. Hunter's reaction makes my chest tighten. It's like he thinks I should've served my suspension too. Then he says, "Okay. Come in during lunch today. See you at eleven fifteen."

I'm relieved to have somewhere to go during lunch. Raleigh and Nick aren't exactly greeting me with open arms, so the number of people to sit with is like zero. Even though I'm well-known because I win games for our school, I'm not entirely popular. I've made some enemies and haven't exactly been nice to others. My regrets are adding up like missed free throws. How do I make regrets go away?

As I walk to my next class alone, I'm distracted with thoughts of tonight's basketball game, at 7:30. Are we gonna look like a team? Or like one of the athletes—me—weaseled out on a suspension?

CHAPTER 8

MISS HEATHER HALDEN

"Hey, Alonzo. I'm going to heat up my dinner. Feel free to help yourself to the fruit and granola bars." I point to the bowl on my teacher's desk. Alonzo, sitting in the front row working on his math homework, looks up and nods.

I enjoy the solitude of the staff lounge as I heat up my leftovers, mesmerized by the whir of the microwave and my spinning spaghetti and meatballs.

In walks Mr. Mark Johnson. What, for the love of Shakespeare, is he doing here after hours? I quickly turn back to the microwave and stare at my twirling dinner in the hopes he'll just ignore me.

No such luck. I sense Mark slithering toward me. "I think you'll have a few of mine."

I turn but do it slowly to show how disinterested I am in him. "What was that?"

"I'm pretty sure two of my AP students are joining you for the AP Club."

"That's nice." I open the microwave to stir my spaghetti, turning my back on him.

"They don't need your club. They're two of my best students."

I know he's baiting me, so I resist engaging. I close the microwave door, punch in another thirty seconds, the longest thirty seconds ever, and wait for my dinner without another word. I hear Mr. Mark Johnson step out of the staff lounge.

With my dinner, fork, and paper towel in hand, I stroll back to my classroom and replay Mark's words: *They don't need your club.*

My stomach churns with visions of looking like an idiot, believing that I can guide these juniors to success only to find out I've led them to a place where hope goes to die. I especially worry about Alonzo who probably won't be able to go to college. Whenever I bring up college, he evades my questions. He said something about his dad not being on board. I wonder if I should call his parents to discuss the AP Club and applying to colleges. My thoughts are interrupted as I spot Jax Lourde walking toward my classroom.

Yesterday, Mr. Pency sent me an email explaining that Jax is required to attend my AP Club. I suspect Jax is one of the students who was suspended last week, though I'm pretty sure he's been at school every day. What kind of deal was brokered? Sports before justice and integrity … another reason to transfer to the high school across town. My AP Club is, no doubt, a form of community service. Just what I need, a student who doesn't want to be in the club. Will he sabotage my and the other students' success? My heart rate speeds up imagining this possibility.

Then, as I enter the classroom and set the bowl of spaghetti on my desk, I see Alonzo and Adele sitting in adjacent seats. They're laughing about something. Alonzo is crunching into an apple, and a granola bar sits atop his desk. Adele is eating an apple too. Seeing this slows my heart rate. I'm here for them, I remind myself.

Jax saunters into my room and I watch as Adele and Alonzo exchange barely perceptible arched-eyebrow glances. I pierce the awkwardness by saying hello to Jax.

He lifts his chin, I assume as a substitute for "hello," plops into a seat, and stretches his legs into the aisle. I notice he doesn't have paper or pencil. Okay, Jax, you're showing me you don't want to be here. Got it.

It's a quarter till six, so I hurriedly eat my spaghetti. As I'm doing so, seven more students enter my classroom, including Emma and another cheerleader who is hobbling in on crutches. Four are mine, two are Mr. Johnson's, and the student on crutches must have Mrs. Alstad's grade-level English class.

Ten students so far. Not too shabby.

Written on the white board is: *Everyone wants to live on top of the mountain, but all the happiness and growth occurs while you're climbing it.*

— Andy Rooney.

At six o'clock, I invite students to turn and talk about a connection they've made, whether they agree or disagree, and what they know about Andy Rooney. I notice this naturally forces a few students to move closer to their peers, which is my goal. I hold up a stack of index cards. "Will you all please write your name and cell number? I'll send out text alerts to update you on what to bring to our sessions."

As students complete the contact card, I walk toward Emma. "Who's your friend?"

"This is Natalia." She smiles as she turns to her.

I point to the crutches and ask Natalia, "What happened?"

"Just a stress fracture in my ankle," Natalia says.

"I'm sorry to hear that. Will you be on crutches for long?"

"A few days. Then I'll be in a boot, but I can't cheer for at least a month," Natalia says with forced pouty lips and puppy-dog eyes. I laugh at her facial expression despite myself. Having an ally might be why Emma joined the club after all.

"Are you here because you aren't doing cheer right now?" I ask Natalia and she nods.

Thank you, stress fracture.

"I love to write," Natalia quickly adds as she sits up straighter. "I have Mrs. Alstad."

"I'm so glad you *all* are here," I say as I look out at the ten students. "You don't need to answer this, but I ask, are you here for the top of the mountain or for the growth?" I make eye contact with each student. "There's no right answer." Though, my vote is with the humility and joy of growth. I tell the students the session plan and offer to loan iPads to students that need a device for the online quiz. "You all need to use your real first names for this." No one gets to hide behind a fake name.

The game-show-like music playing in the background adds a sense of urgency. A bursting bubble sound blurps as each name pops up on the screen. Emma, Adele, and Alonzo's names appear, then we see Jax's name. I'm surprised by this. I doubted he was going to participate. Must be the competition that appeals to him. I feel a faint glimmer of hope as I notice he's sitting up straight. Maybe I judged him too quickly and he won't sabotage this club after all. I watch as unfamiliar names like Judy, Samesh, and Crystal pop up and connect names to faces.

All students are leaning forward after the first question, which is a softball. Everyone gets it right, so the standings are based on who clicked their answer the quickest. The second question is more challenging, which increases the club members' intensity. Club members are cheering and bantering as if they're at a sports competition. I hadn't anticipated this level of excitement and am basking in their involvement and my relief, at least for now. The third question about Arthur Miller's *The*

Crucible, a play they all should have read in the fall, elicits a few frowns. Judy and Jax, in particular. We all watch their names drop. Judy shrinks a little into her seat and Jax grunts. After five questions, Jax and Alonzo are neck and neck. Their names lift and drop, vying for first place with each question.

"Oh, hi, Mr. Johnson," Judy says to the door.

I turn toward the door and see Mr. Johnson leaning on the doorjamb. My stomach plummets.

"What's all the ruckus?" he asks with a smarmy grin.

The game-show tick-tock emanates from the speaker and our competition is suspended momentarily as we turn our attention toward our intruder.

Judy offers, "We're having a little too much fun with this quiz game!"

"Interesting," he says with his arms folded across his chest and leg casually crossed over the other.

Jax twirls his finger in the air, like a coach rounding up his players, and says to the room, "I'm on a roll. Let's play."

I suppress my smile at Jax's urgency and unintended rescue. "Thanks for stopping by, Mr. Johnson." I walk toward the door and close it.

After four more questions, the game ends with Alonzo in the lead and Emma in second place. Two of "my" students beating Mr. Johnson's Jax, Judy and Samesh, finishing in third, fourth, and fifth place, respectively. Take that, Mr. Johnson!

"Miss Halden," Jax says, and everyone turns toward him. "There were two trick questions in there. The one about *ad homin ... ad humin...*"

"*Ad hom-i-nem*?" Adele says.

"Yeah, that. Who could possibly know that?"

"Um ... me?" Adele says, then tilts her head toward her friend. "And Alonzo?"

"And equivocation?" Jax says with increasing volume. "That was just a confusing, vague question!" As a teacher and a professional, I try to hide my amusement with the irony of his statement.

Adele stands and says with her palms open toward Jax, "We're here to have a little fun. Maybe learn something. No need to get your blood pressure up. It's. A. Game."

"Thank you, Adele." I gesture for her to sit down. Sometimes, students say the perfect thing and I can count on Adele to tell it like it is. "She's right. This was meant to be fun and to help you—and me—determine what you already know and what we need to work on." I'm worried about their sparring. Though, it's evident these students care about their knowledge.

Jax folds his arms across his chest and stares out the window, breathing hard like he's just run basketball drills.

They don't need your class. Mr. Mark Johnson's words echo in my mind, and I'm gratified I've proven him wrong already. And it's not two AP students; it's three that need my club. I suspect Judy and Samesh, Mr. Johnson's two "best students," stumbled from the top of the mountain this evening. Their faces pale when I glance toward them, and my gloating is replaced with sympathy. I've read that highly intelligent children are often complimented on being smart and, doing so, adults cause them to become perfectionists. We should, in fact, compliment them on persevering. Fourth and fifth place probably don't sit well with perfectionists.

"Take out paper and pencil, please. We're going to complete a quick-write." I place a piece of paper and a pencil on Jax's desk. As club members transition, I sit at a student desk in front of Samesh and Judy.

"What threw you off the most in the game?" I whisper.

Both say in unison, "The logic terms."

"Would you like a handout to study?"

"Yes," they chorus.

"Please," Samesh says.

Students begin writing to the prompt: *What would your friend say about you?* I pull five logic-terms sheets out of a folder and hand them to Samesh, Judy, Natalia, Crystal, and Jax. Jax sneers at the handout. My glimmer of hope tarnishes a bit.

Chapter 9

Alonzo Hernandez

"I knew you'd come in first!" Adele squeals as we push open the doors to exit toward her car. I asked her to drop me off at the Metro transit center, a quarter mile away from school. Adele offered to drive me home, but if my neighbors see me getting out of a car they don't recognize, an interrogation will follow, and I'll have to lie again and risk Papá finding out I'm attending the AP Club.

"Shh! Not so loud," I say through a grin, glancing around to make sure no other club members hear us. I don't want to gloat, but a first-place win makes lying to my parents worth it. "I just got lucky."

"No way."

"Yes way. Last weekend, I happened to review logic terms in the AP study guide I'd just checked out from the library. That's luck." I don't tell her that I hide the book inside a pillowcase under my bed and hope Mama doesn't get a burst of energy, vacuum under there, find the book, and ask a bunch of questions about what I'm doing with an AP book.

Adele loops her arm through mine and leans in close to my face. "Who cares why? You beat Jax!" She fake laughs maniacally. I laugh, too, but for real.

Finishing in first place feels good, especially beating a star basketball player who's in AP Lang. When I think about it, though, it's terrifying. It's sort of like Andy Rooney's quotation today. When I'm at the top of the mountain, fear of falling clutches at my throat, and I struggle to breathe. I kind of prefer to be on solid ground, climbing and sweating.

We arrive at her car and as I'm about to open the passenger door to get in, Adele sets her arm on the roof of her car and says, "You know today's quick-write about what our friend would say? I wrote what I thought you'd say about me." Then, she climbs into her car.

My stomach tightens, my hand rests on the door handle, and I'm frozen for a moment. I wrote about what my neighbor friend, Rosie, would say about me. She knows me best because our families have hung out since Rosie and I were little. Rosie goes to Aloysius High School across town and I'm taking her to the Aloysius prom in early May.

"Maybe during lunch we can study the logic terms," I say as I plop into the passenger seat, buckle my seatbelt, and hope she doesn't bring up the friend essay again.

"Sure."

As Adele drives us toward the transit station, I wonder if I should just come out with it and tell her I wrote my essay from Rosie's point of view, not hers. I've never told Adele about Rosie. I'll say things like "me and my neighbor" and leave it at that. Adele doesn't even know I'm talking about a sixteen-year-old girl who celebrated her quinceañera, an event I attended more than a year ago.

We're at the transit station within five minutes of school, and I'm relieved to say goodbye because I'm not ready to try to explain to Adele how she's my school friend and Rosie is something else entirely. It's like two different worlds.

What would Rosie say about me? I recap my essay as I ride the bus home. She'd say I was always curious and taking the world in through all my senses. I had a temper in grade school showing that I'm passionate and I've since learned to channel my emotions into something productive. She'd say that I share everything I have with her, even when it's my favorite churros, which we used to dip in our hot chocolate for breakfast when we were in elementary school. She'd say I'm the real me when I'm with her, like I can let my guard down.

I notice the familiar cross street with my auntie's small grocery store on the corner and pull the lever above my seat for the next stop. Even though I'm exhausted, after I step down from the bus, I switch back to drop by the store.

"*Hola, querida!*" my auntie says, as the bell hanging above the door chimes.

"*Hola, tía,*" I say, as she presses my cheeks between her hands and kisses the air in front of my mouth, saying, "Mwah." I told her a few years ago that I was too old for kisses on my lips. Mama was horrified by my rudeness. Auntie didn't mind and told Mama she understood.

"You look happy," my auntie says in Spanish.

I wish I could tell her about my first-place finish in the online quiz and enjoy the warmth of her praise. If I do, though, she'll tell my parents I'm attending AP Club. My conscience feels as heavy as the box I lift from the floor. Ignoring her observation, I ask my auntie, "Where do you want this?"

I've been helping my auntie at the store in exchange for prom limo rental, though tonight is an unexpected visit. If my parents ask why I was at Auntie's store this evening, I'll tell them the Sudsy Auto wasn't busy, and my boss let me leave early. Dad gets home late most evenings, so I usually avoid his hundred questions. I also avoid lying.

My uncle drives a limo, and his boss is letting him chauffeur Rosie and me to her prom at a huge discount. I try to help in the store as often as I can. I take out my phone, put my earbuds in, and open my VoiceMemos app to listen to the recording of my science vocab so I can study for our quiz tomorrow. As I'm listening, I unhook a feather duster from a nail behind the cash register and run it over the canned foods, and then I pull cans to the front of the shelves.

Something at the end of our session worms its way into my brain. I shut off my recording and straighten my back. *"I plan on sharing excerpts from your quick-write essays on Thursday. If you don't want me to share, please write at the top: 'Don't share,'"* Miss Halden had said.

I did not write, "Don't share," at the top of my essay, but I should have. Adele is going to have a fit.

CHAPTER 10

JAX LOURDE

M y stomach always jumbles before every basketball game but tonight it's worse than ever. It's after AP Club and I'm jogging through the commons toward the gym. My phone vibrates and it's a text from Dad.

> Good luck! Can't make it. Security issue. Need to stay.

Why am I not surprised? At least he was there for me, appealing my suspension. That's something.

I step into the locker room and every team member is dressed in their uniforms. Late to the party because of stupid AP Club. I spot my three buddies, and my stomach settles a little. We high-five but it lacks the snap and excitement that's needed before a game. I pull my uniform out of my sports bag.

Coach pokes his head out of his office and hollers, "Finish suiting up, guys. We're warming up in two."

Raleigh says, "Coach, can I talk to you a sec?" He lowers his voice, glances at me, and adds, "In private?"

"Is this about the team?" Coach asks as he steps toward us.

"Yeah," Raleigh says.

"Then you need to say your piece right here," Coach says, and he crosses his arms.

It's like in the movies when all action stops. Everyone freezes. We faintly hear the pep band warming up, playing "Rockstar" in the gym. I swear my heart stops beating for a few seconds; then it starts up again like I'm on the court. Raleigh is making this a me-versus-him thing. Go ahead and say what's on your mind but ... in front of the rest of the team? To talk to Coach? That's low.

Raleigh swallows, and I see his Adam's apple bob up and down. He points at me and says, "I'm worried about us not playing as a team."

I hate that he's looking at me like I'm an idiot. Like it's my fault.

Coach says, "What do the rest of you think?"

A few players shrug, trying to stay out of this. What I should be saying is if we could move past the suspension, then we'd be solid. We've played well all season and shouldn't let something unrelated to basketball ruin us. Raleigh is separating us, and my opinion doesn't matter so I don't bother saying anything.

"If no one else has anything to say, then let's go!" Our coach claps and points toward the gym door. Coach could've shut down the conflict, but he's letting us squirm in our own pile of crap. My buddies and I glance at each other, then glare at Raleigh. I slam the metal door of my locker and hustle onto the court.

After warming up, a mix of rage and humiliation continues to squeeze my chest, and I force it to fuel my jump shot at tip-off. I scan for open players and Raleigh is staring me down. He wants me to tip it to him and that's not gonna happen. Not tonight. I hear the crowd's collective groan as an opponent gets hold of the basketball and Coach is yelling at me from the sidelines, "Raleigh was open, Jax!"

I don't care.

By the first-quarter buzzer, we're down by seven points. Coach benches me for second quarter so I can "cool my jets," he says. The tight-ass ref has given me two technicals already. As I walk off the court, Raleigh clips my shoulder with his and mutters, "We need this win and you're screwing it up."

I mutter back, "I'm not the dorkwad who went crying to the coach," and ignore my fear of permanently losing my friend and teammate.

As the second quarter continues, I can't even watch as Raleigh surges our team ahead by sinking the ball and assisting. It should be him and me: Raleigh-Jax.

In the locker room at halftime, my allies and I huddle while the rest of the team surrounds Raleigh. I know all it would take is for me to tell my buddies we need to join Raleigh and the rest of the team. I know it's Raleigh serving his suspension that holds me back, and I shove down doubts about not paying my debt. I wonder if the guys in my huddle are with me because they would've wanted their parents to get them out of a suspension and ignore rules too.

We're back in the gym, and I'm sitting on the bench, twirling my thumbs clockwise and counterclockwise to release the anger that's building. I'm about to explode. Not only is Raleigh not my friend, but he's also acting like my enemy instead of my teammate. I can't go back in time and serve my suspension. Raleigh doesn't need to shut me out because of it. He doesn't need to take down the team over this. I see Coach talking to Raleigh. Then, Coach yells at me to get ready for a substitution and I stand, shake my arms, and rotate my neck to loosen up. Coach takes hold of my jersey, his eyes boring into mine, and shouts,

"You ready?" He pushes his arm to the side as if shoving away an obstacle. "You ready to let it go? Play like a team?"

I nod, even though I'm not sure.

I'm on the court, and Raleigh passes the ball to me, like he used to. I pivot to check my openings. It feels good to be trusted with the ball, and I dribble to get used to the idea that Raleigh might be ready to put the whole suspension thing behind us. I tell myself this isn't the time to being thinking about that. "Just play ball," I whisper.

We hold our lead as the third quarter buzzer blasts. The crowd is chanting, "Raleigh-Jax! Raleigh-Jax!" Proof that it's on again. Raleigh and I are playing like we're reading each other's minds, anticipating a pass before we see the ball coming. This is how it's supposed to be.

The final buzzer pierces our eardrums and the team huddles, jumps, and hoots. We've won by a landslide. I'm scanning the crowd, taking in the power of a win, of being on top. I spot Mom giving me a thumbs-up and wave. Her expression wears a question. One that I can't interpret or don't want to. She thinks I should have followed rules and served my suspension. But I'm attending the AP Club. That's something.

I see Emma and the other cheerleaders running toward the team.

"Great job, guys!" Emma says to us.

I turn and head toward the locker room. When I get there, Raleigh is stuffing his jersey into his gym bag, and I shout across the locker room, "That was some second half, man!"

As Raleigh smooths deodorant into his pit, he turns away from me without a word.

CHAPTER 11

ADELE QUESTIN

"**O**h my god! We almost didn't pull that off!" Payton, one of the Pep Club members, says to me after the final buzzer blares.

"What was going on with Jax during the first half of the game?" I ask Payton as I step down from the bleachers, removing the pom-pom from my ponytail and tucking stray hairs behind my ears. "That was cringe!"

"Yeah," Payton says. "I heard Jax and Raleigh aren't friends anymore. They were caught dabbing and got suspended."

"Oh. Wow." I don't care enough to ask for more. Two more games then I'm done with ... What's a good word? These trifles? But maybe I care a little. I hate to admit that tonight's game felt unusual for me now that I've seen Emma and Jax in a different light in AP Club. For starters, they're smarter than I thought. It's as if sports and cheer matter to me now. Go figure. I wonder what they wrote in their AP Club essays. Wait. What do I care? Turning my attention back to Payton, I ask, "Are you heading home after this?"

"I'm gonna grab some pizza with a bunch of cheerleaders and basketball guys," she says with a huge smile as we both walk out to the parking lot.

Even though I'm not interested in spending time with most of the people going out for pizza, feeling like an outsider is worse. "I can't go because my parents make me get home early on a school night," I say as if I'd been invited.

"Oh." After a pause, she adds, "Bye. See you later."

I climb into the driver's seat and pull out of the parking lot. If Payton, Emma, or Jax had invited me for pizza, would I have gone? I've been outside that inner circle all my life. It's familiar. Preferred even. And what was up with Alonzo when I drove him to the Metro station after AP club? He was quiet. Too quiet. Sometimes it feels like we're in different worlds.

What would Alonzo say about me? He would say I'm seriously loyal. That I react on both ends of the emotional continuum: really calm or really excited. Not much in between. He would say I like his poetry, am open to new experiences, and am curious about humans. I ask him about Hispanic traditions and foods, and sometimes he likes answering and sometimes he gets distant. One time, he told me I'm like Adela Quested, in *A Passage to India*, because I'm curious about other cultures but say ignorant things sometimes. I don't mean to be. In his essay, he might even say that I depend on him too much and I'm pretty sure this stresses him out. He'd say I should branch out and make more friends. I'm pretty sure I annoy people being bossy and opinionated. Maybe it's because I'm used to being alone a lot, being an only child and all.

I turn into our driveway and see that Dad's office light is still on. I should go in there and see what he's doing. Then again, he's probably busy and doesn't want to be interrupted.

I head straight to my room, sit at my desk, and pull out my planner to see if I have any homework due tomorrow. I flip to the following week to check on projects and tests and, in the Monday section, *National Merit Scholars Announced* is written in cobalt blue with stars next to it. I pick up my phone and text Alonzo.

> National Merit Scholars on Monday!!!

I flip back to this week, uncap my turquoise Sharpie, and draw a smiley next to AP Club on Thursday.

I hope Miss Halden reads my essay out loud, or at least parts of it. Alonzo will love hearing what I wrote and will see what a good friend I am. I wonder what he wrote about me.

CHAPTER 12

MISS HEATHER HALDEN

Nestled against my plush couch cushions with my tired teacher feet settled on my ottoman, I unclip my hair and shake my head to release the strands I'd held in a low ponytail all day. I remove the two *Don't Share* AP Club essays from the stack of ten.

I pick up one of the remaining eight and am distracted by something I overheard when I was making copies in the teacher workroom before lunch.

Some of Mr. Johnson's AP students have started a petition against our AP Club. I replay their claim that juniors not enrolled in a "legitimate" AP course should not be allowed to take an AP exam. My forehead sprouts a few beads of sweat. This misguided elitism is beyond offensive. Should I just let the petition die a natural death? It'll never succeed. Or should I speak with Mr. Johnson about the petition and put a stop to it now? What if he initiated it?

I can't do anything about it sitting on my couch, so I turn my attention back to the essays. A hint of adrenaline surges and I'm more excited to read these than I am to read junior English essays. Is it because these club members have a choice to write? A choice to attend the club?

Emma's essay is at the top.

Natalia would tell you we've been friends since the third grade and, even then, I loved to dance to whatever music was popular at the time. It's no surprise that I'm a cheerleader now. She'd tell you I wear the pants in our friendship, if you know what I mean. I'm the decider. Like which movie we should go to, which makeup to buy at the mall, who Natalia should like … You get the picture.

I think of the character, Emma, in Jane Austen's novel and smile at the similarities between the two. Both Emmas are influential with their friends, and I overheard Emma and a few friends outside my classroom door talking about setting up a friend with a boy. Just like Emma Woodhouse in Austen's novel.

English is our favorite class (and I'm not just saying this because you're reading this, Miss Halden). If there's a movie based on a novel I've read, that's my choice. Hands down.

I notice Emma often seeks the approval of others, including me. Probably because her mom died when she was twelve. I continue reading her quick-write describing how she enjoys having crushes. Emma probably enjoyed today's quiz with quotations about relationships.

I know I'm supposed to be writing from Natalia's perspective, but what she doesn't know about me is that I'm thinking about quitting cheerleading next year and, instead, figuring out who the real me is.

My pen is poised above the page, and no passage jumps out at me as something that I could share. All her thoughts seem private and would be awkward, especially for Natalia.

Next, I read Adele describing her loyalty, her curiosity about human nature, and her emotional spectrum. No wonder she enjoys literature.

After all, it's an examination of people and situations. I underline a few introspective passages to demonstrate interior monologue and wonder how much time I should devote to just reading these essays during Thursday's AP Club session.

I pick up Alonzo's essay and smile as I read: *She knows me best since our families have hung out since Rosie and I were crawling and putting rocks in our mouths.* Teachers are not supposed to have favorite students, but Alonzo commands a spotlight on my class rosters. He's an eloquent writer in a simple way—the best way—and an extremely hard worker. I've underlined several passages in his essay to demonstrate to the AP Club members the writing techniques of showing instead of telling and sense of voice.

The club members are going to love hearing each other's essays.

CHAPTER 13

ADELE QUESTIN

I settle in for our Thursday AP Club session and it's feeling like a regular thing. I'm actually excited to be here and for Miss Halden to read my essay. Alonzo's going to love it, and I want to hear what he said about me.

I'm curious how I didn't notice a couch Miss Halden has in the back of the room. I've always been focused on getting to my seat in third period and have never taken the time to appreciate the colorful posters and brightly hand-painted end tables next to the couch. We're all sitting in the same seats as the previous AP Club session but it's not like a class. It's chill. Real.

Miss Halden waves our essays at us, which gets our attention. "I enjoyed reading what your friends would say about you and getting to know you better. See if you detect the literary devices being used as I read excerpts from three of your essays. This first essay is Alonzo's."

"Craaap!" Alonzo hisses.

"What?" I lean toward him. Alonzo doesn't swear often, and if he swears, he's upset. Like really upset.

"Nothing. It's just that…" Alonzo shakes his head, sits back, and looks straight ahead. I sit back and look forward too. I don't want to miss a word of his essay.

"She knows me best since our families have hung out since Rosie and I were crawling and putting rocks in our mouths," Miss Halden reads and smiles.

What? *"She knows me best?"* Who is Rosie? He didn't write his essay from my perspective? I know him too! And how could I not know he has a… a secret friend! I look at Alonzo, *my* friend who's always there for me, who's still looking straight ahead. I can't even concentrate on the rest of Alonzo's essay, or the next one Miss Halden reads. When AP Club members give their theories on literary devices being used, all I hear is muffled whooshing like water's stuck in my ears.

Just breathe, I tell myself. Then, I hear Miss Halden reading a familiar passage about an emotional spectrum. My emotional spectrum! My fingers rake up my cheeks and then comb through my hair. I think I might have smudged my eyeliner on my right eye. Then, I pull my hands into my lap. I'm going crazy, but I don't need to look like it with lopsided eyes. Does Rosie have emotional extremes? Probably not. Miss Halden reads the part about my loyalty. Is Alonzo loyal to me? Is Rosie loyal to Alonzo? Probably. Why did he choose Rosie and not me? Just as a pity party is settling in, Alonzo raises his hand and guesses the excerpts are examples of interior monologue and, as usual, I'm impressed with how smart he is.

Is this Rosie girl planning on taking my place as his best friend? Has she already? Alonzo is the reason I can tolerate all this ridiculous social stuff at school. I can't lose him. I don't want to be second best. I'm his bestie best friend.

As Miss Halden hands out sample questions from previous AP Lang and Comp exams, I turn to Alonzo, plaster on a smile, and ask, "Who's Rosie?"

Alonzo whispers, "I'll tell you later... in the car."

Torture! I don't want to have to wait. We're in a club. We can talk in a club.

The sample questions land on my desk like a boulder, shifting my focus. I'm not riding the crazy train right now, I tell myself. I need to read the questions in the handout. Choose the correct answer from a list of choices.

The major purpose of the statement (in lines 7–8) was to... My reading level has just dropped to third grade. I reread the passage and feel my heart race as I weigh the choices and struggle to narrow my answer. Guessing, I circle the letter *C*.

All of the following antitheses are found in the excerpt, except... I can't even remember what an antithesis is! I hate questions that ask me what isn't or doesn't belong. Why not just ask us what is! My IQ has dropped twenty points. And there I go again tucking my hair behind my ear, an area that is probably calloused by now. I pick up my Pusheen eraser to give my hand something to do. This usually calms me down, but my brain, like a locomotive without brakes, keeps careening through the very last question.

After we review the correct answers, Miss Halden says, "Raise your hand if you missed more questions in Section A," and then she hands us Section A study guides. She does the same for Section B.

I ask for both study guides. "You can never study too much," I say, trying to give an off-handed laugh, but it comes out as a snort.

Alonzo gives me the side-eye and Miss Halden is looking right at me, so it was an audible snort. Rosie probably never snorts.

"Okay, you're all set for now. See you next Tuesday and happy Thigh-day or should it be Fursday?" Miss Halden says, laughing at her bad joke.

"How about neither," Jax deadpans. "Furs? That's cringe, Miss Halden."

I watch him walk out of Miss Halden's room and think, *I like Jax's sass.* Then, I laugh out loud.

Alonzo gives me another side-eye. "What's so funny?"

I shake my head. "It's nothing. Just having a moment." I realize that "Jax's sass" sounds like "Jax's ass" and giggle again.

"Okay," Alonzo says. "Enjoy your moment."

As we walk out of school, I strain to keep from asking about Rosie. He said he would tell me in the car, but I'm about to burst.

I'm backing up out of the parking spot, exploding with curiosity, and say, "So. Rosie," as if I've asked a whole question.

Alonzo sighs and starts in, talking fast as an auctioneer. "I completely forgot to write 'Don't share' on my essay and then I meant to ask Miss Halden not to read my essay earlier today. But you know how that turned out." He sighs again and then says, "Rosie is my friend. She's been my friend since—"

"Since you both were crawling and putting rocks in your mouth. Yeah. I heard."

"Since we were very little," Alonzo says, glaring at me.

We drive a few blocks in silence. Still torture! Then, finally, he continues. "Rosie knows me best."

"Got it. Heard that too." I know my tone is spicy, and I should take it down a notch. But this is me sliding up and down my emotional spectrum. Unlike calm and sweet Rosie.

Alonzo says, "You know how when whole families hang out and know each other's history and stuff?" His face looks pained.

I pull into a parking spot at the Metro station so he can finish. I nod, though I don't really know what that's like. I don't even have cousins that live nearby let alone good family friends. Long driveways separate us. It's not easy to just pop over to the neighbor's house for a cup of sugar or chat over the backyard fence like in the movies or make friends who have known me since I was crawling.

"It's like this," Alonzo attempts. "Rosie is my at-home friend. She speaks Spanish."

I speak Spanish, I think, but don't say.

"You're my at-school friend," he adds as he gets out of my car and swings his backpack over his shoulder.

His at-school friend. Is that better or worse? I'm going with worse.

I've been demoted.

CHAPTER 14

JAX LOURDE

I'm *glad I wrote 'Don't share' on my essay,* I think as I pull out of
the school parking lot after our second AP Club session. My essay
is from Raleigh's point of view, and I didn't want the AP clubbers being
all weird about Raleigh and me not being friends right now. I wrote it as
if we are.

Raleigh would describe me as competitive, at all costs. He'd say I'm a
natural leader that some people follow because they're a little bit afraid
of me, and some follow because being around me gives them status and
a backbone.

I have a mischievous streak. Raleigh is usually following rules, always
standing up for the underdog, and helping others. Raleigh will say that
opposites attract, and that's why our friendship works.

Or worked.

I'm driving home and hesitate at Westminster Street. If I turn right, I'll head toward Raleigh's house. Going left takes me to my house.

I turn my tires to the right.

Raleigh's mom answers the door and all she says is, "Oh." She turns to look up the stairs and pauses a beat or two. She finally says, "Raleigh's upstairs. Let me go check with him."

She said, "check with him," instead of her usual, "go get him." She leaves the door open a crack, but doesn't invite me in, so I just shuffle my feet and wait on the porch. She probably knows about me not serving my suspension.

I've been waiting for what feels like five minutes. Why did I come here in the first place? I head down the porch steps.

"Hey."

I pivot, look up, and see Raleigh, with his arms crossed, standing on the porch.

"Hey yourself." My voice is unexpectedly raspy, which is embarrassing.

"Why are you here?"

Raleigh's tone stiffens my back. I hadn't thought this through. I don't know what I could say to make things better. So, I answer, my voice barely audible. "I honestly don't know."

"Fair enough."

I feel my shoulders and back relax a bit. "Here's the deal." My voice gains strength and I walk toward the steps. "Can we just sit down?" Him towering over me and me a few steps below is too intense.

We both sit down on the top step, with our elbows resting on our knees and heads facing out. Twins.

"Here's the deal," I say again and realize I don't know what the deal is. I want to say I miss him and that I'm sorry. But maybe I'm not sorry. My dad appealed and won. End of story. If his dad didn't appeal his suspension, that's his problem. It shouldn't mean we can't be friends anymore.

"What's the deal?" Raleigh asks, rerouting my thoughts.

"I want things to go back to the way they were—"

"Before the suspension?"

"Well... yeah."

"Look, we all got caught," Raleigh says. "But you got away with it. Nick and I didn't."

"Dude! Why are you so salty about it? I never touched that dab pen." My voice raises an octave. "I didn't get away with it. I was in the principal's office too. The principal called my parents too."

"You just don't see it," Raleigh says. "And for the record, I didn't touch the dab pen either. The right thing to do would have been to serve your suspension and be done with it."

"Right thing!" I lower my voice to add, "What does that even mean?" I look Raleigh in the eyes and say, "Maybe you're just being righteous. Have you thought about that? ... Maybe *I* did the right thing." I hadn't come here to say all this but realize this is what's been eating at me. "You and Nick have been actin' like you're the better guys. Why? Because you had to stay home for a few days? As if! Like you have a right to be mad at me. Why can't we just move on?"

"We should've been in this together. We had the dab pen together. We got caught together. We should've gotten suspended together," Raleigh says as he's counting off on his fingers. He pauses a moment. "Not being able to play basketball? That should have been together too."

It's like I've been slapped but I recover. "I don't see why we can't still be friends." I get up and descend the stairs. I've said enough. My visit was pointless.

"Hey."

I turn around to face him.

He says quietly, "Even if we're not friends..."

Even if we're not friends? It's like a punch.

He continues. "At least, let's work together on the team."

"Yeah. I can do that." Defeat and isolation close in on me like eerie mist in a jungle.

CHAPTER 15

ALONZO HERNANDEZ

I sit in the bus seat on my way home from AP Club, my elbows resting on my thighs and my face resting in my hands. I'd groan but it would make me look like a total loon and scare the little kid sitting across the aisle with his mom. I should've remembered to write *Don't Share* on my essay. If I had, Adele wouldn't be asking me a bunch of questions about Rosie. Then again, I should've just told Adele about Rosie all along. I've told Rosie stories about Adele so why not the other way around? Yeah, but my life with my family and Rosie is personal. I don't want... or need to share this with other people. Should I have to be so careful not to slip up and say something, or write something, that drums up more questions?

I lift my head out of my hands and look out the bus window. I don't have time to be obsessing about this stuff.

I open my backpack and pull out the study guide for Section A that Miss Halden gave us. Antithesis totally stumped me. I used common sense to answer that question but probably got it wrong. I read the definition, which is a person or thing that is the opposite. Yeah, Rosie and Adele.

Just stop thinking about them and concentrate.

I read examples of antitheses and am surprised to learn that some of the most memorable lines in literature are antitheses. There's Dickens's "It was the best of times, it was the worst of times." And "to err is human; to forgive divine," from *Paradise Lost*. Cool.

My bus stop is fast approaching, so I tuck the study guide in my backpack and pull the lever to let Chuck, the driver, know that I need the next stop. Chuck's been driving my Metro bus for at least two years.

Chuck says as I exit, "You been gettin' home at a different time this week."

"I've been going to AP study sessions." Then I catch myself and hope he doesn't see Papá and tell him about the AP Club. First with *Don't share* my essay and then lying to my parents. I'm living a secret life and feel like I'm strangling from my lies.

"Oh yeah? Study sessions? ... Smart kid. Good for you!"

"Thanks," I say as I step down onto the pavement. I text Rosie.

> U at home?

> Yes. C U soon?

I text a thumbs-up.

"*Querido mio*," Rosie's mom says to me as she opens the door. I lean in to hug her, and I see Rosie sitting at the dining table hunched over a spiral notebook with a textbook open. Her thick lashes swish as she looks from the textbook to her paper and my heart skips a beat.

"Hi there. Just stopping by for a sec," I say to Rosie, turning the chair so I can lean my arms and chin on the back of it.

"National Merit Scholars are announced on Monday," Rosie says with a huge smile, her dimples making it hard to concentrate on her words.

"I know."

"Are you nervous?" Rosie asks.

"A little. It's complicated. If I get it, colleges will get in touch with me, which is a no-go." I run my hand along one of the spines of the chair and return my gaze to Rosie. She cocks her head, her long, wavy hair falling onto her homework and table. "You know how it is. Why dream about something that's impossible?"

"Anything is possible with hard work," Rosie says, as if it's that simple.

"Papá says that too," I say, running my fingers through my hair. Hard work according to Papá's definition, according to where he wants me to work. Not hard work at college. I told Rosie about AP Club, and she promised to keep the secret and cover for me. I hate that I've pulled her into my lie. I hate that I'm angry with Rosie for forgetting that my papá doesn't want me to go to college. Only for a split second, though. I hope my parents will change their minds and let me go to college, like new waves coming into shore and receding, washing away all the *"nos."*

We're both quiet for a moment. The stuttering hum of a sewing machine floats from the kitchen and I turn my head toward the sound. "What's your mom making in there?"

Rosie smiles and blushes. "She's sewing my prom dress. She wanted to get started early, especially with her work hours."

I blush too and look at the floor. It's been awkward between Rosie and me lately. We used to be like friends but ever since I offered to take Rosie to her school prom it's like we're boyfriend and girlfriend, but without the kissing part. Yet.

She told me she couldn't imagine going with anyone but me. I liked hearing that. Her school, like ours, has a junior/senior prom. A lot of schools have only senior proms, but we get to pay for prom two years in a row. Lucky us.

Adele told me she and her mom are going to the city in March and staying the night at a swanky hotel—that's how she said it—to shop for her prom dress. She'll go to a sewing lady to get the dress fixed. A bunch of girl stuff and a whole lotta money spent on one night. I don't get it.

I lift my head. "Hey, Rosie. Do you talk to your school friends about us?"

She sets her pencil onto her textbook. "That's a weird question. Why are you asking?"

"Just wondering, that's all."

"Course, I do," Rosie says, pulling her chin back, like everyone talks about their friends except me.

"Okay." This conversation makes my stomach hurt, so I change the subject and ask her about her homework and what's happening at her school. Then, after about five minutes of small talk, I lift out of the chair. "Well, I gotta go."

Rosie cocks her head at me. "You alright?"

"Just thinking about stuff. That's all."

As I head out the door, I wonder who Adele's going to prom with. She doesn't think it's me, does she? Two proms in one year? I can barely pay for one.

I'm still stressing about prom as I open the door to our house.

"Alonzo."

I turn toward the voice and Papá is sitting straight up on the couch, not relaxed; more like he's waiting. "Where've you been?"

My mouth drops open. *Crap!* I close my mouth and point my thumb toward Rosie's house. "At Rosie's." I slot my hands into my jeans pockets.

Papá leans his elbows on his knees, looking like an older version of me. "I stopped by your work to get my car washed."

Oh my God, what did my boss say? ... My boss doesn't work on Thursdays. He couldn't have said anything. "I didn't work today, Papá."

"Noticed that."

"My schedule changed. I work more hours on Saturdays now."

"I left the auto store early. Headache." Papá rubs the back of his neck.

"Sorry about your head."

"I'm asking again. Where've you been? If you weren't working, you should've come home. Helped with chores."

"Sorry, Papá. I was studying at school." This isn't a lie. "Then, I stopped by to talk with Rosie but just for a few minutes."

"I saw you go to her house. Next time, study at home." Papá stands and sighs. "Let's get dinner."

We walk toward the kitchen table. I replay what just happened and hope there aren't any holes in my story. I'm pretty sure Papá suspects something's going on. He's never stopped to get his car washed at Sudsy Auto.

Chapter 16

Jax Lourde

I weave through a bunch of crowded tables trying not to feel awkward as I pass Raleigh and Nick. I walk up to a guy and girl—AP clubbers—at a table near the commons windows. I should remember their names from the quiz game we played on Tuesday, but I don't have a clue. "Okay if I sit here?"

I see them look at each other, and the dark-haired guy says, "Sure. Have a seat."

I set down my backpack and as I'm sitting down, the guy holds out his hand. "I'm Alonzo and this is Adele."

"I'm Jax."

"Yeah. We know," they both say at the same time.

I set my basketball on the floor and shake the guy's hand. Then my eyes widen as I remember that the too-much-eyeliner girl debated me on Title IX in social studies. Awkward. The whole basketball team hates her. Me included. As I take out my lunch sack there's a cringy silence, so I start talking to fill the air. "AP Club is kickin' my butt! The logic terms and AP Lang practice questions make me glad I'm at the club. And you!" I hold out my fist for a bump with... What was his name? ... Alondo? Or was it Alonno? "You're awesome!" I envy his first-place finish and am maybe a little intimidated by him... and his sidekick.

"I wouldn't exactly say that," whatever-his-name-is says, barely grazing my fist and kind of ruining our bro moment.

"Sorry. Could you say your name again?" I pick up my basketball and am batting it back and forth between my hands. I set my basketball back on the floor because Eyeliner Girl is staring at it, looking supremely annoyed. Besides, I need to take a bite of my sandwich.

"It's Alonzo."

"Got it. Alonzo. Did I say it right?" I say with a mouth full of my sandwich.

Alonzo nods.

"His name's not that hard," Eyeliner Girl says.

Her snotty tone is totally unnecessary. I've forgotten her name too. This seemed like a good idea a few minutes ago; now I'm not so sure. My scalp and pits tingle with sweat and I rotate my neck to loosen up.

"I'm just not good with names. I've forgotten yours too. Sorry."

"It's A-dele," she says. "Adele... like the singer."

"Got it," I say with what feels like a weak smile.

"Hey, Jax."

I turn toward the deep voice and see that it's Eric, one of my teammates, standing next to me with a clipboard in his hand.

Eric says, "Some of us AP students are putting together a petition to protest the AP Club. Students that aren't in the AP class shouldn't be able to take the exam."

I glance toward Alonzo and Adele; Alonzo's eyelids are lowered, and Adele looks like she's going to punch someone. "Dude," I say to Eric, "I don't have a pen. I'll check with you later." I turn away from Eric and say to Alonzo, "That was awkward."

"Awkward?" Alonzo pauses a moment to let his eyes pierce mine, which makes my stomach churn.

I was just getting their names straight, maybe making a few friends, and Eric had to come along.

Alonzo sits up straighter in his seat and says in a calm voice, which is almost worse than yelling, "I wouldn't call it awkward. I'd call it total bull crap."

"It's not just bull crap," Adele says. "It's illegal. They can't deny our Fourteenth Amendment rights! No one can deny our right to an education. And while we're at it we're entitled to due process. A one-sided petition isn't due process!"

My eyebrows raise. "Look who's been paying attention in social studies."

"This isn't a time for a joke, Jax," Adele says.

"Hey now." I hold out my palms in defense. "I'm not the one who started the petition. And I agree with Alonzo that it's bull crap." I take a bite of my sandwich to give Adele and Alonzo a minute to cool off. "Look, we all know the petition is totally bogus. It's gonna lose momentum."

Alonzo cocks his head like he's thinking about what I just said. Adele looks at Alonzo like she's waiting for him to say something.

She turns to me. "Why aren't you sitting with your... um... pack?" Adele glances toward Raleigh, Nick, Eric, and a few other guys.

My *pack*? ... Just ignore it.

"Oh, yeah. Your 'friends,'" she says with air quotes, "are mad at you. Why is that, exactly?"

I see what she's doing. She's turning her anger on me. I've seen my teammates do this sometimes. I pause trying to decide if I even want to get into this with Adele. I just needed a place to sit and eat lunch. It didn't need to be so complicated. I'll explain to my new buddy, Alonzo, but not to her because she looks ready to pounce on anything I say.

"See," I say to Alonzo with my shoulder hunched to block out Adele, "a few of us got caught with a dab pen and my parents wanted my suspension overturned. It's their right to do that, you know." I sound really defensive. "Anyway, my buddies—"

"Former buddies," Adele interrupts.

"Former buddies," I continue, "are salty because they served their suspensions."

"Interesting dilemma," Adele says.

"No need for sarcasm." I attempt to give her a warning glare.

"I wasn't being sarcastic," Adele says. "Ethical dilemmas are intriguing."

"So true, Professor Adele," I say. Adele laughs and I notice her blue eyes sparkle. She's pretty when she smiles. The tension at the table loosens up a bit. "So, what about ethical dilemmas?"

"Well... you all got caught. Weren't all your parents called into the principal's office?"

"Yeah."

"Who cares if the other two guys had to stay home for a few days, and you didn't," Adele says. "It doesn't sound like a big deal. Your parents exercised their rights."

Finally, someone who sees my side! "That's exactly what I said to my bros!"

"Was there proof?" Alonzo asks with an edge, erasing my imaginary victory lap. "I mean, I see how you exercised your rights. I also see how the other guys felt like they were taking the hit. You didn't."

This is an interesting debate happening here but couldn't they both've been on my side? Alonzo's kind of intense. And maybe this Adele chick isn't as bad as my basketball teammates thought.

"Yeah, there was proof. Joey caught us in a car with a dab pen in the parking lot. Someone else took a hit, though, when Joey saw us. I didn't."

Alonzo is staring me down, getting all social justice about this. I squirm in my seat and wish I hadn't joined them for lunch. I pick up my basketball and set it down again. Then, Adele chimes in.

"Just let it go, Alonzo."

Adele to the rescue. The girl did me a solid.

I pick up my basketball again. God, I'm fidgeting a lot. "Actually, Alonzo, I can see how my bros are salty over a served suspension."

Alonzo's giving me this look and I don't quite know what it is. Respect?

Chapter 17

Adele Questin

I watch Jax leaping into the air after their landslide win and I actually care that we'll compete in the State Championship next Friday, a week from tonight. Every Pep Club member is screaming, including me, piercing each other's eardrums. My unexpected, yet genuine, glee about our team winning is freaking me out. Even though I joined the Pep Club and have attended more games than I can count, I've never been this enthusiastic about sports. Ever.

Also, I've been freaked out about Jax joining Alonzo and me for lunch today. My emotional pendulum is swinging back and forth between suspicion that Jax was desperate for friends and giddy anticipation of adding a friend to our duo. Jax is smart and a smart-ass. My kind of person. Though, is he? Jax is in AP classes, his friends are getting signatures for a petition, and he's an athlete. We're not the same. Although, I don't want to read into it, but Jax didn't sign the petition.

I see Jax scanning the crowd, then waving at his mom. A confident guy who can do that in front of his teammates? Impressive. Then, he spots me and waves. Waves at me. If I was capable of a backflip, I'd do that right now. Should I smile and wave back? As if possessed by an outside force, my arm lifts and I look like a bobblehead doll. I'm pretty sure I'm smiling like an idiot. I've sworn off guys this year. I mean why bother? It's pointless to even try with someone as popular as tall, muscly Jax. Jax has temporarily made me forget my oath to avoid romance and I have no idea how I feel about it. To distract myself I text Alonzo.

> U awake?

> Kind of.

Kind of? What is that? Is that a yes or no? I pause and take a breath.

> Phone call?

> Just a second.

> How bout 5 minutes.

Alonzo texts a thumbs-up, and I head to my car. Once seated, I dial him, and I say over the car speakers, "How weird was it that Jax joined us for lunch today?"

"Not that weird."

"No. It was weird. Weird for a popular guy to sit with us. Admit it." Obviously, I can't stop thinking about Jax and his wavy, jet-black hair and his buff arms in his basketball jersey.

"Yeah, maybe," Alonzo says. "We're in the AP Club together, though, so we have something in common... What's going on? Why are you calling so late?"

"I dunno. I was just thinking about how people are separated into categories and how it throws us off when those categories get mixed up."

"Meaning?"

"It's like we have a caste system. Like Miss Halden explained the caste system in *A Passage to India*. We're not much different from one hundred years ago."

"You and I have a caste system?" There's an edge in his voice.

Is he annoyed that I said this? I need to think before I speak. "I'm mostly talking about the whole school... The petition is proof that there are elite people who want to keep us down."

"I wouldn't use the word, 'elite,' because they're not. Just different." Alonzo blows out a blast of air from his nose. "We all are the same. It's like that quote about education being the great equalizer."

"I can see how at school, we're the same," I say, pausing to think. "You know, neither of us talk about our home life. Did you realize that?"

"I hadn't thought about it as hard as you, but yeah. I guess so. At school, we make fun of the same people, we like the same books, we discuss characters and talk about what we're learning in social studies. Think about it. If we talked about our home lives, there'd be... like, a canyon between us. We have different lives."

A canyon? That's intense. I was talking about a caste system but wasn't picturing a whole canyon. I'm trying to make it seem like our home life isn't a big deal when, I guess, it is a big deal. "So, did I wake you?"

"No, but you might've woken up my little brother."

"You share a room with your brother?"

"Yeah, Bennie. It's really Bernardo, but we call him Bennie. He's a pain in the butt sometimes, but I like him. Right now, I'm sitting outside on our porch and freezing." Alonzo pauses. "See? I just shared something personal, and you can't relate, right?"

"I don't have any brothers or sisters." I sound sad and I can't relate. It's lonely not having someone that's a pain in the butt. I perk up my voice. "The upside of this is that I don't have to talk on the phone outside..."

I hear the fake airy sound of my voice, which I hate. "I better let you get inside to warm up. See you Monday." I'm about to hang up, and then say, "Alonzo?"

"Yeah."

"Would it be okay if I invite Jax to join us for lunch again?"

"Sure thing."

"I think we should talk to him about the petition."

Alonzo sighs. "I think we should let it die a natural death."

Miss Halden, standing at the front of the room, says, "Last Friday, we read an excerpt from the French play, *Cyrano de Bergerac*. I'm going to read you a quotation and I'd like you to respond. 'There was the allegory of my whole life: I, in the shadow, at the ladder's foot, while others lightly mount to Love and Fame!'"

These kinds of assignments are my jam. Literature has a long shelf life; not much changes with human beings.

When we're done writing, I'm paired with a cheerleader named Emma to read each other's quick-write. I hand her my notebook paper, she hands me hers, and we both read silently.

Being behind the scenes for the benefit of others happens all the time in modern society. Politicians have speechwriters that make them look smarter than they are. Newscasters are the same. These two examples are related to fame.

Emma is actually a good writer. Her quick-write is good, and I wrote a long ol' whine-fest about being in the shadows—shadows cast by people who think they're elite but they're not. Why couldn't I have been paired with Alonzo? He already knows I'm a complainer. Will Emma figure out that my quick-write is about the petition? I'm pretty sure she's friends with Eric and might tell him what I wrote.

I refocus on Emma's words.

The pursuit of love is another motivator for people to seek a proxy to make them look better than they are or to increase their chances of finding love. For example, let's say someone writes an online dating profile for someone who isn't a good writer. That's just false advertising if you ask me.

It wasn't fair for Cyrano's skills to be exploited. He deserved love and fame too. In present day, people should earn their own fame and their own love.

The bell rings and Emma whispers, "I heard about the petition. I think it's—" she mouths, "bull crap." A canyon of separation just narrowed, and my mouth drops open in surprise. Who would've guessed Emma would criticize an athlete like Eric? I wish we had more time to talk about the petition. If it wasn't for her being a cheerleader and the ridiculous caste system that Alonzo and I were just talking about, I could be friends with her.

CHAPTER 18

ALONZO HERNANDEZ

"**J**ax is straight ahead. That table near the windows," I say as I bob my head in their direction, holding an empty lunch tray. "Jax is sitting with Emma."

"Isn't that a cliché? A jock and a cheerleader."

I smirk but try not to. Sometimes Adele is hilarious and sometimes she's not. As usual, she's being snarky, but why?

The lunch lady hands me a plate of spaghetti that smells pretty good, and I set it on my tray. "Why be mean?"

Adele lowers her head. "I don't know. Stuff just blurts out."

"Are... are you jealous of them or something?"

"No. Nothing like that. Just trying to be funny... Let's go join them." Adele pulls my elbow in the direction of Jax's table, almost tipping my tray.

"I don't think that's such a good idea. We might be interrupting something."

"We're all in the AP Club. Can't we have lunch together?"

"I guess so." We arrive at the table. "Hey, Jax," I say.

Jax holds out his fist for a bump. I balance my tray on one hand, and I meet his hand with my fist.

Jax pulls his arm back. "Hey, bud. How was your weekend?"

"Worked a lot." I shift my tray to get more comfortable. "Did some homework yesterday. You?"

"Probably should get a job for some extra cash," Jax says. "Had a lot of homework too."

My feet are shuffling, and my arms are getting tired from holding my tray. I was hoping we'd be invited to sit down but that's not going to happen in this lifetime. I give Adele a questioning look to hint that she needs to ask if we can sit here. I wait another few seconds, but I guess I need to take charge. "Okay if we sit here?"

Emma says, "Um... okay." She looks at Jax for confirmation.

I set my tray down. "So... Emma, right?"

"Yeah, I'm Emma. And you are?"

Is it me or is she being kind of snotty? We sit next to each other in English; she should know me. Though, I can't blame her for being snotty since we interrupted their, um, hookup, maybe? With my hand on my chest, I say, "I'm Alonzo, and this is my friend, Adele."

Adele is already seated. Bold as always. Adele waves since her mouth is full of a bite of her sandwich.

"I'm gonna go get more dressing for my salad," Emma says.

After Emma steps away, Adele says, "A cheerleader eating a salad. Shocker."

Jax laughs.

I don't laugh. "C'mon, Adele. Be nice." I twirl my fork into my spaghetti.

"Nice?" Adele says. "Nice is boring."

Jax laughs again and nods. I glance from my friend to Jax. Maybe Adele has met her equal.

"What'd I miss?" Emma says as she sits down, and tears open a dressing packet without spilling a drop. Usually, Adele's dressing packets explode on her shirt or jeans. I stifle a laugh as I picture my friend.

"We were just talking about salad, Em," Jax says.

Emma beams. "I'm Em, huh?"

"Yeah." Jax smiles.

"I like it."

"Are we interrupting something here?" Adele asks. Her voice is flat, and I hope she doesn't blurt out something rude again.

"Interrupting us?" Jax says. "Nah. I'm glad you're here."

I believe him and feel a little bit of pride being at Jax's table. Emma gives Jax a salty stare. We *are* interrupting something, but Adele wants to be here, so I'm here too. I'm kind of enjoying this social experiment, especially since Adele mentioned the caste system earlier. I set the tray on the bench next to me. "So, Jax. How do you like AP Club?" I hope this will give us all something to talk about.

"I don't know how long I'll stay, actually."

"Why's that?" I ask.

"Mr. Pency made me join."

Adele kicks me under the table though I'm not sure why. I keep my facial expression neutral, though my shin is throbbing. "I don't understand," I say to Jax.

"I do," Adele says, and all eyes turn toward her. She's retreating, leaning away from the table. "Never mind."

I've just witnessed a historical moment. Adele has never backed down on anything and she's very, very quiet right now. Why is she not pressing Jax for more information, making him tell the truth?

"No, go ahead," Jax says. "I'd like to hear your theory."

Adele shakes her head and says, "It seems like it's related to what you told us on Friday, that's all." Then, she clasps her hands in her lap.

Adele not taking a stand and ratting someone out? This is a first. I hope Jax joins us for lunch from now on because Adele needs another person, and not just me, calling her out.

"So," Adele says, "what are we doing about the AP Club petition?"

No small talk, no polite "How are you?" She just dives in and is off swimming in the deep end.

Jax says, "I've been asked a few times already to sign it." He shrugs his shoulders. "I'm trying to stay neutral and pretending I don't have time or a pen."

"How diplomatic of you," Adele says.

I'm about to jump in and call her out on her sarcasm, when Jax says, "Yeah. Diplomacy can get stuff done too, you know." He leans toward her. "Think about it. Who are they giving the petition and signatures to? Mr. Pency? He approved the club."

Adele doesn't have anything to say about this because she knows he's right. It's like I can hear her brain working overtime, trying to find fault in his argument.

Emma perks up and pivots to Jax. "What if you're wrong? What if the petition grows? Won't it be harder to stop it then?"

"You have a point," Adele says to Emma.

"You said you hate being in the shadows," Emma says. "You know. In your quick-write?"

"True. I hate being overshadowed," Adele admits.

Emma says, "Then, fight back."

Jax jumps in. "If it doesn't die in the next week or so, we'll do something about it." With a huge smile says, "We'll step out of the shadows and take a stand."

"Yeah," Adele says to Emma. "Maybe Jax can be our Cyrano."

"Maybe not," Jax says.

CHAPTER 19

MISS HEATHER HALDEN

My prep is shorter today because we have an assembly to recognize academic achievement. The bell rings and I sigh because I haven't completed half of what I'd planned. I'm tempted to stay in my room to use this time to catch up. Mr. Pency never notices if we're at the assemblies or not. Or at least he doesn't say anything to staff members who miss assemblies. However, when I picture Alonzo, Emma and Adele's names being announced and me not being there, I drape my key lanyard around my neck and head to the gym where I find a spot to stand along the west wall.

I see that Mr. Pency; Mrs. Annatol, one of our counselors; and Mr. Johnson are seated next to the podium. Why is Mr. *Creepers* Johnson sitting up there? After Mr. Pency's welcome, I get my answer.

Mr. Johnson booms over the mic saying something about 1.5 million high school students entering to qualify for the National Merit program ... blah, blah, blah. I tune out his self-important voice.

"We have ten juniors this year to honor—an unprecedented number," I hear Mr. Johnson say. He continues, "When I read off your name, please come down to stand next to me. Mr. Pency and Mrs. Annatol will shake your hand."

I scan the junior section and see Adele and Alonzo glance at each other, shifting in their seats, and Alonzo runs his hand through his hair.

"The National Merit qualifiers are: Jax Lourde."

Many juniors erupt into whoops, "Yeah, Jax!" and shrill whistles. I notice that Raleigh and Nick are not cheering. Jax, with his confidence and grace, lopes down the bleacher stairs. Guys like him make everything seem so easy as he wears an "Aw shucks" grin. When he arrives next to Mr. Johnson, they high-five like they're friends.

"Good God," I mutter under my breath. Mrs. Parson, our librarian, glances at me, and raises her eyebrows. I whisper to Mrs. Parson, "Over the top, right?" She nods.

"Samesh Jai." Mr. Johnson pauses a moment. When Samesh arrives next to Mr. Johnson, he adds, "Jai means victory, by the way," and he holds up Samesh's arm as if he's a boxer who's just won a match.

I sigh. Are these theatrics necessary?

Mr. Johnson reads off four more names, some I don't recognize, with more theatrics and more applause.

"Alonzo Hernandez." The junior section erupts almost at the same volume as Jax's. I had no idea Alonzo was so well-known and supported. I guess students have affinities for friendly, humble, and hardworking people. My eyes fill with tears. I wipe them and clap until my hands are stinging. My tears blur my vision, but I can make out Mr. Johnson shaking Alonzo's hand. No high five? No fist bump? Is it because Alonzo is my student? Before I can stop myself, I'm heading out onto the gym floor to give Alonzo a side hug.

"I'm so proud of you," I say.

"Thank you, Miss Halden. I couldn't have done it without you."

"Nonsense! This was all you." I look away from Alonzo to see Mr. Johnson smiling at me.

"Whenever you're ready, Miss Halden, for the next name," he says into the microphone.

Heat rises up my neck and into my cheeks but my glare at Mr. Johnson is pure ice. "Carry on," I say to Mr. Johnson, returning to the wall.

"Emma Woodburn."

During the applause, I return to the gym floor to greet Emma and congratulate her with a side hug too. No other teacher is stepping in to congratulate these students, but my urge to imply to Mr. Johnson and the crowd that he isn't the only person responsible for juniors' success overrides my self-consciousness.

"I knew you could do it," I say to her.

"Wow! A cheerleader!" Mr. Johnson says into the mic, and I hear some gasps with sprinkles of laughter from the student section. Mr. Pency steps up to the mic to add, "I think what Mr. Johnson means is that our cheerleaders are very busy with year-round practices and community service, so it's commendable that Emma finds time for academics too."

Good save, Mr. Pency.

"Adelay Questin."

Mr. Pency whispers in Mr. Johnson's ear.

"Correction. Adele Questin."

During the applause, I step out again for a side hug and back to the wall.

"Lastly, Judy Weston." Mr. Johnson shakes her hand. No high five for her either.

The program ends and students are dismissed from the assembly.

Mr. Johnson is standing in the middle of the gym floor, wrapping the mic cord around his hand and elbow to put away the sound equipment. I approach him, red-hot fired up, with the intention of telling him he needs to apologize to Emma.

Mr. Johnson smirks. "Hello, Miss Halden. Next time we'll add your hugs to the agenda."

I feel like I've been slapped with cold water and my fire extinguished. All I can muster is, "No need, Mr. Johnson." I start to walk away. Why did I think I could reason with this arrogant, insufferable man? I turn back toward him. "Actually, you do need to add hugs and handshakes to the agenda. Did it occur to you that other teachers have played a role in these students' success? Did it occur to you that other teachers might have wanted to congratulate the scholars?" I pause to glare at him and wait for an answer. "One more thing. You think you're being funny? It's not working."

He looks down and perhaps is remorseful. "You're right." After shuffling his feet and running his fingers through his thick hair, he adds, "Humor gone bad. Sorry."

My cheeks are still flaming and my desire to defend Emma collides with my desire to get far away from Mr. Johnson. I leave the gym and march toward Mr. Pency's office. By the time I arrive, I've cooled down a bit and, surprisingly, Mark Johnson's apology helps, but I'm still upset for Emma. *Humor gone bad.* What kind of excuse is that?

Mr. Pency, miraculously, is available, and I launch into my complaint. "I found Mr. Johnson's comment about Emma offensive." My hands grip the bottom of my chair to stop them from visibly trembling. Teachers need to stick together, but Mr. Johnson's failure to think of anyone but himself is egregious. My complaint is fair game.

"Let me stop you right there, Miss Halden. I'm not at liberty to discuss personnel matters with you, so you'll just have to trust I'm taking care of it."

"It's just that I'm very fond of Emma and worry about her perception of herself... as a scholar."

"Noted."

"I have another thing to ask as well." I pause to make sure it's okay to proceed. Mr. Pency nods at me, so I say, "Could you tell me where we stand with Jax? He's been an important member in our club."

Mr. Pency slaps his forehead. "I'd forgotten to call Jax in to let him know he doesn't need to attend your club anymore."

My hand flies to my chest. Lose one of my AP Club members? I've grown to like Jax, and it won't be the same without him. If he quits now, how will it look to staff and students? People will gossip. Say the club isn't worth Jax's time. Maybe say the club isn't worth anyone's time.

"I'll call Jax in tomorrow," Mr. Pency says. "He and I had an agreement that he'd bring up his AP grade and let's see..." He peers into his computer screen and clicks a few times. "Jax has a B minus in his AP Lang class," Mr. Pency says, smiling. "Hmm... He's exceeded my expectations."

Mine too. "Thank you for your time and for your support of Emma, Mr. Pency. And thank you for making Jax attend AP Club as his community service. I hope he chooses to stay."

CHAPTER 20

ADELE QUESTIN

"W e did it!" I squeal to Alonzo as we exit the gym in the swarm of bodies after the assembly. I must've squealed too loudly because several students turn around to glare. *If it bothers you, plug your ears*, I want to say.

"Great job, Adelay," Alonzo says with a snort.

I punch Alonzo's shoulder. "Not funny."

"National Merit. Another thing we have in common," Alonzo says, rubbing his shoulder.

Now, when he brings up our commonalities, it automatically makes me think of Rosie, which makes me want to ask Alonzo about her and how much they have in common, and by comparison, how little we have in common. I'm his "at-school friend," which keeps repeating in my brain. When he brings up what we have in common, is he convincing himself that we should be friends?

"We need to celebrate with ice cream," I say.

"Can't. I have to work."

Does he have to work? Or is he going home to celebrate with Spanish-speaking, sweet Rosie? It's times like this when I wonder, Am I temporary?

Alonzo continues. "In fact, I need to get going or I'm gonna be late." Alonzo pulls me in for a side hug. "Congrats, my friend." He jogs toward the main entrance door and is gone. I still need to walk through the two hundred wing to get to the student parking lot on the other side of campus.

"So," a deep voice behind me says, and I turn around. Jax says, "you and Alonzo are tight."

"If by 'tight' you mean we're close, then, yeah. We've been friends since our freshman year." Maybe Alonzo and I are better friends than I think and Jax surprises me. I never thought he'd be the type to pay attention to anyone but himself.

"Mr. Johnson's comment about Emma was pretty shady, right?" Jax says.

"If I'm being truthful, I was surprised she made the cut." I shrug my shoulders. "I tend to stereotype people." As soon as I say this, I slap my hand against my mouth. I drop my hand and add, "Actually, Emma is smart."

"You probably thought I was just another stupid jock until today."

"Of course not. You're in AP classes." I can't believe I just told him this. He probably thinks I'm a creepy stalker or something.

His eyebrows raise. "So, you noticed." He smiles. And he has a great smile.

I clear my throat. "You're tall and hard to miss coming out of classes." Did I seem normal enough right there? Maybe I still sound like a stalker.

"Fair enough," Jax says.

We both exit to the parking lot.

"Well," Jax says, pointing to a Tesla. "This is me."

I point toward my Beemer two rows away. "That's me over there."

"Okay then. See ya," Jax says.

"See ya." As I walk away, I wonder if I should've asked him if he wanted to get ice cream with me. Ridiculous idea. Not in this century would he want to celebrate with me. Just because we've eaten lunch together, go to AP Club, and disagree with the AP petition doesn't make us besties. I pull out my phone from my pocket and scroll to Dad's contact info as I walk to my car. He's told me not to text him during work hours unless it's an emergency. Is finding out I qualified to be a National Merit Scholar an emergency?

Probably not. Then, I scroll to my mom's number and text her the good news.

I step into our entryway and holler, "Maria! I qualified as a National Merit Scholar!"

Maria strides out of the kitchen into the entryway. "What's this? What is National Merit?"

"It's *importante*. An honor. There are scholarships. Um... *la beca*."

Maria wipes her hands on a kitchen towel draped over her shoulder and places them on both of my cheeks. "Such a good girl. So smart."

As I'm heading up to my room, I realize that telling someone who doesn't have high-school-aged children, and who doesn't know about the College Board and PSATs is like sharing a delicious meal with someone who doesn't have taste buds.

I pace my bedroom floor. Who can I text or FaceTime? Are any National Merit qualifiers in my contacts, other than Alonzo? Hardly. I could text Payton, from Pep Club, but what would she care? I sit at my vanity table and pick up my brush to run it through my hair. After sixty strokes or maybe closer to fifty, I set my brush down. I open my playlist to find a song that'll match the euphoria I want to feel. I press play and turn up the volume for "Happy" and bounce around my room for about ten seconds, then hit pause. I switch to "Can't Stop the Feeling" and my body wants to dance but my mind won't let me. Besides, I dance weird. So what if I am alone in my bedroom? It's still weird.

I head back downstairs and open the fridge for a snack. Nothing in there grabs me either. I pick up my wallet and keys from the entryway table. "Maria, I'm heading to the Chilly Swirl."

"Perfect. Ice cream for the smart girl. *Buena*."

The moment I enter Chilly Swirl, I see Emma sitting at a table with two guys. I think one is her brother. I get in line behind a couple of elementary kids with an adult.

"The mango's good."

I recognize Emma's voice and am glad she joined me in line. I was starting to feel awkward standing here solo. I say, "No salad today?" *Crud!* Why did that burst out of my mouth when she's being nice? "Sorry. My mind can't keep up with my mouth sometimes."

"You're forgiven." Emma smiles at me, which is generous considering what I just said. She adds, "I'm here celebrating National Merit with my brother and his friend. Want to join us?"

"Sure. I'm celebrating too... Congratulations, by the way."

"You too!"

I say to the clerk, "I'll have the mango. In a cup, please."

"Mine's in a cup too!"

The more I hang with Emma the more I realize we're alike. When we both arrive at the table, Emma says, "This is my brother, Pete, and this is Greg, his obnoxious friend." She smiles at Greg, and he winks at her. "This is Adele."

"You're seniors, right?" I say.

"Yeah. They're both football players, so they think they're all that," Emma says, puffing out a laugh.

"Why is it that being an athlete gives students more status?" I ask, cringing at how sassy I just sounded.

"Fair question, I s'pose," Greg says. "Admit it. There was an entire assembly today showing off smart people."

"Do you really think the ten students standing in front of the entire student body increased their chances of getting a prom date with their National Merit status?" I ask.

"There's a lid for every pot, Mom used to say," Emma says.

"I'd ask a smart person to the prom," Greg says.

Is his comment for Emma or all smart women?

"Were you surprised by any of the qualifiers?" I ask, then shove a spoonful of ice cream into my mouth.

"I was surprised by Mr. Johnson's comment about Emma." Greg turns to Emma and points his spoon at her. "You should complain to Mr. Pency."

"Mr. Johnson owes you an apology," Pete echoes.

Emma says to Pete, "I hate it when you say what is so obvious."

I laugh, surprised that nice ol' Emma is speaking up for herself.

"Actually, I'm still stunned by all of us from Miss Halden's," Emma says. "We're not in AP Lang. Not in calculus. I'd call us average."

"Average? Nuh-uh," I say. "Alonzo's the smartest guy I know. He's anything but average... You ever think about signing up for AP?"

"Sure, I've thought about—"

"Cheerleaders aren't supposed to be smart," Pete says.

"That's so wrong!" I say as I scowl at him.

Emma says to me, "Thank you."

I say to Pete, "How can you be upset with Mr. Johnson but say that to her?" *That's total crap!*

"At least I'm not saying it to the entire student body," Pete says.

"That's a weak argument," I say.

Emma points her spoon at her brother, then Greg. "Both of you have said I shouldn't be smart."

Greg shakes his head. "I've never said you shouldn't be smart. In fact, I've told you to sign up for AP."

"He's right, Em," Pete says. "Greg never said that. I have. Doesn't mean I believe it. I'm just repeating what guys say."

"Why would you repeat something so stupid to your sister?" I ask.

Emma says to me, "You sure don't hold back, which is awesome."

Pete frowns at me and Emma jumps in for the rescue. "Adele has a point. Why repeat something mean and, like Adele said, stupid?"

Now Pete is scowling at Emma. He says to Emma, in his bossy older brother tone, "I'm just trying to protect you. People are supposed to be predictable. When they don't do what people expect, it throws off things."

This conversation is so weirdly like what Alonzo and I have been talking about. I say to Pete, "Even though what you're saying is true, it doesn't mean it's right or okay. Your thinking has flaws. Stereotypes are usually wrong."

Emma says, "Exactly! What if people change? What if someone is two stereotypes?"

"Yeah." I crumple my napkin and get up to throw away my garbage. What kind of awesome would school be if students and teachers didn't stereotype each other? What kind of awesome would a whole community be?

Chapter 21

Alonzo Hernandez

"**Y**ou look tired and cranky this morning," Adele says to me as we walk into the back entrance. "Did you work too many hours?"

"That's not it." I rub the back of my neck. "I don't want to talk about it right now."

"So, not now. Maybe later?"

I wish she'd just let it go. "Something happened at home. That's all I'm sayin'." I press my palms toward her and watch as Adele's eyebrows lift. I shouldn't have said it was about home.

"Did something happen with Rosie?"

My eyes squeeze shut. "No." We stop at our lockers, which are near each other, so I can't avoid her. If I tell her, she won't understand. The first bell rings, and I'm relieved to head to class and get away from the questions.

First- and second-period classes are behind me, and I don't remember squat. All I heard was like the Charlie Brown teacher, "Wah, wah, wah, wah," in the Charlie Brown Valentine movie my elementary teachers made us watch every year to teach us to give everyone a Valentine's card. Adele and I have third period with Miss Halden. Adele's questions are going to start up again. I can't handle an interrogation right now, so I walk slowly so I'll arrive at Miss Halden's as the bell rings. This way, Adele can't pound me with cross-examination.

When I reach the classroom, Miss Halden greets me at the door, and we walk in together to applause. At first, I'm confused, then I see on the board: *Congratulations, Emma, Adele, and Alonzo!* Our classmates must've applauded Emma and Adele when they arrived earlier.

"Thanks, everyone," I say, then quickly take my seat.

Miss Halden hands out a few pages from *The Crucible*, a play by Arthur Miller that we'd read in the fall. After we reread the pages and write in the margins, we organize our desks into a circle, preparing for a Socratic Seminar about accusations and revenge.

Could today get any worse?

After about ten minutes, the seminar discussion slows down. "Alonzo, what do you think?" Miss Halden asks even though I've kept my head down, trying to be invisible.

"Pass," I say, because we're allowed one pass per month. I've never used my passes and shame burns my cheeks. I just can't get into accusations with these people right now.

The discussion finally and mercifully ends, and I'm loading my binder into my backpack.

"You must be having a bad day," Adele says as she arrives at my desk, "because you usually love Socratic Seminars." As much as I'd like to hide in the bathroom for lunch to avoid the conversation we're about to have, I'm hungry. My basic needs are forcing me to be with the most curious person I know.

Once we're settled at our lunch table, Adele asks, "What's up with you today?"

I decide to just jump in. Here comes the canyon of separation, the reminder that the caste system is alive and well.

"My mom has a housecleaning business."

"Okay," Adele says with a shrug.

"Rosie's mom works for my mom."

"Okay," Adele says, again with a shrug.

I take a bite of my ravioli, which is a little rubbery, so I chew more than usual. This buys me time to decide how I want to roll out this story. "Last week, Rosie's mom was cleaning a house... More like a mansion. And this lady that lives there has more crap than she can keep track of." I hear the bitterness in my voice, and I don't want to disguise it.

"Okay," Adele says.

"*Stop* with the 'okays.' Just listen." I glare at Adele.

Adele nods and bites into her sandwich. I can see on her face that she wants to say "okay" again, just to be a smart-ass.

"This lady thinks Rosie's mom took a necklace... A very expensive necklace."

"The lady doesn't keep her jewelry locked up?"

"Why should she have to do that?" If this was a chemistry experiment and I was a beaker, I'd be boiling over right now. Adele probably can see my chest expanding. "If Rosie's mom isn't a thief, then why would that lady have to lock her crap up?" I'm holding my voice steady to cover my seething anger.

Adele just shrugs and takes another bite of her sandwich. I shove in another bite of ravioli.

When Rosie and I talked about her mom last night, Rosie was like, "My mom works hard. Gets to work on time. Does more than is expected and then this is her reward for hard work? That lady just can't keep track of all her jewelry!" We both know her mom's honest and wouldn't steal anything. Adele? She's been shaking her head like a bobblehead doll for the last few minutes. And that shrug? Why wouldn't she believe me? Does she think Rosie's mom took the necklace? My teeth are gritting; my jaw is starting to throb.

"Hey, guys."

I look up to see Emma standing there. Adele and I were so intense in our conversation, I didn't notice Emma walking up to us.

She says, "Okay if I sit with you?"

"Sure," is all I say. I should be more welcoming, but I can't worry about other people's feelings right now.

Emma sets down her bag and sits. "The timing of today's Socratic Seminar in Miss Halden's class was weirdly coincidental, right?"

You have no idea.

"Weird how?" Adele asks Emma.

"Well, Mr. Johnson's slam about cheerleaders was kinda like an accusation," Emma says. "I complained to Mr. Pency before school today."

"You talked to Mr. Pency? That's awesome," Adele says, nodding. "Accusations *are* like stereotypes. What Mr. Johnson said was shady. A lot of people were shocked."

I wonder if Mr. Johnson had made a comment about me qualifying for National Merit, would I ask for an apology? I wonder if Adele sees the similarities between the accusations and stereotypes with Rosie's mom and Emma. Why is she so eager to defend Emma and not Rosie's mom?

Emma says, "Did you see Miss Halden's face when Mr. Johnson said, 'Wow. A cheerleader'?"

"No," I say. I was too nervous waiting for my name to be called to notice much.

"She was pissed!" Emma says.

"Miss Halden's got our backs," I say, then take another bite of my overcooked ravioli. She's been on my side for as long as I can remember, encouraging me.

I'm glad Emma showed up. When Adele and I were talking about Rosie's mom, I was about to blow up and yell at her. I want us to be friends and all, but there's a canyon separating Adele and me, and a bridge connecting Rosie and me. Sometimes, I'm not sure how to build a bridge with Adele.

CHAPTER 22

MISS HEATHER HALDEN

Today, I wonder if I'll see Jax at our AP Club session today. And what was up with Alonzo during third period's Socratic Seminar? I hope he's not worn out from school, work, and AP Club. I'll check in with him at today's session. If he's at the session.

I'm nervous about the prospect of my club members dwindling. I interrupt my thoughts realizing I'm engaging in slippery slope and hasty generalizations. I chide myself for falling into this faulty logic trap. Human nature, I guess. For the AP Club members this evening, I'm reviewing examples of faulty and exemplary logic using excerpts from some of our great thinkers, like Aristotle and Karl Marx, who thankfully help us to be rational. I guess I need to apply their logic to my own thinking.

I'm preoccupied, skulking at every corner, hoping to avoid Mr. Johnson. I know it sounds crazy, but I've locked my door so no one, namely Mr. Johnson, can barge in on me during my lunch. With my bagel and cream cheese in one hand, I distract myself by scrolling through my inbox. I read an email from an American History teacher telling me he overheard two of his juniors talking about a petition against AP club students taking the exam. He said he supported our AP Club and to let him know if there's anything he can do. I had hoped the petition would have died down by now. Why is it that when someone sticks their neck out, an ax is raised at the ready?

I've made it through the school day without run-ins with Mr. Johnson, though I'm not quite in the clear because I'm still at school for Alonzo and AP Club. It's five o'clock and Alonzo hasn't come to my classroom yet. I furtively poke my head out of my classroom door scanning the hallway left and right, feeling like an idiot. Aristotle would be so disappointed in my lack of rational thought. The coast is clear, so I tape a note onto my door: Be back by 5:10 and head to the staff lounge to grab my chicken and mixed greens salad out of the fridge, which was intentionally a grab-n-go meal to minimize potential contact with the odious Mr. *Creepers* Johnson.

I tamp down my irrational thoughts as I swing open the staff lounge door and take a deep breath. I have an AP Club session soon and need my head clear of worries and frustration. Should I share my worries about the petition with my AP Club members?

CHAPTER 23

JAX LOURDE

It's after basketball practice, and I'm heading out of the locker room, toward the commons to wait for AP Club to start.

Mr. Pency called me into his office this morning to tell me I didn't have to go to AP Club anymore. Imagining relaxing at home on my bed tonight sounds amazing, but the AP Club is amazing too. Maybe it's Miss Halden's way of teaching. Maybe it's the other juniors in the club. Maybe it's the whole mess with me not serving my suspension and feeling like I should pay my debt. I'm not sure why exactly, but I'm staying in the club.

While I was in his office, I considered telling Mr. Pency about the AP Lang and Comp students' petition. This week, at least four times, I've refused to sign it and told them their bandwagon approach was ridiculous. I purposely used a faulty logic term against them. It made me sound like a dick, but it was worth it. Before AP Club, I would have signed the petition and thought the AP Club members were posers. Now I know better. Instead of telling Mr. Pency, I decide it's time to bring it up again to my AP Club friends.

I walk into the almost deserted commons, spot Alonzo sitting at a table reading, and walk toward him. "Okay if I join you?"

"Sure," Alonzo says as he closes his book. It's *Narrative of the Life of Frederick Douglass*, which surprises me because it's an AP book. Why would grade-level juniors be reading that? Then, I stop. I realize I'm acting exactly like the AP Lang juniors with their petition. I'm making a hasty generalization, and the National Merit qualifiers prove this more than ever. There were some unexpected people standing in the gym next to Mr. Johnson and Mr. Pency, me included.

"Working on homework?" I ask, spinning my basketball on my finger.

"Yeah, Miss Halden wants us to choose a quotation and do a quick-write. It's due Friday."

"What quote are you going with?" I grab my basketball with both hands and set it on the floor between my feet.

"I like the one where he says…" Alonzo turns to a page with a sticky note on it. "'I had as well be killed running as die standing.' I like it because it's all about taking action, no matter the cost. And about not standing still and enduring the bad without a fight."

"Being killed, though?"

"Yeah. I mean… I don't want to *die* over something, but I'll suffer the consequences," Alonzo says.

I hate hearing the words, "suffer the consequences." It reminds me of my situation—the stuff between Raleigh and me.

"For example, I joined the AP Club and could suffer consequences," Alonzo says. He twirls his book on the table, then stops and looks at me. "I'm lying to my parents about where I am on Tuesdays and Thursdays. They don't want me in the AP Club."

"What kind of parents don't want their kid to learn more in school?"

"My papá has a different future in mind for me. We disagree and I'm lying because of it."

"You think you'll get caught?" I ask.

"Papá—my dad—is usually at work when I get home. My mama assumes I'm at the Sudsy Auto." Alonzo fidgets with the memoir, spinning it on the table. "Papá came home early last Thursday and asked me where I was. I talked my way out of that, but it stresses me out. To lie, you know?" He raps his knuckles on the table like he's knocking on wood. "I haven't been caught yet."

I can see in his eyes that he hates lying. I think of the times I've lied, like it was perfectly normal. Alonzo's a decent guy... like Raleigh. I swallow a lump in my throat.

Alonzo jumps in. "I have this thing with my neighbor... a friend's mom. I want to help her but don't know how."

"What's goin' on?"

"My friend's mom was fired on Friday," Alonzo says as he's looking at the table. "She's a house cleaner and the lady that lives in the house accused her of stealing an expensive necklace."

"That's intense," I say.

"But she didn't." Alonzo looks directly at me. "Didn't take the necklace."

Why is he telling me this?

Apparently, Alonzo has the same thought. "I don't know why I'm telling you about this. It's not your problem and, besides, what can you do?"

"I dunno. Two heads are better than one, right?" I'm like a fish on a hook when it comes to a problem to solve. "If she didn't do it, then is there another house cleaner? Someone that can look for the necklace? It sounds like the lady misplaced it or something." I bounce in my seat. "Ooo, maybe the husband took the necklace and gave it to his side squeeze." I might be right.

"What? No! That didn't happen," Alonzo says.

I can tell he's wondering too.

"Anyway, my mom owns the housecleaning business. She lost the job completely, so there's no way Mama could look for the necklace now."

"Could you go to the lady's house and tell her she's wrong? That Rosie's mom didn't steal the necklace?"

Alonzo's eyebrows press together. "Why would she believe me? She already made up her mind."

"Is there a way to protest a bogus firing? You know, like a labor department or—or a Better Business Bureau?"

"Again, why would any of them believe Rosie's mom? It would be her word against the lady that owns the house."

I swear, every muscle in Alonzo's body is flexed. "Sometimes people get justice," I say.

"When? Where?"

"I dunno. In the movies." I admit my answer is lame. "Maybe we—you and I—could do something?"

"Yeah? Like what?"

"Where's this house? We could stake it out, watch for the new house cleaner, and then ask her to look for the necklace." I feel like I'm picking up speed with this, and ideas are flowing. "What if we replace the necklace? I mean, how much are talking here?"

"Why would we buy this lady another necklace? Like she needs more jewelry."

"Sure, the lady doesn't deserve the necklace, but your friend's mom deserves justice."

Alonzo's shoulders lower away from his ears and his breathing slows down. "Rosie's mom does deserve justice," he says.

"At least it would clear her. Prove she didn't do it." I pick up my basketball, place it on the table, and lean my hands and chin on it. "You've already shot down the other solution, so…"—I smile at Alonzo—"this is what we're left with."

"Where're we getting this money?" Alonzo's glare is killing my optimism.

"I dunno. Just brainstorming."

Alonzo sighs and puts his book and notebook in his backpack. "Let's just go to Miss Halden's room. My head's gonna explode if we keep talking about this."

We start walking toward Miss Halden's room. I can't stop thinking about Alonzo's neighbor and want to keep talking but Alonzo is done with that conversation. Justice for Rosie's mom makes me think of justice for the AP Club members. "Onto another topic. The petition is still alive. Eric and a few others are still asking for signatures."

"What I don't get is what difference would it make to them if I take the exam?" Alonzo says, his eyes darkening.

"Maybe they're worried you'll earn a five and they'll earn a four," I say, the corners of my mouth lifting.

Alonzo stops, nods, and then he smiles. "You might be right."

I set my hand on Alonzo's shoulder. "How about we talk to Adele and Emma tomorrow at lunch?"

"Yeah. Let's figure out how to put a stop to the petition."

CHAPTER 24

MISS HEATHER HALDEN

With my chicken salad in hand, I return to my classroom, and Jax and Alonzo are standing near my door. Just seeing them there makes my heart somersault and my grin stretches to my ears.

"Look who's the canary that ate the cat," Jax says. "What's up, Miss H.?"

"Don't you mean the cat that ate the canary?" Alonzo says, giving Jax a sideways glance.

"It sounds better the way I said it, right?" Jax says with that winning grin of his.

"You guys crack me up," I say, unlocking my door. It occurs to me that the AP Club members and I have relaxed into a rhythm that feels like joy and fun. There's no way an AP-student petition can dismantle this.

I'm tempted to express my surprise at Jax being at this session, but I'm afraid I'll ruin this moment. Instead, I turn to Alonzo and say, "You're usually here around five o'clock. Everything okay?"

"Yeah, Miss H. I was just in the commons. Sorry I didn't let you know," Alonzo says.

I smile at his use of Miss H. "It's okay, Alonzo. You probably had plenty to talk about... I'm glad you're here."

Alonzo doesn't look as angry as he did during third period. Jax probably had something to do with that.

CHAPTER 25

ADELE QUESTIN

I arrive at Miss Halden's room a little early for AP Club and see Alonzo and Jax sitting near each other, looking like they've been besties since grade school. I'm not sure how I feel about this. Happy? Jealous? Both? I tuck my hair behind my ear as I bend over to set my backpack on the floor. "Hey, guys." I sit next to Alonzo. "What's up?"

"Nothin'," Jax and Alonzo say at the same time.

I swivel so I can see both of them, my chin lowers, and I stare at them through my eyelashes. "You guys are up to something."

Jax looks at Alonzo.

"I'll tell you later in the car," Alonzo says to me. "I promise..." His eyes burrow into mine. "And it's not about Rosie, so *don't even* wonder."

My head shakes a little. "Okay..." There's no point in pressing him for more information. I change the subject. "I watched *The Crucible* with Winona Ryder last night since Miss Halden said we were going to have a Socratic Seminar today during class. It's geeky, I know. But I wanted to refresh my memory. Movies mess up storylines, but this one did a pretty good job."

"Right?" says Emma as she sits down behind me. She obviously heard our conversation as she arrived. I turn around to face her and she says, "I have to read the book before I watch the movie."

"Me too!" The more I get to know Emma, the more I like her. "Where's Natalia today?"

"I think she's coming." Emma shrugs.

Hm. I thought Emma and Natalia were besties.

"Three more minutes and we're getting started," Miss Halden says.

I turn in my seat to face Miss Halden.

She holds up a stack of handouts and points to a stack of small whiteboards. "Could I get a volunteer to hand out this faulty logic cheat sheet, these whiteboards, and the markers?"

Alonzo stands to help and Jax does the same. Alonzo pauses to chat with Judy and Samesh as he's handing out the boards. Somehow the AP Club makes us all sort-of friends. I smile as I look around at us sitting in Miss Halden's room. After school!

Jax asks Miss Halden, "How come we work on logic so much?"

"It's usually a weak area for juniors taking the AP Lang exam. It helps you with your argumentative skills."

Jax laughs. "I like being good at arguing." He sits down.

I have a flashback of Jax and me debating in our history class. He's different from the fall. It's like, now, he'd debate to know the truth instead of just win. I don't know. I'm probably overthinking stuff again.

"Let me state that differently," Miss Halden says. "Helps with your persuasive *essay* skills." Her eyes twinkle like she's messing with us.

Before I can stop myself, I turn to smile at Jax. I swivel back around. Cringe. Why did I just smile at him? We both like to debate. Both are sassy. But it's not like I'm interested in him.

Natalia hobbles in with her plastic boot still on her foot and sees us sitting together. She smiles and sits next to Emma who is next to Jax.

Miss Halden projects quotations and situations on the screen one at a time and we write as quickly as we can on our whiteboards whether we think a statement is logical or faulty logic, plus we identify the faulty logic term. Then, we wave the whiteboards like we're brokers on Wall Street or something. My brain is working on overdrive and some of the faulty scenarios embarrassingly describe things I've done or said. My impression of Emma? A hasty generalization. And when I debated in history class with Jax? I was attacking him, *ad hominem*, more than I was attacking the issue. I always thought I was more logical than I actually am. I need to work on that.

When our logic session ends, Jax says, "Coach wanted us to rest today but I feel like I just worked out." I turn around and he's slumping in his seat, hanging his arms to his sides. I blurt out a laugh and look around to check if other people laughed too. I hate it when people don't have the same sense of humor as me.

Thank God Alonzo laughs and adds, "I broke a sweat."

I'm not as weird as I thought.

"That was hard, Miss Halden," Emma says with a smile.

"I have another ... um situation that might be hard as well," Miss Halden says as she sits down in a student desk, looking grumpier than I've ever seen her. We scoot our desks into a lopsided circle. "I've heard from a few teachers that there's a petition being circulated regarding you all taking the AP exam." Miss Halden blinks a few times, like she's blinking away tears. "I'm sorry to share this with you but I thought you deserved to know."

"It's all right," Jax says. "We already know." Everyone nods.

"How do you all feel about it?" Miss Halden asks.

"It's bogus," I say.

"Definitely bogus," Emma agrees.

"When students asked me to sign, at first, I said I didn't have a pen, but then I just came out and refused." Jax smiles. "It felt good."

Natalia shrugs, saying, "Sorry, guys, but I signed it. I didn't know how to say, 'no.'"

"God, Natalia," I say. "Didn't know how to say, 'no?' Have some self-respect."

"Adele," Miss Halden says with a warning glare.

"Sorry, Natalia," I say, though I don't mean it.

Natalia shrugs again. "I thought they might be right. Maybe we shouldn't take the exam."

"That's absolutely not an option!" Miss Halden says, her voice loud. Like basically yelling. She takes a breath. "What would you all like to do about the petition?"

Samesh says, "We could write a letter to the editor."

"Yeah," Alonzo says, "in the school newspaper."

"I could talk to Mr. Johnson and Mr. Pency," Miss Halden says.

"We could ask to be on the school board agenda," Emma says. "Last spring, cheerleaders had to give a presentation about our community service, and the board members really liked it. Why not give a presentation about this club? About our goals and what the club means to us."

For about ten seconds, I swear you could've heard a mouse fart, then Jax and Alonzo break the silence with applause and the rest of us join them.

"That's a brilliant idea, Emma. I'll talk to Mr. Pency about getting on the agenda," Miss Halden says.

"Having the board on our side should shut down the petition," Alonzo says.

There's a remote chance that the board will agree with the petition. I decide not to say this out loud. Everyone looks so happy right now.

The moment Alonzo and I are at my car, I ask, "So, what's going on?"

"You know how I told you about Rosie's mom being fired?" Alonzo sets his backpack in the seat behind him, and we both climb in.

"Yeah. Over the missing necklace." I start the car, and we're on our way.

"I told Jax about it, and he was saying we should replace the necklace or ask the new housekeeper to find it."

"Wait. What? That makes no sense."

Alonzo sighs. "Jax and I were sitting in the commons before AP Club and he said he wanted to help, so he started brainstorming. He thinks if the new house cleaner finds the necklace, whether for real or we ask the house cleaner to plant one in the house to be found, then it clears Rosie's mom's name."

"What are we? Elliot and Olivia in *Law and Order*?"

"I know it sounds out there, but isn't it better to do something than do nothing?"

Why would we do something? "Who's the new house cleaner that's planting this necklace?"

"We don't know yet."

"What do you mean, 'don't know yet?'"

"Jax thinks we could stakeout the lady's house and figure out who the house cleaner is."

"Oh, sure, you're going to look for a person pulling into the driveway with a mop and bucket in the back seat?" I say a little too sarcastically. Doing nothing sounds like a better option.

"Pretty much," Alonzo says as his brows meet in the middle of his forehead. "Do you have any other brilliant ideas?"

"Figuring out what kind of necklace you're replacing and somehow returning it to the lady sounds impossible. Why not find a lawyer who would take this on pro bono?" Leave it up to the professionals instead of a few students.

"What's pro bono?" Alonzo asks.

"Law firms have to donate hours of free legal service."

"Rosie's mom won't accept something for free. She's proud that way. Besides, what's more interesting," Alonzo asks with a huge grin, "staking out a house looking for a house cleaner or contacting a law firm?"

"What's more interesting: Going to school or going to jail for tampering with a situation where you have no business putting your nosey nose into it? Ever hear of fraud?" I pull into the bus station and Alonzo climbs out of my car. I lean out of my window. "You're crazy talking, my friend."

Alonzo just smiles and says, "I know, but isn't it great?"

What the hell is Jax thinking? Staking out a house? Someone could call the police, thinking he's casing the place. Replacing a necklace? A housekeeper helping us? Jax and Alonzo are insane.

CHAPTER 26

ALONZO HERNANDEZ

I sit down at our lunch table and am struggling to open a ketchup packet.

Emma says, "Here. Give it to me." She opens the packet with one swift tear.

"Thanks!" I squeeze ketchup onto my paper plate.

Jax says, "I was just telling Emma about our necklace idea."

Emma and Adele share a glance.

I ignore their skepticism. "I talked to Rosie last night, and she showed me the type of necklace that was lost." I pull out my phone and click on a link for a David Yurman site. "I guess the lady who owns the house showed Rosie's mom a picture when she accused her of stealing it."

Adele whistles when she sees the necklace. "David Yurman is top-of-the-line. My mom has a few of his designs."

His designs? What is *that*?

"It's beautiful!" Emma says.

"This piece of string with a medallion costs a ridiculous thirteen-hundred dollars," I say, trying to hint to Adele that calling a piece-of-string jewelry *designs* is obnoxiously bougie.

"Small enough to lose," Adele says, bringing my thoughts back into the conversation.

Jax says, "So far, our ideas are to find the house cleaner and ask her to find the necklace. Or buy a replacement necklace and give it to the house cleaner to 'find' and give it to the lady." Jax uses air quotes as he says find. He makes his voice high-pitched. "Look what I found in the laundry hamper. A piece of string with a medallion."

Adele chimes in. "First of all, I don't think she's going to sound like that. Second of all, I think we should talk to a lawyer." She looks at each of us with a lopsided grin. "Did I mention that my mom is a defense lawyer?"

I drop a tater tot back onto my plate.

"I didn't want to say anything until I talked with my mom," Adele explains. "She says it would be difficult to prove that Rosie's mom didn't steal the necklace. My mom asked what if she *did* steal it?"

I can't believe Adele just said that and now I'm squeezing my napkin to keep from saying something that'll ruin our friendship. She's practical and looks at both sides of an issue. I get that. But this is Rosie's mom. I *know* she didn't steal.

Adele says, "There might be a lawyer that would take this pro bono, but my mom wonders, 'Where's the proof?'"

"Whatever pro bono means." Jax shrugs.

"It's free legal help," I say, like I've known what this means all my life.

Jax leans over toward Adele. "I'm gonna ignore that you're thinking Rosie's mom might be guilty. If Alonzo says she didn't do it, she didn't do it."

I like that Jax is challenging Adele. It saves me having to debate her, which is exhausting sometimes. And Jax? The way he handles Adele is surprising.

"I didn't say that. My mom did." Adele crosses her arms, which means she knows Jax called her out.

Jax glares at Adele. "It's harsh and you know it."

"Jax is right." I'm looking straight at Adele. "Rosie's mom is innocent. It's that simple." This is tense, which I predicted. It's quiet for a few minutes while we take bites of our lunches. At least Jax is standing up for what's right. I bet Emma believes me too, even though she's not saying anything right now.

If Adele knew Rosie's mom, she'd know she once found a wallet with two hundred bucks in it. She didn't take a cent, and she took the time to contact the guy's company because his employee badge was in the wallet. She helps old ladies in our neighborhood carry their groceries into their homes. People trust her. I wipe my mouth with my napkin. "Let's get back to buying the necklace."

Jax says, "Yeah. Where are we with getting the money?"

I'm thankful Jax helps shifts the conversation, which changes the energy. I loosen my grip around my napkin and pop a tater tot into my mouth.

"Not that I think your idea of replacing the necklace is a smart idea, but the Pep Club is having a car wash next weekend," Adele says. At least she's moving away from talking about Rosie's mom so my heart rate can slow down. And does this mean she believes Rosie's mom didn't steal?

"In March? Brrrr!" Emma fake shivers, which is kind of funny.

"People have dirty cars in March too," Adele says. "Anyway, Jax and Emma, you could come work at the car wash, take on extra cars and, since you're not part of the club, keep the money you earn for the necklace."

"Yeah. I could take off my shirt and we'd get a lot of extra money," Jax says, throwing his head back and laughing. I don't think I could say that and get away with it. This guy's got *cojones*.

Emma's nostrils flare and Adele sticks her finger in her mouth like she's going to throw up.

"Maybe not," I say to Jax, pointing to Emma and Adele. Jax just keeps laughing. I like having another guy around. It keeps Adele in check and the shock value is a bonus. *Take his shirt off.* He's funny.

"Mrs. Parsons is the Pep Club advisor, right?" Emma says.

"Yeah," I say.

"When it comes to library books, she's a maniac about keeping track of everything," Emma says. "She'd probably be a maniac with car wash money too. There's no way you could keep the extra money you make. She'd notice."

I know we're just brainstorming but they must know they can't do that. I'm not in a club, except for AP, and I know that. "Even if Mrs. Parsons doesn't notice, it's against the law to take money from a fundraiser."

"True," Adele says. "Sad. I thought we had something going there for a moment."

"Let's put the money issue aside for a second," I say. "The necklace is probably lost and inside the lady's house. Let's start with staking out the house and talking to the new house cleaner." I can't believe I'm actually saying this. Jax's idea that he shared in the commons on Tuesday is growing on me. Adele's facial expression is 100 percent disbelief, and it doesn't look like it'll change.

Jax says, "Tomorrow's our championship game, so I can't go to the lady's house after school."

Emma says, "Me neither."

Adele says, "I think you're nuts. I'm out." She lifts her arms in mock surrender.

"I can't. I don't have a car to sit in for the stakeout." I'm glad everyone laughs at my joke. It takes away the awkwardness of me not having a car.

Adele says to me, "Hypothetically, if a person were to stake out the lady's house, what day and time did Rosie's mom clean? The new house cleaner will probably go at the same time. This'll save someone sitting in a car when no one's showing up."

"Good point," I say to Adele. Does her question mean she might be up for staking out the lady's house?

Chapter 27

Miss Heather Halden

The end-of-the-day bell has rung, and, like every other teacher on a Friday, I'm relieved that students will head home or to the basketball game. Too many were distracted with the evening's championship game, and I'm exhausted from attempting to keep students' attention and from AP Club.

The extra AP Club hours are worth it, though, because it gives students a chance to prove to themselves how scholarly they are. Maybe apply to colleges. I'm still afraid that I'll lead them down a road with too many barriers. My stomach clenches as I stuff students' quizzes and free-writes into my bag to read over the weekend.

I think back to the first AP Club member essay from their friend's point of view. Samesh wrote what his dad would say: that he needed to be a doctor like his older brother. Judy wrote her essay from her therapist's perspective, instead of a friend's. These are two kids who already have enough pressure without joining a club to strive for more. Jax wrote from Raleigh's perspective. I've overheard students' conversations about how Jax and Raleigh aren't friends anymore. Heartbreaking. And Alonzo. He's juggling a part-time job, school, and AP Club while still maintaining impressive grades.

To finish my week on a positive note, I open my laptop and compose an email to the AP Club members' parents telling them that we've successfully completed our fourth session, and that each member has brought scholarly energy, skill, and camaraderie to the sessions. I outline what we've accomplished so far and what we'll work on in future sessions, including our board presentation. I talked to Mr. Pency and we're on the next agenda.

With my work bag slung over my shoulder, I walk to my car and imagine the parents reading my email and complimenting their children on their efforts.

CHAPTER 28

ADELE QUESTIN

My numb butt from the bleachers vibrates, and I pull my phone from my back pocket. It's a text from Alonzo telling me that Rosie's mom used to clean the lady's house on Mondays, between noon and four so the new house cleaner will probably be there on Monday. He's sharing this information as if I'm the one staking out the lady's house. Not unless I get a lobotomy and can't make good choices.

I tuck my phone back into my pocket and look up to see Jax pass the basketball to Raleigh and Raleigh score a three-pointer. Payton and I high-five. I'm still getting used to this I'm-interested-in-basketball new me. I don't think I've high-fived over sports. Ever.

The Pep Club members and cheerleaders will ride the bus for two hours after the game. I'm excited to talk to Emma without Jax and Alonzo next to us. I haven't felt this excited about anything since... since I got to see *Hamilton* on Broadway in New York City when I was twelve.

We're in the fourth quarter of the championship game and it looks like we might lose. I've never played sports, so I don't know what it feels like to win or lose.

The end-of-game buzzer startles me and as predicted, we've lost. The eleven-point margin feels better than losing by one point. But what do I know? I try to imagine what Jax must be thinking but can't. What'll I say to him on Monday that isn't a cliché? *Better luck next time. You played your best.*

It would be weird for me to sit near the front of the bus with the rest of the cheerleaders, like a total outsider. Emma and I find a spot in the middle—a neutral zone—where seats are open, and it gives us the privacy we need.

I open my phone and show Emma my text from Alonzo. "I'm trying to wrap my head around helping Rosie's mom," I say to Emma. "I mean, Alonzo and I have talked about social justice before but I'm not sure how far I'd go for justice."

Emma nods. "I'm not sure either."

"Jax and Alonzo's crazy plan could blow up in their faces—our faces if we go along with it."

"I've never gone out and protested, waved a sign, or whatever," Emma says. "But actually doing something that matters?" She lays her hand flat on her heart. "It would feel pretty awesome, wouldn't it?"

"Probably." I've never joined a protest either. I shift in my seat to face Emma. "We're kind of protesting with our board presentation."

"True." Emma smiles. "With the necklace, Alonzo is your best friend. Helping Rosie's mom is important to him and friends show up for each other."

I blink hard and a mix of guilt and fear pour over me as I replay Emma's words. *Friends show up for each other.* "Do you think I should go on that stakeout on Monday?"

"It's up to you, but, yeah, I'd go." Emma sits up straighter. "I have news too. My dad has an eBay account. You heard of it?"

"Of course," I say.

"Anyway, he showed me how it works, how to search for stuff. You're not gonna believe this... The David Yurman necklace is on eBay. It's selling for seven hundred and fifty dollars."

"It's still a lot of money, but way better than thirteen hundred." I pause a moment. "Emma? Why'd you look up the necklace if you're not sure about the plan?"

"I guess... even though I'm a little bit scared and a little bit doubtful, I'm still an optimist." She shrugs, and her lips lift into a crooked smile. "I guess I felt like I needed to do something." She squeezes my arm. "Let's talk to Jax and Alonzo about this on Monday."

I rub my sweaty palms on my jeans. "Now, it's getting real."

"Can I ask you something?" Emma says, and she gives me the side-eye. "And don't judge."

I laugh. "I can't guarantee I won't judge."

Emma laughs too. "Try not to judge." She pauses a moment, then says, "My brother, Pete, says Jax is bad news. Says he's a jerk and can't be trusted."

"Seems trustworthy enough to me," I say, though I barely know the guy.

"That's what I said to Pete. I told him people change. But he said, 'You don't know him like I do,' and I said, 'You don't know him like I do.'"

"Sounds like a stalemate."

"A what?"

"Stalemate, like you're both stuck in your opinion and can't listen to the other side."

"Then it's not a stalemate because I kinda agree with my brother that Jax *was* a jerk. Don't think I'm weird, but last night I was flipping through our sophomore yearbook. Jax looked like a jerk in his sophomore picture and basketball pics. There's one of Jax and Raleigh, with their arms resting on each other's shoulders. Jax's chin is tilted up, and he looks so cocky."

"So... what's your point?" I ask, shaking my head.

"My point is that what my brother says about Jax isn't fair. The Jax we know is helping his friend and wants to help a lady he doesn't even know."

If a guy who barely knows Alonzo is jumping in to help, what would that say about me if I didn't? I sigh, pull out my phone, and text Alonzo to tell him to give me the lady's address. "I guess I'm going on a stakeout."

CHAPTER 29

JAX LOURDE

I hate that a game we lost is a game Dad finally attended. Mom was there, too, sitting as far away from Dad as possible.

"You all played your hearts out," Coach says to the team as we sit on the locker room benches, sweaty and spent. The hardest part about losing a game is that people don't know what to say, except lame stuff that doesn't help. *"Played your hearts out"* is a weird expression, but I know Coach means well.

An urge to barf sits in my throat and I squirt water into my mouth. Nope. Shouldn't have done that. I gulp deep breaths into my lungs, and this helps a little. I bury my head in my towel and try to listen to Coach but the voice in my head is too loud telling me it's my fault we lost.

Maybe if I had served my suspension, Raleigh and I would have played more in sync. Maybe if I hadn't been required to attend AP Club, I would have felt more rested. Maybe if I hadn't been so nervous with Dad in the stands—

Coach stops talking, so I lift my head out of my towel. The guys are moving around pulling off their shells and shorts, showering, and changing into dry, comfortable clothes. It's a relief to have something to do that doesn't involve rehashing the game. When I pull on my jeans, I feel my phone vibrate and pull it out of my back pocket. It's a text from Emma. A text I do not want to look at right now, so I slide the phone back into my pocket. It vibrates again once my jeans are on, which is a nagging reminder that there's a whole school's worth of students to face on Monday. Raleigh and I leave the locker room at the same time, and I continue walking next to him rather than avoiding him.

"Sorry, dude." I'm not sure what I mean by this. Sorry for the suspension? Sorry we lost? Sorry we're not friends anymore?

"I'm sorry too," Raleigh says, and I wish I had the guts to ask what he means.

We board the bus and most of us choose seats by ourselves. I pull out my phone to queue up music and figure, what the hell, I should read Emma's text.

> Monday's gonna be tough. What do U need from us?

I feel my shoulders and back relax. I don't know what I expected to read, but it sure wasn't someone just being honest... and kind. I reply:

> Maybe just don't bring up the game? Thx

I picture sitting at a table during lunch on Monday with Adele, Emma and Alonzo and read Emma's text again: *What do U need from us?* I feel a hint of a smile on my face, and I realize I have friends who have my back. Would I call them friends? Yeah, my AP Club friends pull me away from the old Jax that, let's face it, was a jerk. The kind of guy who yelled at team members for missing a shot. The kind of guy who dances with some girl and doesn't thank her when the song ends. My AP friends push me into being what? I'm not sure yet, but I'm figuring it out.

I'm looking forward to working on our presentation to the board and standing with them to defend their right to be in the club and take the AP exam.

After the bus drops us off at school, relief floods me. Basketball is over. I remember last year after our final game. I was sad for the season to end. This year, I can't pull out of the parking lot fast enough.

Then it hits me. I'm with Dad this week, starting tomorrow morning. Here comes the interrogation about what happened in tonight's game. How do I begin to explain that the season took a downturn, starting with our appeal to Mr. Pency? That's where it all went wrong.

CHAPTER 30

ALONZO HERNANDEZ

As I buff a car door with a chamois, Papá's car pulls behind two others in the car-wash line. What's Papá doing at Sudsy Auto on a Saturday? We meet eyes, and he's pissed about something. He must've come here on his lunch break. And my brother is sitting in the passenger seat. Did something happen at his auto store? At home?

My stomach churns like the gyrating brushes inside the waterlogged tunnel. After at least ten minutes, Papá's car emerges dripping water. With wipers squeaking away condensation, it veers to a parking spot. I jog over to it and Papá's window lowers.

"Hey Papá. Bennie," I say into the open window. Bennie's face looks drawn, stressed.

"I got an email from your teacher." Papá's mouth is a straight line and his eyes are flat.

Sweat begins to gather at my hairline and dribbles down the back of my neck. "Yeah?" My mind accelerates through my assignments and test scores, but I can't come up with anything I'm missing. I have all *A*'s right now.

Papá says, "I figured I'd come by to make sure you're really here."

Really here? ... Holy crap. "Which teacher?"

"Miss Halden."

I swear my heart stops for a moment.

"Miss Halden told parents what committed scholars the AP Club members are." Papá is quiet. I hate when he's like this. But who needs words? His facial expression says it all. He's here because he knows I've lied about being at work when I wasn't.

"Papá, I can explain." I'm tempted to tell him that Miss Halden must've sent the email by mistake. But every lie I tell my parents separates me from them and I crave their comfort and approval. I want the lying to stop.

"Like I said. I came by to see if you were really working today." He shifts his car into drive. "We'll discuss this tonight." His window whirs closed.

I nod and return to the car I was detailing. Papá and Bennie pull into traffic. Bennie must be going to hang out at the auto store; he loves cars and being with Papá. I lean over the car's hood to continue buffing it to a shine. Sweat rolls from my forehead to my cheeks and I swipe away the dampness. My chest is caving in; it's hard to get enough oxygen, and I stand a moment to catch my breath. A whole day of wondering what Papá is going to say to me spans ahead. Whatever Papá has to say, it's not going to be what I want to hear.

Seven hours later, Papá is waiting for me at the kitchen table. Mama and Bennie must've already eaten dinner. Walking to the kitchen feels like I'm in a courtroom, approaching the judge towering in the bench. Damp fabric clings to my underarms and I swallow as I take a seat.

"Alonzo. Mama and I raised you to be honorable."

I pick up my fork to dig into my Spanish rice and diced chicken that's already sitting on a plate in front of me but I'm not hungry right now. I wait to speak, predicting Papá has more to say.

"You've been lying. Lying about where you are on Tuesdays and Thursdays."

Sometimes, I wish Papá would just yell. His calm voice scares me more than yelling. "I—I wanted to be in the AP Club more than... more than anything."

"More than obeying me, I guess."

Before the school day starts, I wait for Adele to arrive, standing at our usual place. I'm replaying Papá's and my discussion last night and trying to decide how I'll break the news to Adele.

Adele looks like she's in a good mood as she approaches, so maybe she'll take my news without too much drama. We fall into step with each other and enter the back entrance. "There's Jax ahead," Adele says to me as we walk to our first-period classes. "I hadn't realized how much taller he is than everyone else." She heads in his direction.

I see Jax hanging with a few of his teammates and notice Mr. Buccio, the campus supervisor that some kids call Joey, leaning against a wall nearby. It's almost like Mr. Buccio wants to catch Jax breaking a rule. We shouldn't approach Jax; it's a bad idea to go up a bunch of people we don't know. But I'm going along with Adele.

"What are you going to say to him?"

"I don't know," Adele says as we arrive near the cluster.

One of the teammates is saying something I can't hear, and the four guys laugh. Jax glances up and tips his chin at us. Adele and I stand awkwardly a few feet away from him for about ten seconds and it's obvious he's not going to turn to face us or open the circle to let us in.

"We need to get to class." I grab Adele's arm and lead her down the hall.

Adele shakes her head. "What was *that*?"

"You know how it is. We're not tight with Jax."

Adele shrugs her arm away. "Us and Jax. What are we, AP lunch-bunch friends?"

I laugh, though I'm not sure why I think it's funny.

Adele and I separate. Me to chemistry and Adele to yoga. As I walk to class, I replay my words, *"not tight with Jax,"* implying Adele and I are tight. This may not be entirely accurate. Maybe I'm more like Jax than I want to admit. If Adele were to show up in my neighborhood where me, Rosie, and some friends are talking in a circle, would I invite Adele in? Or not know how to blend my two worlds?

Adele was in a good mood earlier, but now she's upset about Jax ignoring us. How am I going to tell her what Papá said?

Adele and I meet outside our third-period English class before heading into the classroom.

"You want to eat somewhere else today, or with Jax?" It's best to check on her mood before assuming anything.

"Maybe we should see what Jax does." The whites of her eyes are showing near her lower lashes, kind of like sad, puppy-dog eyes.

"It's not like he was rude or anything," I say, and Adele's facial expression stays the same. "He just didn't stop and talk to us. It's only a big deal if we make it that way." I nod, hoping to convince her.

Adele shifts her backpack. "I can't help but wonder if this morning was a reminder of our place in this school."

"But is our place so bad?"

Adele's mouth turns up into a small smile. "I guess I like our place." We both enter Miss Halden's classroom a moment before the bell rings.

I'm paying attention to Miss Halden but I'm also thinking about Adele's and my place. The more I take it in, the more comfortable I am with being just me. Who would want to be a guy like Jax with the pressure of winning, a whole school watching me as I succeed and fail? Standing in the gym as National Merit Scholar qualifiers were recognized last Monday was pressure enough and that was just for a few minutes. Soon enough, people will forget about that assembly. But Jax? People will be talking about the championship loss for a long time.

In English class, we finished reading Frederick Douglass's memoir. Douglass's wisdom and truth inspire and enrage me at the same time. I want to be wise and fearless. Instead, I'm just enraged. Why bother with inspiration when Papá said I can't attend the AP Club anymore? Why bother with inspiration when other students want to tear me down with a petition? I guess I have one purpose in life—to work at Papá's store—but I don't see how I'll get over the injustice of this. When I try to talk to Papá, he doesn't listen. When I try to lie, he finds out. I might as well give up. But Frederick Douglass didn't give up. I should figure out a way to convince Papá I'm creating the right path for me.

First, though, I need to break my bad news to Adele.

At the start of lunch, Adele and I see Jax walk into the commons, and we both freeze in anticipation of what he'll do. The tension breaks as Jax waves at us and points to a table, nodding like a question mark. We arrive at the table, and Jax holds out a fist bump. I meet it and feel his morning snub fade.

Jax says, "So, what'd you find out about the house cleaner?"

His eagerness is obvious, and it rubs off on me.

"The house cleaner should be at the lady's house this afternoon," I say. "I gave Adele the address and she's going to watch for the cleaner when she leaves."

"Wait," Jax says as he turns to Adele. "You've decided our plan isn't nuts? Last Friday, you said, 'I'm out.'"

"Now, I'm in. I'm leaving right after school to park across the street from the house." Her eyes are downcast. "I'm kind of nervous."

I've never seen her like this—rattled and reserved.

She continues, "Rosie's mom says the house cleaner will probably leave at around four."

"Want me to come?" Jax asks. "Would that help you be less nervous?"

Adele looks at me for approval and I nod. Jax wants to be part of the stakeout? Cool.

"Sure." Adele wipes her hands on her napkin and doesn't make eye contact with Jax.

Did Adele's cheeks just turn red? I see Emma approaching our table and wave her over.

"Hey guys!" Emma says.

"What's got you so happy?" Adele asks her. "Too happy."

"Be nice," I say to Adele.

Emma laughs. "It's okay. I like Adele's sarcasm."

"Someone who likes her sarcasm? That's a first," I say, and Adele squints her eyes at me like she's pretend mad.

"I dunno why I'm so happy... Maybe because cheer is done for the year," Emma says.

"Basketball is done," Jax says. "What a relief."

"Timing is perfect," Emma says. "Now we can focus on clearing Rosie's mom's name."

CHAPTER 31

ADELE QUESTIN

I tuck my hair behind my ear again, then drop my arm at my side. I don't want to look like some flirty cretin that plays with her hair all the time. "So, you know what car I'm in? Same area as you?" I say to Jax as he, Alonzo, and I walk out of the commons after lunch. I just told Jax I know where he parks. If he didn't think I was a stalker before, he does now.

"Yep." He's all casual like we always meet in the parking lot.

"See you at my car after school." I sound like a dork, and OMG! Jax knows my car. I'm pretty sure my cheeks are about to burst into flames.

It's happening. We're not just talking about helping Rosie's mom, we're actually doing something. I think of our housekeeper, Maria, and try to imagine her stealing one of Mom's necklaces. My brain can't get there. Maria is honest and has been loyal to our family since I was maybe eight. She would *never* do anything shady, so why am I so skeptical about

Rosie's mom? I'm just practical and looking at this from a legal stand-point. That's all. It's not like Alonzo is taking my skepticism personally.

"Are you even listening?"

"What? What are you saying?"

Alonzo says, "I need to tell you something." The bell rings to get to our fourth-period classes. "I'll tell you tomorrow since you're meeting Jax after school."

It's hard to focus on my afternoon classes. What did Alonzo need to tell me? And I'm distracted by what Emma said last Friday about Jax not being a jerk anymore and our stakeout. When I see the house cleaner, how will I approach her without spooking her? Will she be willing to, at least, talk to me? Will she be willing to look for the lost necklace? All my questions swim in my mind like goldfish in a fishbowl, around and around.

I'm standing at my car so Jax can easily see me. I spot Jax and Natalia walking toward a Mini, which I assume belongs to Natalia. I didn't know they were hanging out, but what do I know? Natalia gets in her car and Jax turns and sees me. He waves, and his mouth widens into a smile. I'm pretty sure he didn't smile like that for Natalia. I ignore my heart pounding like a marching band and, instead, press my key fob to open both front doors.

He climbs in and I start the engine, then turn off the blaring music. Cringe! He's going to think my taste in retro music is geeky! I plug the address for the lady's house into my GPS.

"Style Council?" Jax says.

My eyes are as wide as they'll stretch. "You know that band?"

Jax sings in a falsetto, "You're the best thing that ever happened."

I laugh at the surprise and relief of Jax knowing a British band from the '80s.

Jax gives me a sideways smile. "My mom loves this kind of music, and I was basically raised on it." He opens his phone and shows me part of his playlist and I can see artists and bands I recognize.

"Okay then," I say. Jax becomes more like the rest of us mere mortals the more I get to know him.

"Okay then." Jax smirks and turns in his seat to face me. "What's our plan?"

"If we see the house cleaner and it's a woman, I should approach her by myself." I back out of the parking space and head toward the exit.

"Do you think you should just come out with what we want from her? Or should we act like we're just walking in the neighborhood and are curious about house cleaning?" Jax asks.

"Personally? I think we just come out with it. If we make chitchat at first, she's going to see right through us once we explain about the missing necklace." The GPS interrupts with directions and I flip my turn signal.

"You have a point."

"I'm going for her emotions," I say. "Let her know she's helping another house cleaner. That it could have happened to her, and she'd want someone to help her."

"That's good."

"Can I ask you a question not related to housecleaning?" I pause to listen to the GPS directions while my hands massage the steering wheel. I can't believe I'm asking Jax this.

Jax cocks his head. "It depends. But go ahead."

"Don't take this the wrong way, but you don't seem like the kind of guy that would stay in AP Club... You're a busy athlete and all." I'm trying to soften what sounds like an insult.

"Is there a question in there somewhere?"

"Oh. Right. How long did Mr. Pency make you stay in AP Club?"

"He told me—maybe a week ago—I didn't have to go anymore," Jax says.

I wait to allow Jax to say more but he doesn't elaborate. I blurt, "But you attended last week."

"Yep." He looks out the passenger window at businesses and reader boards zooming past. "It was like instinct took over and I just ended up there on Tuesday," Jax says to the window.

We're at a stoplight, and I turn to Jax. "Do you think you'll continue until the end of April?"

"Mm." Jax shrugs. "Probably... I'm just taking it one day at a time."

"That's such a guy thing to say."

"No, it's not."

"Yes, it is." I'm laughing now. His I-don't-know-how-I-got-there explanation is *woo-woo*. "Alonzo encouraged me to attend; I encouraged him to attend. That's how I ended up at AP Club. Probably Natalia and Emma encouraged each other too. Just think, if Mr. Pency hadn't made you go, you and I wouldn't be driving to this lady's house."

Jax's mouth tilts up on one side. "So, basically, he did me a favor."

My stomach leaps into a backflip. He's glad he's in the club with me? Glad he's staking out the house cleaner with me? I blow out a breath to rein in my emotions. "It looks that way." I smile, though I want to squeal. I pull to the curb and park my car. "Here we are." I point toward a driveway, set my emergency brake, and turn off the engine. The car is uncomfortably quiet as Jax and I sit for ten minutes staring at the driveway.

Breaking the silence, Jax says, "Too bad it's such a long driveway and we can't see the house from here." He leaps out of the car, pulls off his shirt, and throws it in the passenger seat. "I'm going for a jog."

"Wait... what?" I watch as he jogs down the sidewalk away from the lady's house. A jog? Now? I gawk at his flexing back muscles, shake my head to pull my brain back into gear, and return my attention to watching for the house cleaner.

Maybe this is what Emma's brother, Pete, was talking about. I can't trust Jax to stick with our plan. He's out jogging instead of staking out the house with me. This is going to be the most boring thing I've ever done. How do police stake out a place without falling asleep or going crazy? Jax is jogging down the other side of the street and into the lady's driveway. What is he doing? He's going to blow our cover! I press the button for the window and remember windows don't open when the engine is off. I start my car so the windows will work and then shut off the engine. "Just stay in the car and don't yell out the window," I say to myself. Laughter bursts out of me at the absurdity of what we're doing, and my stomach feels like a mop being wrung out. Finally, I see Jax jogging down the driveway toward my car. He opens the door, grabs his shirt, pulls it back on, and climbs in.

"There's a Toyota sedan parked in the driveway with one of those magnetic signs on the door. Guess what it says?"

"First of all, you could have been caught! How would you explain jogging on someone's private driveway?" I'm yelling, aware of how hysterical I sound.

"Guess. What. It. Says," Jax coaxes, ignoring my outburst.

"Something about housecleaning?"

"You got it. It says Southwest Cleaning."

"You scared me, Jax!"

"Sorry. But I couldn't just sit here and do nothing. I needed to know if it was even possible that we'd see the house cleaner. I figured I could look like a jogger who's lost his way."

"Lost up someone's driveway?" My eyes are wide.

Jax smiles. "Now we know."

Surprisingly, Jax is right. Now that we know the house cleaner is, for sure, at this house, we're able to relax and talk about our classes, our upcoming board presentation, and students at our school. I was hoping Jax would mention Natalia, but he doesn't. My curiosity needs to chill.

"Wait." I don't know why I didn't think of this before. "How are we going to talk to the house cleaner if she's in a car when she leaves?"

"You have a point there." Jax gets out of the car again.

Communication would be good here. Jax leans and knocks on my window. I open my door, and he says, "Open the hood of your car."

"Why?"

"Open the hood, then I'll walk down the driveway to ask for jumper cables."

"You're good at this. Were you, like, a detective in your former life?"

CHAPTER 32

JAX LOURDE

It's kind of eerie walking down a private driveway. You never know if some crazy person is armed and dangerous or if there's a slobbering, angry dog hoping for a snack.

I ring the doorbell, which is as elaborate as cathedral bells. A simple ding-dong would do the trick. A woman wearing rubber gloves holding a sponge in one hand answers the door. Ya gotta love clues like this and I try not to laugh at how easy this is.

"Good afternoon," I say with the friendliest smile I can produce. It helps to be a clean-cut guy, so people aren't suspicious of me. Plus, I don't have a button-down shirt, black tie, and black pants, so she doesn't think I'm at the door to talk about the Lord, our savior.

She smiles back, which is a good sign.

"My friend's car won't start, and I was wondering if you have jumper cables."

She hesitates. "Hang on." She grabs her keys out of her purse on a table in the entry hall. "Where're you parked?"

"The end of your driveway. It's a silver BMW. I can meet you there." I head down the porch steps and jog down the driveway.

She's pretty trusting. I would not have helped someone, worried it might be a trap. By the time I get to Adele's car, the woman is pulling her car next to the curb, her engine facing Adele's open car hood.

The woman gets out of her car and with her hands on her hips, peers at the engine. Does she know what she's doing? "Try starting your car," she says to Adele.

Adele gets into the driver's seat and, in seconds, the engine purrs like a lion cub. Why didn't Adele pretend to start her car? Act like the battery was dead?

"It's a miracle." The woman is being sarcastic and who can blame her? We're faking a car problem, and she knows it. She turns to get into her car.

"Wait!" Adele reaches her arm out like she's drowning in a lake or something. "The house cleaner that used to work here was accused of stealing this necklace." Adele swipes, points at her phone screen, and walks slowly toward the woman. "But she didn't steal it and thinks it's just lost somewhere in the house you're cleaning."

The woman looks confused and maybe a little pissed.

I hold out my hand. "I'm Jax, by the way."

The house cleaner looks at my hand, doesn't shake it. "I'm Elizabeth, and I should get back to work."

"I'm Adele. If this were you being accused of stealing, wouldn't you want someone to help you?"

Elizabeth looks across the street like she's thinking, then turns to Adele. "I might want someone to help, but I wouldn't want them to lose their job." She throws the jumper cables into the truck of her car and slams the trunk closed. "I don't know what you're up to, but you need to leave."

Adele and I are back in our car and neither of us move. We watch Elizabeth's Toyota disappear up the rich lady's driveway.

"Even though it didn't work, that was amazing!" Adele says.

"I know. Right?"

"When you went jogging off, I thought you were crazy!" Adele says.

"It pretty much scared the crap outta me jogging down their driveway."

Adele laughs. "And Elizabeth."

"She could've called the police on us."

"She could've slammed the door on your face when you asked for jumper cables."

"She could've shot me!"

We both laugh at my exaggeration, which settles our adrenaline.

"What do we do?" Adele asks. "The house cleaner won't help us; what now?

"I haven't thought that far in advance."

"Oh, right. You're taking it one day at a time." Adele shoves my shoulder.

"I'll think of something."

CHAPTER 33

MISS HEATHER HALDEN

I'm standing at my kitchen sink and all I can think about is my AP Club students. I've lost Alonzo. His parents have pulled him from the club. I should've seen this coming. I should've asked questions about why he was staying after school and why he was reluctant to talk about college. Alonzo is not the type of person to lie.

I rinse dishes, set them in the strainer, and sigh. No sense in hashing over it. What's done is done. It just goes to show that you really don't know a person. Jax is just as much of a surprise as Alonzo, showing up last week when he wasn't required to attend. He usually struts around school like a peacock. In AP Club, though, I see humility and maybe just comfort. It's the cocky students who are most insecure but, in AP Club, he genuinely seems proud of himself instead of always having to pretend like he's on top of everything.

I tidy the kitchen and think about this week's AP Club lessons. The club members need to finalize their board presentation tomorrow, without Alonzo. Wednesday is our board presentation.

With prom arriving soon, for Thursday and the week following, the AP Club students should debate whether women could successfully make the first move. To start, I'll pull some quotes from twentieth-century literature about the plight of women waiting for love and marriage. Then, the club members will cut loose on research and their own common sense.

When I arrive at school the following morning, prom theme posters cover the walls throughout our school. Students are asked to submit ideas for the theme. They'll vote for the winner next Thursday, and the theme will be announced next Friday. The timing is perfect. Prom equals dating rituals, equals females waiting for males to ask them out. Such an infuriating tradition. A regular Jane Austen coming-out ball where women had to receive permission to attend at all.

The board president raps his gavel on the wooden sound block which startles us all to attention. "We'll start with public comments," the board president says into the microphone, "and, after that, we'll hear from some AP Club students." Even though I'm sitting in the front row, I can't read the president's expression. He could've smiled at my students but didn't. He could've said they were happy to have us here but didn't and now my heart races even faster. I can't concentrate on any public comment and, instead, silently rehearse my opening statement.

"AP Club, we're ready for you," the president says. Still no smile.

Jax, Adele, Emma, and I approach the podium and microphone, and I start with introductions and thank the board for making time to hear about our club.

"When I approached Mr. Pency in February about starting an AP Club, I had my doubts because this was a risk. Why not just keep my head down and teach my classes? I thought. But this isn't how school works. Or should work.

"When the ten students showed up on that first Tuesday and kept showing up, I knew without a doubt that I'd made the right decision. It is my pleasure to hand over the microphone to Jax, Adele, and Emma. They will explain the AP Club far better than I."

Emma sets her index cards on the podium. "Like Cyrano de Bergerac, I was hiding in the shadows, not wanting to own my inner scholar. Miss Halden invited..." Emma laughs and looks at me. "Actually, she *told* me to join the club. She saw in me what I didn't want to see in myself. Once she opened the door, I walked into a world where I want to achieve more. The AP Club is the best thing that's happened to me this year."

The board president's face transforms from stern to soft. Is that the start of a smile? I scan the rest of the board members, and they're intent. Most are nodding and one board member's arms are folded across his chest.

The microphone squeaks as Jax pulls the flexible stand to his height. "Hi, I'm Jax." He waves at the board and the audience. A quiet ripple of laughter fills the room. He clears his throat. "Truth? Mr. Pency made me attend the AP Club."

My heart lurches and eyes widen. I hadn't anticipated that Jax was going to reveal this private information; my protective instincts are on high alert.

"When I took a seat in Miss Halden's classroom that first Tuesday, I was pissed." Jax lifts his hand. "Sorry. Shouldn't cuss at a board meeting." More ripples of laughter. How does Jax do it? He's won over the crowd in less than a minute. "But by the end of that first AP Club session ... I can't believe I'm going to say this publicly ... I was glad Mr. Pency made me go. Don't get me wrong. My AP Language and Composition teacher, Mr. Johnson, is teaching me stuff, but Miss Halden and the members in the club? I'm feeling more prepared to take the AP Lang exam and feeling more like a scholar in this club than in any other classroom. Maybe I'm not supposed to say this, but you need to know that some students started a petition against AP Club members taking the exam. I'm here to say that no petition is going to stop us." Jax takes a step back, pauses, and leans toward the microphone. "Thank you."

"I'm Adele." She places her palm on her sternum as she steps to the mic. The lime green, long-sleeve top brings out her eyes, and she's wearing less eyeliner. "Even though I had the grades and test scores to be eligible for AP classes, I was afraid to register for them." She swallows. "Afraid I didn't belong. Throughout high school, I've been trying to figure out where I fit, trying different clubs and classes. And finally, I'm in a club where I'm the real me. Then AP students had to come along and tell me I don't fit there either." Adele blinks and shakes her head. She's not looking at her notes and instead scanning the audience and board members. "Taking an AP exam isn't a zero-sum game. It's not like there are limited exams available; that if I get a 5—which I hope I will—it'll deprive an AP Lang student from also earning a 5. What difference does it make if I want to achieve more than I thought possible? What difference does it make if I'm taking extra time to go to a club that makes me happy? The petition needs to be shut down." Adele steps away from the microphone and I take her place and say, "As you can see, these club members are very passionate about being part of something that allows them to explore their capabilities."

The board member with his arms folded leans into his microphone. "I appreciate that you want to give your students opportunities, but how might it look if one—or some—of your students earn a score of two or one on the exam. How does that look for our district?"

A hand raises above the audience. "I'd like to answer that, if I may."

I crane my head to see who just said that and Mr. Mark Johnson stands. "I know I'm stepping out of protocol, but this needs to be said."

"Go ahead," the president says.

"If you review our district's scores, you'll see that we already have ones and twos. And those are from students who are enrolled in AP classes." Mr. Johnson turns his head and makes eye contact with me. My face burns. "You have my word that I will speak with my students about the petition. The AP Club students deserve to take the exam."

What just happened? Mr. Johnson has had a change of heart?

It's Thursday after school, and I'm still stunned by the board member's question about scores and Mr. Johnson's retort. Does Mr. Johnson typically attend board meetings? Was he there out of curiosity? Or was he there to defend us?

I've written *Date Debate* on the whiteboard, and club members are whispering about it. I scan the nine club members, pushing away my sadness that Alonzo is not here. "What do you think this title is about?" I ask.

"We're going to debate about historical dates and their significance?" Judy says.

"Maybe." I wait for more ideas.

Emma says, "Probably something to do with dating."

"Yeah!" Natalia says. "We're gonna debate the ideal age for kids to be allowed to date without a chaperone."

"A chaperone?" I say. "That's very Victorian!" I regret my comment immediately as most of the club members laugh. "Sorry, Natalia." I hold up my hands like a surrender. "I didn't mean that to be a joke."

"I don't get it," Natalia says, and she is not laughing. *Crud.*

Adele turns to face Natalia. "Victorian Era? Like from the nineteenth century? When really uptight people protected women's respectability by always chaperoning them."

"That about sums it up," I say. "Any other ideas?"

"I have an idea," Emma says. "Should it always be the guy that goes after the girl?"

Natalia glares at Emma like she's telepathically saying, *Of course the girl can go after a guy.* What is going on between those two?

"Yeah! We should debate that!" Adele, a hardcore feminist, says.

I try not to smile.

Adele adds, "Should a woman always have to play hard to get?"

Samesh and Jax look at each other. Jax mouths, "Yikes!"

"How do the rest of you feel about debating this topic?" Adrenaline is tingling in my arms and spine. I had a hunch the students would be invested but didn't anticipate this level of passion.

Samesh shrugs.

Jax is beaming. Oh, he's on board. "It could be educational." He turns around to fist-bump Samesh.

"Okay then," I say. "Organize into two groups and decide on your debaters. All of you will research the topic and provide support during the debate deliberation periods."

Samesh raises his hand.

"Samesh, you don't need to raise your hand in here. But go ahead."

"Could we have judges," Samesh says, "who have to research both sides and then after the debate decide the winner?"

"I wanna be a judge," Natalia says.

"Samesh, would you like to be a judge too?" I ask, and Samesh nods. "Okay. Anyone else interested in being a judge?" No one else volunteers. "Natalia and Samesh are judges and the rest of you need to decide who's on the two teams. Everyone okay with this?"

Everyone nods but Emma shrugs. I need to check in with her after our session. "Okay, then. Get started on your research."

Natalia is sitting shoulder to shoulder with Samesh. I wonder if they'll end up going to prom together. Teachers notice things. It's our job to be aware of dynamics and possible upsets, which impact their learning.

By the end of the session, both teams have submitted their resolutions. "Okay, everyone. Our Date Debate will probably be in a few sessions. A lot is happening right now. How are you all feeling?"

Jax gives me a thumbs-up. Samesh and Judy nod. Emma beams and says, "Excited."

"I miss Alonzo," Adele says.

I nod. "Me too."

As club members prepare to leave, I step toward Emma. "Could I speak with you for a moment?"

Natalia bobs her head and smirks at Emma. "Later gator."

Adele walks toward the door and says, "In a while, crocodile," which makes me laugh, then I cover my mouth. I should not be reacting to this.

"I notice some tension between you and Natalia," I whisper since Jax is still stuffing materials into his backpack. "Is this going to be a problem with the debate?"

"I don't know... maybe," Emma says as she watches Jax leave the room.

"Is there anything I can do to help?"

"It's just that..."—Emma glances toward the door—"Natalia asked me to help her with some guy and I said, 'no.' Now she's mad at me."

I laugh again, trying to rein it in, but failing. I wonder if the guy is Jax.

"What's funny?" Emma starts laughing too.

"It's just that it's ironic our debate topic is so timely!"

"I know. I thought the same thing."

We both stand still for a moment, then Emma says, "It's just that I wonder if Natalia being the judge is the best idea."

"You think she won't judge fairly because she's mad at you?"

Emma nods. "And she thinks girls... um... females can make the first move."

"Wouldn't that give you an advantage? Isn't your team arguing for equality with asking for dates. Making the first move?"

"That's true. I hadn't thought of it that way." Emma tucks her notebook into her backpack.

"My offer remains, Emma. If there's anything I can do to help with you and Natalia, let me know."

"Okay. Thanks." Emma starts to leave.

"One more thing," I say.

Emma turns back to me.

"Just curious. Did Mr. Johnson apologize after the National Merit announcement?"

Emma nods. "Actually, he did. Mrs. Annatol called me in last week and Mr. Johnson was there. He said he was really sorry for his comment. Told me he was insensitive."

I feel my eyebrows dart up. "Oh! That's good." Mr. Johnson apologizing to Emma and defending the AP Club at the board meeting. Surprising.

CHAPTER 34

ALONZO HERNANDEZ

"We missed you at AP Club last night," Emma says to me as the four of us are seated at our usual lunch table.

"We missed you" is like a knife in my heart. It's not like I had a choice. It's not like I didn't try to convince Papá to let me stay, despite lying to my parents. The bite from my burger congeals in my mouth. I sip some milk to coax it down my throat.

"How come you weren't there?" Emma asks.

"It's complicated." I gaze out the commons window. I told Adele yesterday as we were walking to lunch, and I had to blink away tears as I explained that Papá caught me in my lie.

Adele sets her sandwich on her napkin and says to Emma, "You know the email Miss Halden sent to our parents?" I'm glad Adele is explaining this; saves me from tasting my bitter words.

Emma smiles. "My dad printed it and pasted it on our fridge. Like I'm in third grade or something." In a perfect world, Papá would have done the same.

Adele continues. "Well, that email let Alonzo's parents know he was attending the AP Club when they told him he couldn't."

Emma places her hand on my arm. "I'm so sorry."

I shift my gaze from my burger to my friends. "Thanks. I told my parents I was working. I wanted to be in the club badly enough that I lied."

"It's not the same without you," Emma says.

I blink and pull a breath through my nose pushing away my disappointment. Pride is mingled in there too. I like hearing that I'm missed. Adele said the same thing yesterday, in addition to how angry she was with my papá.

Adele says to Emma and Jax, "We need to change his dad's mind."

She doesn't get it. "It's not that simple. Let it go," I say, even though I haven't let it go either. "Enough about me." I tell Emma that the house cleaner won't help us.

Jax says, "I'm workin' on a few ideas."

"You want to let us in on it?" I ask.

"Not yet," Jax says, one side of his mouth tilting up. This guy and his crazy ideas. When I think, "game over," Jax wants to stay on the court, which makes me want to stay in the game too.

After school, Adele and I exit the building toward the parking lot. I don't have to work today, so I'll catch the Metro bus and stop by my *tía's*

grocery store. My *tía* promised Papá she would confirm that I'm there. I hate that Papá doesn't trust me, but I did this to myself.

"How's Rosie's mom doing?" Adele asks as we walk toward her car. "Have you told her that we staked out the lady's house on Monday?"

"Hell no. If Rosie's and my mom knew what we were doing, they'd make us stop. They'd say something like, 'Don't make waves.'" Another deception with my parents. Will Papá find out about this too?

"That's annoying!"

Adele finds a lot of things annoying. She unlocks her car doors.

"Annoying? How?" I throw my backpack into the seat behind me and climb in.

"Nothing would change for the better if people didn't make waves. I wouldn't take an accusation without a fight!"

"Me neither... which is why we're figuring out a way to help Rosie's mom." Has Adele done a one-eighty on Rosie's mom? Even though she can be a lot sometimes, I'm glad her usual badass is back.

"Even though we haven't figured out how to get the necklace into the lady's house," Adele says, "I've been thinking how we might come up with the money to buy a replacement." She turns out of the parking lot. "You know how my mom and I are going to the city to shop for my prom dress in a few weeks? I can spend four hundred dollars."

I whistle. That's a lot o' nuts for one night. "Girls spend that much on a dress?"

"Some do. Anyway, I looked into used dresses online. I think I could save like three hundred dollars. I don't need a new designer dress."

"Designer dress? Instead of a regular dress?" I know what she means but she's being all bougie about designer this and designer that. I'm just giving her a chance to explain herself so she can hear how ridiculous she sounds.

"Trust me. There's a difference." It's stone silent for a few beats, then she scrunches her face. "I sounded like a snot, didn't I?"

"Kind of." This is what I like about Adele. One minute she's a bougie snob, and the next she's aware of her attitude. "You keep it real. It's all good."

"I was thinking... maybe I could pitch in whatever's left over from the four hundred to go toward buying the replacement necklace."

"Adele... that's—it's really generous." Generous and awkward, like she's giving Rosie's mom money. "Generous and over the top."

"You and Jax said we're brainstorming, so I'm brainstorming. For prom, you could just wear one of your dad's suits instead of renting a tux."

"For Rosie's prom, I'm renting a tux. I wouldn't fit into my dad's suits. Her mom is sewing her dress."

"What about our prom? Are you renting a tux for that too?" Adele's face looks like a kid on Christmas morning.

"I... um... wasn't planning on going to this prom."

Adele's smile drops. "What? ... We're not going to prom together?"

Oh boy. Here we go. It's like Adele's face has been wiped with bleach. "Adele. I—I never said I was going to our prom." I'm stuttering and sounding like an idiot.

"I thought you were my date. We hang out all the time. Who will I go with now?" Her voice is in the Minnie Mouse range.

"It's about six weeks away. You'll find someone."

"Find someone? You make it sound like I've lost someone."

She's not going to start crying now, is she? I can't handle crying, not with what I'm dealing with already.

"Couldn't you just go with me? I'll buy the tickets."

"No. ... Just no. Adele, you're not buying tickets and I'm not paying for two proms this year." Disappointment is etched in her face. "But if I had planned on going to our prom, you would've been my date, as friends." I'm looking into her eyes to make sure she knows I'm being sincere. "I had to choose, and I chose Rosie's prom. Please say you understand."

"I don't know. I'm just really confused right now. First, you're not at AP Club anymore. And now we're not going to prom." Adele looks down at the steering wheel and sighs. "You're gonna miss your bus."

I'm relieved she mentioned my bus, but I don't want to leave her like this. If I stay, though, what would I say that would make this any better?

"Adele? Are we still friends?"

"We're at-school friends. Isn't that what you said? I guess at-school friends don't go to prom together." She takes a huge breath like she's trying to calm down.

I grab my backpack, hitch it over my shoulder, and watch her car drive away. *"At-school friends."* Like it's a bad thing.

CHAPTER 35

ADELE QUESTIN

It's Friday morning, and I'm sitting on my yoga mat in first period, ignoring morning announcements projected on a large screen in the gym. I usually don't care all that much about what's happening at school socially, but a slide with Emma's name catches my eye. I look up at the screen and the senior class president is speaking.

"Emma Woodburn's theme, More Alike Than Different, is the winner for this year's prom," the class president says. The students in yoga erupt in cheers.

At this point, I don't want to think about prom and Alonzo not being my date. If two people go as friends, is it called a date? Two days have passed since he dropped the bomb that he's not going with me, and I still feel like I just got the news.

On Wednesday evening, I talked to Mom about shopping for my prom dress and asked her if it would be okay if I shop with my friend, Emma. I haven't talked to Emma about this, but I think she'll be up for this. This way, Mom will give me four hundred in cash, and I can keep whatever's left over. Mom will think we're insane if I tell her about our necklace plan. I can't wrap my head around the crazy plan myself. Lying to Mom is my only option. But friends show up for each other, right?

Jax, Emma, and I sit at our usual lunch table and Emma has her spiral notebook out. Alonzo approaches us holding his lunch tray and says, "It's French fry-day!"

I shake my head at his corny joke that he has said almost every Friday and point to Emma's spiral notebook. Alonzo nods and sits down.

"Okay, so if you and I buy gently used prom dresses," Emma says to me, "we'll save maybe three hundred dollars. Maybe more. The lady's necklace costs seven hundred and fifty dollars on eBay, so we need another five hundred, more or less. Tax and stuff." She writes figures on the paper.

Alonzo and I know we're not going to prom together, but Jax and Emma probably assume we are. I'm not setting the record straight. At least not until it's necessary.

"Speaking of prom dresses," I say to Emma, "do you, like, think we could shop for our dresses together?"

Emma's mouth spreads into a huge smile. "Yes! I'd love to shop with you. We'll figure out the deets later." She's nodding so fast her face is a blur. I thought making friends and hanging out would be so difficult, and here's Emma smiling and saying, "Yes." Who knew?

Jax pulls Emma's notebook in front of him. "Let's say the average dinner costs seventy bucks."

"Seventy bucks!" I say, tucking my hair behind my ear.

Jax waves his hand dismissing his thought. "Let's call it an even fifty. What if me and my date just have dinner at my house out on our patio? I could put up twinkle lights. We could save a hundred bucks that could go toward the necklace."

"Twinkle lights?" Alonzo says, smiling.

"Yes. Twinkle lights," Jax says to Alonzo.

"That's an idea... but your date would expect a dinner out," Emma snaps.

Was her tone sharper than it needed to be?

"You never know," Jax says with a smile.

"We're just brainstorming here," I say, holding up my hands like a referee. This whole conversation would have been so much easier had we debated last night at AP Club. Neither team was ready, and we asked Miss Halden for more time to research and finalize our arguments. The Date Debate is scheduled for next Tuesday evening.

The whole idea of dating is new to us, and a debate might clear up some of the confusion, such as who pays for prom tickets and dinner. Emma might have different dinner expectations if she hears both sides. We have six weeks before prom, so there's still time for me to "find someone," as Alonzo put it. I need to know if it's better to ask someone or to wait for someone to ask me.

"Jax and Emma, have you talked to your parents about using some of your prom money to help Rosie's mom?" I ask, but I haven't exactly told my mom either. My stomach muscles clench at the thought of lying to my mom. She's a lawyer and an intense cross-examiner. I've seen her in action. It's scary.

Both shake their heads. "Okay, then, that's the next thing you need to do." I know I sound bossy, but this is important, and I can't help it. "Jax, were you thinking about a limo rental?"

"I hadn't thought that far in advance. I'm just taking it one day at a time," Jax says with a wink.

I tuck my hair behind my ear for the second time in less than ten minutes and try to ignore my heart fluttering. I can't believe he remembers our conversation while we were staking out the lady's house. I cover up my nervousness by being even more bossy. "You know you need to reserve a limo way in advance. There aren't enough to go around, especially with a bunch of rentals on prom night."

"All the more reason to put the limo money toward the necklace, right?" Jax smiles at me.

I'm melting into my chair. "Right."

Alonzo says, "I told Rosie about our plans, and she promised not to tell her mom. She asked some of her friends to pitch in and she thinks she'll have about a hundred bucks and I'm pitching in fifty." Alonzo points to the figures written in the notebook. "That's a hundred and fifty from me and Rosie. We've got almost five hundred."

Me and Rosie. Me and Rosie. I can't listen to that another second. I get up to throw away my lunch garbage to calm down.

We all head toward our classes, and I walk next to Jax. "Don't you have a lot of pressure to go to prom as a huge group, like with some of the basketball players?"

"Probably. I guess I need to figure that out, huh?"

We split up and I walk to my fourth period, imagining what it would be like to go to prom with Jax. My brain can't get me there. We are in two different worlds. He didn't acknowledge me in the hallway after the championship game because he was standing with other athletes. He would never go to prom with someone like me tagging along with him and his friends. A pinch in my gut reminds me that I wouldn't belong. I don't belong as Alonzo's date. I don't belong with a guy like Jax. I sigh and my shoulders sink. I guess this weekend, I'll go through last year's yearbook to skim for possible dates to "find someone" I belong with. Someone in the Photography Club or Pep Club, maybe? I laugh at myself for believing I have any control over this. I guess I'll find out at Tuesday's debate.

CHAPTER 36

JAX LOURDE

I'm glad I was with Mom this weekend. She's easier to talk to than Dad. Mom was suspicious, though, when I asked if she wanted to go out for breakfast earlier this morning because usually when I ask her to do stuff with me, I want something. Which is true.

Mom wasn't expecting me to ask to help someone else. "I love your idea to give up something for prom," she said and, though skeptical, she agreed to give me a hundred dollars for a necklace to help someone wrongly accused of stealing. Mom's a social worker, so she gets it. She was grinning like Gengar... but friendlier, of course. She laughed at my twinkle lights idea, just like Alonzo. "You're so cute," she said. What is it with me and twinkle lights? Anyway, Mom said, "I'm so pleased." Adrenaline surged through my body when she said this, like sinking a three-pointer.

Now, I'm just lying on my bed, throwing my basketball in the air and catching it, probably a hundred times already. My belly's full of eggs and fried potatoes, and my head is full of thoughts.

Last year, prom was worse than having my wisdom teeth pulled. Some senior I hardly knew asked me, and I would've looked like an idiot if I'd said no to a hot senior. This year, I like figuring out a way to do prom on the cheap, though it makes me miss Raleigh more than ever. He'd be all in with helping someone.

Mom suggested we have a picnic at a park a block from school, instead of our patio. Maybe. Either way, it's gotta be the right girl who won't care about sitting outside.

Even though all of this is complicated, planning is the easy part. The hard part is figuring out who to ask. And it's a hugely ridiculous circus with juniors and seniors asking people to prom, filling cars with balloons, sticking candy bars on poster boards to spell out messages, delivering bouquets of flowers, and finding other over-the-top ways to ask: Will you go to the prom with me? Of course, everyone posts their "ask" on social media to look all romantic and stuff.

I'm going old school. I'm just gonna ask someone. But who? The obvious answer is Emma or Natalia but they're too vanilla. And probably high maintenance. I need someone who won't mind sitting outside. Someone who doesn't care what other people think about her not going out for a fancy dinner. I push away an obvious answer. Too scary. Too outside the box.

My phone vibrates and it's one of my baseball-basketball buddies.

> We R renting an SUV limo for prom. It holds 8. U in?

Eric knows I'm not responding right away. He can see the three dots, and it's like a timer is about to buzz. My stomach jumbles like I'm at the championship game again, on the free-throw line. Why is it so hard to say "no" to my buddies? I'm sure Mr. Johnson has talked to Eric and the others about the petition. I'm surprised Eric is even asking me to share a limo. I can't tell them the whole story about me using my prom money to help someone I don't even know. They'd think I'm crazy.

> I haven't decided if I'm going. Don't count me in for now.

Letting go of that pressure feels like I'm the Hulk throwing off a ton of boulders from my chest. Then, panic hits me. I bounce off my bed and pace the floor. I just lied to my buddies. What if my bros find out that I am planning on going to the prom and are salty with me?

> Sorry buddy. I hope U find UR 8.

I pace and stare at my phone waiting to get a reply from Eric telling me it's okay.

Ten minutes have passed. No text.

I thought for sure me speaking out at the board meeting and saying no to sharing a limo would be high key, but by this evening, I saw lots of posts about prom stuff, but no mention of me. Am I okay with being ignored? I suppose it's better than people throwing shade. If my teammates are mad at me for not going in on a limo, that's on them. What does it matter if I go or don't go with some of my bros?

What matters is I'm not letting Alonzo down.

I'm upstairs in my room and sitting at my desk, doing my usual Sunday night homework. Our AP Club debate is Tuesday, and I open my laptop so I can look over my group's research. We have a shared Google doc. I can add ideas in there and Emma, Adele, and Crystal—another club member who I don't know well—can read them too. I see that Adele has added a lot of comments to our document and it makes me laugh. She always has a lot to say, and I like that about her. I think back to our debate about Title IX in social studies and remember she was tough. I'm glad we're on the same team this time.

Our debate team members exchanged cell numbers, and I'm tempted to text Adele and Emma to tell them about my mom's offer to give me limo money toward the necklace. Nah. I'll wait till tomorrow to tell Alonzo, Adele, and Emma at the same time.

CHAPTER 37

MISS HEATHER HALDEN

I'm writing learning targets on the whiteboard near my classroom door. I hear a girl's voice uptalking. "Jax ... a limo with the guys." I can't quite catch every word, but her angry tone says it all. The girl continues, "And I know you had something to do with that."

"I don't know what you're talking about, Natalia." This voice is Emma, and clearly, the other person is Natalia. Emma and Natalia have had some tension lately, which is never good. "Jax makes his own decisions," Emma says.

"Whatever, Emma! I know you don't want Jax and me together."

"That's not—"

"Just stop! Don't bother trying to explain."

All three students are in the AP Club. This won't end well. I step over to my desk, sit down, and compose an email to the junior counselor telling her about Emma and Natalia's disagreement. They might need a mediator.

I circulate among the two debate teams as they devour the five minutes I've given them to get ready for our AP Club debate. Jax and Adele are sparring over who should deliver the debate. Jax gives in to Adele's suggestion that Emma, a woman, ought to advocate for the right to ask a guy out. Samesh and Natalia set out their research notes. Their desks are covered with notebook paper and Samesh's laptop is open to a page of notes as well.

I glance from Natalia to Emma trying to detect if there's any residual strain between them. They're sitting far enough away from each other to avoid glaring.

"Miss Halden, before we start our debate," Jax says, "both teams would like to propose a ground rule. We prefer to use the terms boy and girl. Woman, man, male and female, are too formal, and our school's athletic teams still use boys and girls."

I say from my seat in the back of the classroom, "I appreciate how you're negotiating your terms."

Emma begins. "Resolved: Any person, regardless of gender, can successfully ask someone on a date."

I set the timer for five minutes.

"Our team argues for the affirmative. Our grandmothers were limited in their job prospects. They were typically teachers, nurses, secretaries and definitely 'housewives.' And now girls have infinite possibilities. We even get to vote!"

Emma's sarcastic tone elicits some snickers, and I suppress a laugh. Adele's satire has rubbed off on Emma.

"Okay, that was a century ago. But, in our generation, boys and girls have female role models, ranging from astronauts to soccer players, from doctors to rappers, which demonstrate that anything is possible, including asking someone for a date."

Clever for the affirmative team to broaden their argument to all scenarios and not just dating.

"The other team will argue that boys need to pursue and win. This objectifies a girl as a prize rather than someone to just hang out with. When you really think about it? It's offensive.

"We believe people should lean toward their strengths. Some girls are great communicators, more confident, and would feel comfortable asking out a boy. Some boys aren't good communicators, aren't confident, and are relieved when a girl asks them for a date." Emma looks toward Natalia and Samesh. Smooth move to make eye contact with the judges, though I can't see Natalia's expression from where I'm sitting.

"To further illustrate this point of tapping into one's strengths, let's examine same-sex partners. Typically, someone takes the lead based on their strengths and it has nothing to do with gender or societal expectations.

"Stop worrying about what's considered right or wrong and do what comes naturally. And, for girls who ask a boy for a date, and that boy doesn't like it, they're not right for each other.

"For someone looking for the right person to date, why not increase your chances? It's a numbers game, so if everyone shares the burden of asking and paying for at least half or all the expenses, isn't that a win for everyone?

"Rejection hurts. What hurts more is not having a date for the prom, if that's your thing. Or feeling lonely when there's someone out there for you.

"Let's stop hanging onto archaic practices, such as girls playing hard to get or boys having to do the asking. How about just playing to our strengths?"

"Time's up, affirmative team." My lungs fill with pride. Adrenaline courses through my body and I wish Mr. Mark Johnson were here to listen to how intelligent, skilled, and courageous these club members are.

Last Thursday in English class, Alonzo handed me an envelope to give to Stewart, a member of the opposing team. He told me it contained his research and advice for his team. I could tell he wanted to be here this evening.

"For this past week," Stewart begins, "our team members have observed students. Whether we agree or disagree, gender roles are alive and well at school. Actually? Stereotypes are alive and well. We saw boys most often taking the lead in P.E.-class teams and it seemed like girls allowed them to do it. We saw girls taking notes in chemistry as lab partners, more boys in AP Calc and computer science, and more girls in AP Lang and Comp.

"Most of us observe our moms taking care of housework and our dads mowing the lawn. You might say this is 'offensive,'" Stewart says, using air quotes like Emma, "but it's the way it is. As much as we might want equality, we're not there yet. A girl risks asking a boy for a date and failing when, had she been patient for another day or two, that boy might have asked her to go to prom, for example.

"As long as these conditions exist, why would a girl choose to be a pioneer and, consequently, be left with no date?

"Boys play sports more often and stay with sports for a longer period, demonstrating that most boys like competition more than most girls. If a girl asks a competitive boy for a date, he probably is going to say, 'no,' or he'll say 'yes' and lose interest after the first date. If a girl is attracted to strong-willed, competitive boys, she needs to be patient and wait for the boys to ask her for a date.

"Oh, and the soccer player role models the affirmative team mentioned? People still talk about the sports bras they wore more than their soccer skills. Offensive? Yes. Reality? Yes.

"Physiologically, boys are stronger than girls. Girls want protection and for boys to take the lead."

I hear Adele sighing loudly and Jax quietly telling her to be respectful.

Stewart continues. "We polled girls at our school, and we found that three out of four said they wanted boys to ask them for a date. We haven't come as far as we could or should. To be successful, we need to follow the social norms that have been set for us. Girls, just wait and see. And boys? Have some guts and ask someone out for a date."

I hold up my hand. "Time's up for the negative team. You all have five minutes for deliberation, and we'll have rebuttals."

The two teams erupt in a cacophony of opinions, rehashing the two sides. Samesh and Natalia approach me at the back of the room, and I shift my focus to them.

Samesh says, "We're wondering if Natalia and I could have until Thursday to decide which team won the debate. We're going to meet during lunch tomorrow to go over our notes. We promise we'll keep our decision a secret until Thursday."

"Let's check in with the rest of the club members after the rebuttal."

I glance over to the opposing teammates, Andrew, Stewart, and Cindy. Then, over to the affirmative teammates, Adele, Jax, Emma and Crystal. I hold up one finger to communicate they have one more minute before rebuttal. The clock runs down. "Time."

Cindy stands. "The affirmative team believes that girls ought to ask a boy for a date and that they're modern in doing so. If you're such modern pioneers, why participate in an archaic ritual like prom in the first place? We have one girl on our football team. Two girls that joined the wrestling team. Girls at our school are not clambering to be 'one of the guys,'" Cindy says with air quotes. "In hospitals, 88 percent of their nursing staff are women and 33 percent of doctors are women. Only 10 percent of Fortune-500 companies are run by women. We are not there yet. Until these percentages equalize, high school students should not take risks with changing the status quo."

Adele stands. "Thank you, negative team, for confirming that girls are better communicators, with more of us in AP Lang and Comp, as you say. And the negative team says we girls need protection. Protection from what? What's dangerous at a high school prom?" Adele waits for the laughter to subside. "We heard Stewart and Cindy stating what might be construed as compelling arguments, but some statements were opinions and conjecture—the very mistakes in logic that keep us from changing for the better. We wonder if the negative team had polled boys—three out of four might have said they want girls to ask them on a date. The affirmative team is not comfortable with the status quo, which is why we emphatically believe high school students need to play to their strengths instead of playing dating games."

Adele sits down, and the club members' voices rise to deafening decibels in seconds.

I say to everyone, holding my finger to my lips, "Quiet, please." I wait for the din to die down. The excitement is palpable, which sends a tingle down my spine. "Samesh and Natalia need more time to decide on the winner of this debate." Team members groan loudly, and I hold up my hands to quell their reaction. "They'll announce the winner on Thursday, which will give them time to weigh the strengths of both teams' arguments." Each club member reluctantly nods in agreement.

"These two," I say, gesturing toward Samesh and Natalia, "have a tough job. Both teams debated with integrity, so I expect that you will act with integrity for the next two days. Do not approach Natalia or Samesh about their decision. Agreed?" I scan the club members and see them nod.

Adele says, "So bringing them donuts tomorrow is a no go, then?"

CHAPTER 38

ADELE QUESTIN

Still buzzing from our debate tonight, I'm lounging on my bed and faintly hear Maria in the kitchen singing in Spanish, which makes me smile. I'm in a good mood, which doesn't happen every day. Our board presentation went well, the debate cleared up some things about dating, and I'm pretty sure my team won. We'll see on Thursday. What's left unresolved, though, is the necklace. Even if we were able to buy the necklace and place it in the lady's house, what do we think is going to happen? The lady calls the previous house cleaner and apologizes? It's a long shot, maybe impossible. The lady could just take the necklace and not say anything. My heart squeezes at the thought.

I try to ignore thoughts about the necklace and focus on prom. The reality of finding a date creeps closer. I open my spiral notebook to look at my list of possible prom dates. Eddy Buchmaster and Timothy Turnbaum from photography club are my best prospects. Both are decent-looking, smart, aren't afraid of girls, and Timothy, especially, is funny. My quasi-friend, Payton, knows both, so she could plant the idea of asking me to prom. If I don't ask one of them first. I chew on the end of my pencil, tuck my hair behind my ear, then cross off Eddy, choosing Timothy's humor over Eddy's brains. Besides, Timothy would fit in better with Jax and Emma since we're picnicking together before prom. My Pep Club prospect is the snacky Shin Quan who is smart and a flirt, which can be fun. I'm pretty sure, though, that every girl in Pep Club is dying to have him as a prom date. I don't need that kind of competition. I cross him off my list. That leaves Timothy.

One prospect. I toss the notebook off to the side, flop onto my back, and sigh. The odds are against me. I stare at the ceiling feeling doomed before I've even tried. Then, I think of the odds against my AP Club friends and me. How we staked out a house and talked to the house cleaner—basically a stranger. How we found a replacement necklace on eBay. How we are collecting money. How we're going to prove Rosie's mom is innocent.

I sit up, fluff my pillow, and erase the lines through Eddy and Shin's names. I rank them in the order of preference and pick up my phone to text Payton.

> Any prom dates yet?

Payton is effortlessly beautiful. And nice. I bet she'll be flooded with dates. I stare at my phone waiting for a response and, after a few minutes, I set my phone on my nightstand to go brush my teeth before bedtime. From the bathroom, I hear my phone ping and pick up my phone with my toothbrush hanging from my mouth.

> 2 asks so far. Said I'm deciding.

What must it be like to be Payton? I hate having to make lists, begging Payton to help me, waiting to be asked, and likely being rejected. Do guys go through this turmoil when they're deciding who to ask? Doubtful. If only Alonzo had been willing to let me pay for the prom tickets, he and I would have gone together as "at-school friends." A small lump forms in my throat. I'm not as sad as I was when Alonzo first broke the news about prom but still, I wish I wasn't in this position. No sense in wishing for something that isn't going to happen. Besides, there's another prospect I didn't write in my notebook, which shows me the meaning of butterflies in my stomach. I thought when girls said this, they were idiotic and then I got to know Jax. I push thoughts of him out of my head. It's insane to even think about it. I sigh, look in the bathroom mirror, and then spit out toothpaste.

Back on my bed, I text Payton.

> There R a couple guys I'd like to ask me.

> I'll help you if you help me...

> What do U mean?

> Hoping Emma's brother will ask me. Since you're hanging out with her...

I Facetime Payton and she answers with a bunch of cream all over her face. I'll never be beautiful like her. I don't have the patience for facial care... or manicures. Her nails are always perfect too. I inspect my image in my phone's screen. Would a guy think I was hot? Not hot, maybe interesting, with my dark hair, high cheekbones, and expressive eyes.

"Are you sure you want to go to prom with Emma's brother? He's a senior. And a football player!" I pull my comforter over my feet. "He probably already has a date."

"My intel is he doesn't have a date yet."

"Wouldn't it be easier for you to ask Emma yourself?"

"You know her better. It would be weird for me to go up to her."

It would be weird for me to talk to Emma about her brother. I only met him once at Chilly Swirl. "Lemme think about how I'd bring it up to Emma." I sigh. "Now for my date, could you talk to Timothy, from Photography Club, for me?"

"Sure. I have second period with him. I'll ask him about his prom plans. But if I talk to Timothy, you need to talk to Emma. Deal?"

"Deal." I try to ignore the sinking feeling that our exchange isn't going to go as planned. How awkward is it going to be to ask Emma about her brother?

CHAPTER 39

JAX LOURDE

"Tonight, we find out who won the debate," I say to Emma, Adele, and Alonzo who are already seated at our lunch table. I set my backpack and basketball on the floor, sit down, and look at Alonzo. "Sorry, dude, that you weren't there... Both teams debated well. Some of the stuff the opposing team said made me think."

Adele shakes her finger at me. "Uh, uh, uh! No talking about the debate until this evening at AP Club." She's smiling so I can tell she's just playing.

I smile back at her. "You're right. Change of subject." I bite into my chicken Caesar wrap.

Emma's face is pale, which is not a good sign. "I have some bad news," she says.

It's like the air got sucked out of the commons. All four of us are frozen in time and Alonzo finally says, "What? Just say it! Give us the bad news before I have a coronary."

I'm about to have a coronary too.

"Well... I was checking eBay last night and..." Emma hesitates, her face scrunched.

"Just say it!" I blurt, though I hope I didn't startle her.

"The necklace isn't on eBay anymore. It must have sold."

"Holy crap." My heart is pounding. "Maybe it's under a different title or category?" It didn't even occur to me that the necklace would sell, which I guess is pretty stupid, since it was on eBay. For sale. I set my Caesar wrap down on my napkin. For the first time in my life, I think I've lost my appetite.

"Let's not panic," Adele says. "Emma, could you keep looking tonight and see if Jax is right—that it's under a different category? Could you check other places online that sell merch too?"

Emma nods. "Sorry for the bad news, guys."

Alonzo shakes his head. "You know what, guys? This is a sign it's not going to work. We need to let it go."

"Are you kidding?" My voice is a little too squeaky for an athlete. "No way. We're seeing this through." I grab onto Alonzo's shoulders and look him in the eyes like my coach does when I'm giving up. "We're seeing this through."

Alonzo just nods and shrugs. I look toward Adele and she's smiling at me. How can she smile right now? How can Alonzo just give up like that? We can't give up. I can't give up.

We all pack up our lunch garbage, with discouragement hanging over us like mossy vines.

I have my own bad news to share. I've been with my dad this week and I asked him if I could have the money from the limo rental to help pay for the replacement necklace. He flat-out told me, "No." Said he couldn't support someone he didn't know and who might be lying.

You're giving me the money for the limo anyway, I thought but didn't say out loud.

Dad said, "I'm not giving you money for a stranger."

I never thought I'd say this, but I hated Dad right then. I just walked away and shut myself in my room for the rest of the night. I decided I'd talk to Mom when I'm at her house on Sunday. She'll agree to give me the money. At least, I hope. She doesn't like to contradict Dad. They call it co-parenting. I call it ganging up on me.

After what Emma just said about eBay, I'll just hang onto my bad news for now.

Natalia steps in front of the AP Club members and says, "Both teams made good points. The affirmative team used logos—a logical appeal—effectively, such as girls being able to pursue any career they want, so why shouldn't they pursue a boy? Why shouldn't a friend help another friend pursue a boy?" Then, she glares at Emma.

I glance over to Emma, like what did Natalia just mean with that comment? Emma makes a weird face, crossing her eyes, and shrugs at me.

Natalia says, "In addition, increasing the odds when everyone takes the risks is another example of well-played logos. We also could appreciate the negative team's use of logos and pathos such as girls not being as equal as we'd like so we need to stick with the status quo. In addition, the poll they took and the need to follow social norms were compelling arguments."

I pick up my basketball and shift it from hand to hand. I'm trying to keep my face from showing my impatience. Why the speech? Just tell us who won!

Samesh steps forward and says, "In India, arranged marriages are still the norm. A very small percentage of couples have what are called love marriages, and this is an indication that most young people are following the social norm. Now may not be the time for India's youth to ignore these customs. Marriage is complicated because of religion and caste systems. The US, though, is different. We've come 'a long way, baby' with human rights and other reforms. Now is the time for us to push the norms."

We should have had Samesh on our affirmative team. He's persuasive.

He continues. "The most compelling argument was regarding same-sex couples and how these couples lean on their strengths. This logically made the most sense and is hard to dispute. In addition, although the negative's team cited their poll, the affirmative team had a good point about the limitations of that poll."

"Therefore," Natalia says, "the affirmative team won the debate."

Emma, Adele, Crystal, and I whoop and applaud. The opposing team gives us a golf clap.

I clasp my hands behind my head and lean back into my chair. "Well, it looks like I get to kick back and wait to see which girl," I say with a huge grin, "or girls ask me to prom."

Miss Halden flares her nostrils at me, then smiles. "Jax, I can't decide if you're obnoxious or really likable."

Adele says, "Agreed, Miss Halden."

Maybe I can be both.

CHAPTER 40

ADELE QUESTIN

I 'm sitting on my bed, and I've just received a text from Jax saying he thinks he has a plan for getting the necklace into the lady's house. I begged him to tell me what he's going to do but he wouldn't spill. I guess I need to help Emma find a used necklace.

Facebook Marketplace doesn't have the David Yurman necklace we need, so I search for consignment shops. I researched them for a gently used prom dress last week, so I have a few bookmarked. I dial the closest shop. Luckily, they're open till eight o'clock. I describe the necklace to the salesperson, and she says they don't have anything matching the description.

"If we get a necklace like that, would you like me to call you?" the salesperson asks.

"Yes, please!"

I call the next consignment shop, and the salesperson acts like I'm interrupting her. She's not nice. At all. I apologize for bothering her. Though, I'm not sorry. *No commission for you.*

The third consignment shop salesperson listens to my description and says she'll call me back after she checks.

Agh! I hate waiting! I open Google again to see if there are any options I've missed. I key in jewelers that sell used necklaces and find so many listings I don't even know where to begin. I start with a jeweler closest to me and dial the number. A man older than my great-grandfather answers. I repeat myself several times and I'm practically yelling into my phone. I say "Goodbye," and hang up.

A few minutes later, my phone rings. It's the third consignment salesperson. "We have another store in Hollywood," she says. "I have good news! They have your necklace."

"We'll take it!"

"Can you pick it up tomorrow?" the salesperson says.

I pause to consider if I should skip school tomorrow to drive at least an hour and a half away. Mom would never allow me to drive that far on the freeway. Maybe Jax has driven to Hollywood before. Maybe I should text him, and then we could drive together. Then there's the most important detail: the money. I say to the consignment clerk, "I need to explain something. Do you have a few minutes?"

"We don't have any customers right now. Go ahead."

"First of all, how much is the necklace?"

I hear the salesclerk rustling around a moment and then she says, "It's seven hundred dollars."

"Okay. We can do that." I take three minutes to explain our situation, that we're helping a house cleaner, and that I'm a student and should be at school tomorrow.

"Let me give that store a call and see if they'll hold the necklace till Saturday. Would that work better for you? I'll call you in the morning."

I write the address of the store in the Notes app on my phone and then end the call.

My stomach is jumbling like a dryer full of wet clothes. What if the salesclerk says they won't wait till Saturday? Then I'll have to skip school tomorrow and go buy the necklace. I text Jax.

> I found the necklace but it's in Hollywood. Will you pls drive me to get it?

I'm relieved to see a text pop onto my screen immediately.

> That's great! Sure. When?

My stomach settles a little knowing Jax is willing to drive. I need to be more like Jax. He agrees to things without a lot of decision-making or details. I usually ask a ton of questions before I agree.

> Either tomorrow or Saturday. I'm waiting on a call from the store.

> Tomorrow? During school!? That's a no go.

I text a thumbs up to Jax and hope the store will wait till Saturday. Jax and I will have at least three hours in his car to talk.

CHAPTER 41

ALONZO HERNANDEZ

I'm standing near the school entrance and Adele runs into me like a linebacker and then clutches my arm. "Good morning to you too," I say.

"It is a good morning," Adele says, out of breath. "I found. The necklace."

"What?"

"I called a bunch of places last night," Adele says, "and found the necklace at a consignment store in Hollywood." I swear she's squeezing my arm with every syllable.

"That's amazing!" I clear my throat. I honestly thought nothing would come of our talk about clearing Rosie's mom's name. I mean, who follows through on what they say these days? I guess the answer is me and my friends. "Now we need to pull together money. How much is this gonna cost?"

"You know how the necklace was seven hundred and fifty dollars on eBay?"

I can tell she's waiting for me to answer, so I say, "Uh-huh. Don't tell me it's more than eBay."

Adele says, "No. It's seven hundred!"

"Fifty bucks less than eBay." I whistle. "That's karma. When we do good, good comes back to us."

"Right? Anyway," Adele continues, "the sales lady said she'd call the store to hold the necklace until tomorrow, so we don't have to skip school today. The store opens at nine, so she'll call then. Cross our fingers."

I've made it through first and second periods and have been able to focus, at least a little. I'm sitting in third period, and Miss Halden puts three quotations on the screen for our quick-write: one about hope, one about success, and another about love. I choose the one about hope because I've been thinking a lot about what hope is and what it shouldn't be. Even though I know some things, like college, are basically impossible, in my heart, I at least want to try. My notebook is open, and my pen is pressed against my lower lip as I think.

Last week, our counselor, Mrs. Annatol, visited our social studies classes to talk to us about college. I wanted to ask her why teachers encourage us to go to college when it's so expensive or our parents don't want us to go. But I kept my thoughts to myself.

Mrs. Annatol explained about Pell grants for students that qualify, which could give me up to seven thousand dollars a year for tuition, books, and other expenses. Parents need to sign off on the Pell application, so that might be complicated.

"Many of you have the grades and the standardized test scores to be eligible for scholarships," she said. I swear she looked right at me when she said this.

Mrs. Annatol laid it out for us in hard figures. Somehow, seeing actual dollar amounts made college seem less like a dream and more like a reality.

I raised my hand. "What about a part-time job? Do college students have time for that?"

Mrs. Annatol said, "You could even get a job on campus, if that's what you want." I hadn't realized all of this. It solves the issue of me not having a car.

As Mrs. Annatol explained all this, I couldn't help but wonder about Jax, Adele and Emma. Are their parents paying for college? For sure Adele and Jax's parents are. Maybe not Emma. So many emotions were swirling inside of me. Sitting in that presentation, I felt like Merlin's wand was spinning skepticism, jealousy, optimism, and hope around me.

Today's quick-write gives me a chance to sort out this swirl of emotions. I think about the necklace situation and college, then write about them. By the time I finish my last sentence, hope is the loudest word in my head.

Jax, Emma, Adele, and I are sitting at our usual table in the commons. Adele squeezes dressing on her salad. "Well, this morning, just as I predicted, the salesperson called me at 9:05, and I pretended I need to use the bathroom and called her back. The salesperson said that the Hollywood store will hold the necklace till tomorrow for us." We all exhale at the same time. I hold back a laugh at how intense we all are right now.

"Well... it's not seven hundred and fifty dollars. I can tell you that." Adele's grin stretches across her face. "It's not even seven hundred dollars!"

"What?" I say. "How can it not be seven hundred? That's what you said before." I see something in Adele's expression that makes me think she's messing with us right now. "How. Much?"

"Six hundred and thirty dollars."

I don't think I've ever seen Adele smile this much.

"How can it be so much less?" Jax asks.

"The consignment store was selling it for seven hundred, and they gave us ten percent off because they're impressed with what we're doing," Adele says.

"Good karma," I say. I taste salt and blink to keep tears from pooling. I hope no one notices. I don't cry. Especially not in front of friends.

My friends. Jax's mom. And now the consignment shops are proving that people want to do the right thing. All four of us are silent for a moment and I wonder if they're feeling what I'm feeling. I wish I could tell Rosie's mom about these people willing to help, but I can't. Rosie's mom and Mama would shut down our plan in a heartbeat. The pressure on my chest is crushing. Keeping secrets about the necklace, PSAT, and my senior course registration form is like a piñata about to burst. I learned from my lies about AP Club that these things have a way of catching up with us—exploding and making a huge mess.

"Wow," is all Emma says.

"Wow," Jax echoes. "I didn't see that coming."

Then, Adele bursts our happy bubble. "How are we coming up with this money by tomorrow?"

"I have a hundred bucks in my wallet."

"You carry that kind of money around?" Jax says to me.

"I put it in my wallet last night. I figured we'd probably need Rosie's and my money for the necklace. Anyone else have money on you?"

Jax says, "No, but I'll bring a hundred tomorrow. A week ago, my mom gave me an advance of what I would have paid for tux rental and dinner."

Emma says, "I have a couple hundred that I can bring tomorrow. My brother, Pete, pitched in, so that added a little extra to my dress money."

"Your brother?" Tears sting the backs of my eyes. Add her brother to the list of supporters.

"He's carpooling with a neighbor now and saving his gas money," Emma says.

"Your brother?" I ask again, trying to comprehend. I'm overwhelmed by people's generosity.

"Yeah," Emma says, laughing. "When I told Pete what we were doing, he said he wanted to help."

"That's really cool that he wants to pitch in," Adele says.

"Very cool." I wish I had more words to describe what this means to me. "Adele?"

Jax, Emma and I are looking at her.

"What?" Adele says.

"Can you get money to Emma by tomorrow morning?" Jax asks. "Any chance it could be two hundred and thirty dollars?"

Adele's eyes widen and I wonder why. "I was going to get cash from my mom for my prom dress and use what's left over for the necklace."

Emma says, "Why don't we buy our prom dresses from the consignment shop?"

"Emma, that's brilliant!" Adele says. "We'll have to buy the cheapest dress possible to make this happen."

"The cheapest and most beautiful," Emma says.

"We are some resourceful people," I say.

"What time are you picking me up?" Emma asks Adele.

"I'm not. Jax is."

That'll be a cozy car ride with the three of them driving to Hollywood.

CHAPTER 42

ADELE QUESTIN

The following morning is the first time I've been *happy* to wake up early on a Saturday. I'm sitting on the steps of our veranda and Jax and Emma arrive at my house at nine sharp. I wave them over and climb into the back seat. Jax holds out his palm and says, "Hand me your phone. We need your tunes for our road trip."

"Um," Emma says to Jax, "how do you know what's on Adele's phone?"

I keep my cakehole shut and let Jax sort out that one. I'm no Sherlock, but I think Emma might be jealous. Does she like Jax?

Jax says, "Adele and I staked out the house cleaner and she had some lit tunes. Stuff I like."

"Oh," is all Emma says. No one talks for a few awkward minutes and then she breaks the silence. "So, Adele, are you and Alonzo going to have matching dress and cummerbund for the prom?"

"Alonzo's not going to our prom," I say.

Emma gasps. "Alonzo's not going?"

"Nope." I suppress the urge to ask what was with the dramatic gasp. "He's going to his friend's high school prom and doesn't want to go to two."

"So," Jax says, "you don't have a date?" He peers into the rearview mirror and our eyes meet.

"Nope, but I'd like one." I sound like I'm flirting with Jax, which I'm not.

"I don't have a date either," Emma interjects as she grabs Jax's arm. She's not subtle about the fact that she'd like Jax to ask her to prom. I recall Jax saying that he was planning on waiting for a girl to ask him, so she should just ask him. Move things along.

Jax turns up the volume on his stereo. "I love this song!"

Looks like Jax wants to change the subject. "So, Emma," I holler over the song, "which quotation did you choose in Miss Halden's class yesterday?"

"I thought about writing about hope because I've been thinking a lot about college lately. Instead, I wrote about love." Emma looks at Jax and then widens her lips into a huge lip-glossy smile. Do guys like it when girls do that? Maybe I should take a few lessons from her on flirting.

Emma continues. "Which one did you choose, Jax? ... Oh, wait. You're not in Miss Halden's class. But if you had to, which topic would you choose: love, hope, or success?"

"Love. Hope. What was the third one?" Jax asks.

"Success," Emma says.

"I think hope. Yeah. Definitely, hope." He adds, "What did you choose, Adele?"

I like that Jax is including me in this conversation. Emma sure isn't taking care of the whole inclusion thing. "I wrote about hope. Don't know much about love." I cringe. Should I admit that I'm clueless about love? Whatever. "I wasn't in the mood to try to define success. The concept of success changes every day for me. Hope is just... well, it's hopeful."

"I like that," Jax says. "Hope is hopeful." Then, he laughs at my comment, which makes my stomach heat up like lava.

"I like it too," Emma says.

Girl. You are trying too hard. Disagree with the guy at least some of the time.

We pass the next hour by gossiping, with Emma sharing most of it. A social anthropologist would have a heyday in our school. When we take the exit toward the consignment store, Emma shifts to being a navigator. She successfully guides us to a parking spot nearby.

"You two are a great road trip team," I say to Jax and Emma as we step into the consignment shop.

"You're important too," Jax says.

Warmth rises into my neck.

All three of us enter the shop and stop at the counter. Emma says to the salesperson, "Are you Annette?"

Annette's face brightens when we introduce ourselves. "I just love what you're doing." Then, she reaches under the counter, pulls out a white leather bag, and pours out the necklace.

"I can't believe we're actually doing this." Jax leans on the counter.

I look up at him, tuck my hair behind my ear, and we're both beaming. I think back to what I said to Jax on our way here about not knowing how to define success and I'm certain this, right now, is my definition of success.

"Now, for dress shopping," Emma says.

Jax points toward the door. "I'll be outside while you ladies do your shopping thing."

My brows meet in the middle of my forehead. "Shopping thing?"

Jax laughs as he exits.

Emma and I flip through a rack of glam dresses. I narrow down my choices to six options, all less than a hundred dollars. A year ago, I would have died buying and wearing a used dress but now I feel like I'll never pay full price again. Emma chooses three options and we both enter separate dressing rooms.

I pose in front of the mirror in my favorite option, which is a beaded aqua asymmetrical mini dress with one thick strap. I dance with my arms flailing to make sure the strap stays on and I won't have a Janet Jackson wardrobe malfunction. I wonder what Emma would think of me if she knew I was dancing in the dressing room.

While Emma is changing in and out of two options, trying to choose, I check out jewelry in a display case. As I peer through the glass top, the unfinished part of my friends' and my story prickles my skin. Where is the original necklace?

After our purchases, we walk out of the store. Emma is at the front of our line holding the shopping bag with the necklace and her dress, and Jax falls into line with us. We're looking like the three wise men following the North Star.

CHAPTER 43

JAX LOURDE

I pull into Emma's driveway after dropping off Adele. It wasn't as weird as I thought it would be driving all the way to Hollywood with two girls in my car. Except, what's up with Emma? Is she into me?

"We did it!" Emma says, interrupting my thoughts.

"I didn't think we could pull it off." I'm kind of laughing. "I freaked out when you told us the necklace sold on eBay."

"And the consignment shop. How awesome are they?" Emma is quiet for a moment. "Are you sure you're okay with having dinner outside and borrowing one of your dad's suits instead of renting a tux?"

"I've never been surer. Are you sure about wearing a used dress?"

"Oh, God." Emma turns her head abruptly. "My brother, Pete, and his friend, Greg, are looking out the window at us." She swivels in her seat so she's not facing the house. "I'm a little sad about the dress, but it's for a good cause."

I see Pete and Greg peeking out of a window upstairs and try to ignore them. "I wonder if a girl in a dress is gonna mind sitting outside to eat dinner. I mean, you said my prom date will expect dinner at a restaurant."

"No, I didn't."

"Yeah, you did. I remember."

"You're right. I said that before..." Emma glances away like she's embarrassed or something.

"Before what?"

Emma sighs. "Before the necklace, things like going out to dinner and being on a real prom date mattered."

"Real prom date? Mattered?"

Emma looks at me. "You know. The boy pampering the girl, so she feels good about herself. Maybe having some space away from Natalia and Sara, buying the necklace for Alonzo's neighbor, and our AP Club debate helped me decide what matters. I don't care as much what others think of me," Emma says. "Besides, my used dress is great."

"I know what you mean, though not about the dress." I sputter out a nervous laugh and my hands grip the steering wheel. I look up to the window. I wave to Greg and Pete.

"Jax?" Her voice sounds kinda squeaky.

"Yeah?" I turn to face Emma.

"Will you go to prom with me? Dinner outside's okay."

What can I say? I have someone else in mind but maybe I should just say "yes" to Emma's invitation. Emma is nice and pretty with her reddish-blonde hair and pale green eyes...

"Say something." Emma's staring at me like a fawn.

"It takes guts to ask someone, you know? So... um... thank you." I shift in my seat. "I need to think about it." My throat tightens as I try to swallow.

"You want to take Natalia, don't you?" Emma's voice has an edge.

"No. I don't know." I can see on her face that she's not happy. Of course, she's not. I'm basically saying "no."

"Um... have a good rest of your weekend," Emma says as she gets out of my car. "See you Monday." She closes my car door.

I don't know if she even *likes me*, likes me. Not like that. If I tell her yes, she's not really who I want to go with, and if I tell her no, things'll be awkward in our friend group. Why did prom and the necklace have to happen at the same time? I pull out of Emma's driveway and drive. I don't know or care where I'm heading. I just drive.

Adele's comment about hope being hopeful ricochets in my brain. Everything we're doing with the necklace hangs on hope. We hope we can get the necklace into the house. We hope the lady apologizes. We hope Rosie's mom's name is cleared. I guess prom is hope too. We hope someone accepts our prom invitation and hope we have a good time with that person. And *my* "someone" is a fierce, opinionated girl who used to wear too much eyeliner but who makes me bring my A-game when I'm around her. The question is, does she like my A-game?

Emma's invitation is a sign that I need to do something. My pits prickle with sweat and my stomach spins like the wheels on my car. I've been aimlessly driving for ten minutes, and I look around to get my bearings. I see the Sudsy Auto ahead on the left, turn on my blinker, and pull into a parking spot.

Alonzo looks up with a chamois in one hand.

I get out of my car. "Hey bud." I hold out my hand. "Gimme one of those." He bends down, reaches into a bucket, and tosses a chamois to me. I start to buff the hood of the car that Alonzo is detailing.

"How'd it go?" Alonzo says.

"We have the necklace, and I have a plan for getting it into the lady's house."

Alonzo throws his chamois in the air and catches it. "That's awesome!" He gives me the side-eye. "Should I be nervous about this plan?"

"Truth? I'm nervous, but it is crazy enough to work. If my plan takes a nosedive, I don't want any of you in on it. I've been in my share of trouble, and my parents are used to it. Your dad's already mad at you. You don't need any more drama."

"True," Alonzo says. "Thanks, bud."

We both buff the car in silence for a few minutes, then I say, "Emma asked me to prom."

"Thought that might happen."

He thought that? How did I not see it coming? "I don't know what to do." I rub the chamois across the roof of the car.

"She's a hottie and nice," Alonzo says with a shrug. "What's the problem?"

"I just wonder if it'll make our AP friend group weird," which is part of the truth.

Alonzo's hand pauses on top of the roof. "I said 'no' to Adele, and things aren't weird."

"You guys started out as friends, though." As I say this, I realize Emma and I are friends too. Some guys would kill to have a girl like Emma ask them to prom, and here I am thinking it's a problem.

"It's only weird if you make it weird." Alonzo wrings out the chamois. "Besides, if you're not sure about Emma, then don't go to prom with her. That's not fair to her or to another guy that wants to ask her."

"You're right." How did Alonzo get so wise? Going with Emma would not be fair to her. It wouldn't be fair to me, either, to lose the chance to go with the person who's right for me. "I gotta go." I toss the chamois to Alonzo across the car and he catches it like a pro baseball player. "I need to take care of something now."

CHAPTER 44

ADELE QUESTIN

I've just locked the necklace in our safe. I know it's totally paranoid, but I'm scared I'll lose the necklace, and then we'd be back at the beginning. I had to sneak into Dad's study, remember the combination, and tuck the necklace way in the back so my parents won't notice it in there.

I'm leaving the den when I hear a knock at our front door. I head down the stairs to the entryway and see a shadow of someone very tall through the marbled glass of our front door. Kind of looks like Jax. I tuck my hair behind my ear and open the door. "What're you doing here?"

"I dunno. Just dropped by," Jax says. His feet are shifting side to side, like he's nervous or something.

"Oh my God! What's the matter!"

"Nothing."

"Something's going on. Come in." I open the door wider. Then I remember I changed into my baggiest sweatpants. And I washed my face already. Without my eyeliner, I don't look like me. My eyeliner is my thing. My edge.

"Could we maybe... I dunno... go for a quick walk?" Jax says.

"Lemme grab my trainers." I run up the stairs and am out of breath when I reach the landing. Why is Jax here? Something must be very wrong because guys don't come knocking on my door. Especially not guys like Jax.

We start down our driveway and Jax says, "You look different."

My hand covers my face. "I know. I washed off my makeup."

"I like it."

Was that a compliment? And what is happening with my racing heart?

Jax jokes, "We're not even to the sidewalk and we've already gotten our steps in for the day."

I snort out an embarrassing laugh. "Yeah, it's an obnoxiously long driveway... Not that I'm bragging or anything," I say, holding up my hands in defense.

"Of course not. So."

Why's he being so jumpy? "So?"

"So... Emma asked me to prom," Jax says.

My stomach clenches like a fist. I guess I saw that coming. It's preordained that Emma and Jax would be prom dates. I mean, she's a cheerleader, and he's an athlete. "You said 'yes,' then?" My heart is squeezing, and I wish I hadn't asked the question. I don't want to know the answer.

"I told her I needed a few days to give her an answer."

A loud exhale escapes my lungs. "Harsh." I can't believe I just insulted Jax. I try to recover. "Of course, it's your choice."

"Hey. You girls want equality," Jax says with a lopsided smile.

I laugh.

"You... are a strong-willed person."

"What's that...? Is that a compliment?" I ask, glancing sideways at him.

"Pretty much."

Why is Jax so cute when he's being sassy? "I guess, thank you?"

"My point is... The thing is... I want to ask you to go to prom with me," Jax says.

Did I hear him correctly? Prom?

Jax shrugs, then says, "But you're kinda scary."

I stop walking. What kind of girl wants to be told she's scary? "I'm scary?" What kind of guy wants to take a scary girl to prom? I'm confused.

"Terrifying," Jax says with an exploding-hand gesture next to his head. We start walking again.

Now I'm laughing. "I'm scary to you. A popular, very tall guy." He can't be for real.

"You always say what's on your mind and sometimes it's not very nice."

"I guess that's true."

"But I like it. You say what you mean." Jax bumps my shoulder with his elbow. "I'm pretty sure you're going to say 'no,' but the debate made me think I should have some guts." He stops walking and faces me. "Do you want to go to prom with me?"

I'm stunned into silence, which is rare for me. I don't know where to look. At him? At the ground? I finally tilt my head up and see that he's nervous and waiting for an answer. My smile builds until it's a humongous grin. "Actually, I'd love to go to the prom with you, Jax Lourde." How is it possible that Jax Lourde wants to go to prom with me? How is it possible that I'm excited to go to prom with him?

Jax arches his back and clenches his fists like he's scored the winning three-pointer. Then he says, "Now I just need to figure out how to give Emma the news."

What do I do now? Should I shake his hand like we've just agreed to something? Should I hug him? And how is this going to go with Emma? Too many thoughts are clogging my brain. I have no idea how to accept

Jax's invitation, so I just take hold of his hand and say, "Thank you. This is unexpected." Unexpected? More like someone pinch me and wake me up. Earlier this year, I'd sworn off guys.

I just ended that oath.

Jax and I walk to my door holding hands, which feels awkward and amazing at the same time. "What are people going to say about us going to the prom?" I ask with my other hand resting on the doorjamb.

"When have you cared what people say?" Jax says with a laugh.

I don't care what most people think. I care about Emma, though.

My head is swimming with romance and other gushy stuff that I've avoided for most of my life. It's like I'm in a movie with my bed spinning in a circle and I'm all giddy and staring off into space. Even by myself, I'm embarrassed at how I must look all googly-eyed and sighing. To come back to reality, I pick up my phone to text Payton.

No need to talk to Timothy.

I already did and he's asking U Monday.

I just got asked. Tell him to ask someone else.

Who asked U?!

I'm not ready for the gossip cyclone that's going to rip through school. I don't want to tell her in a text, and, besides, this feels like something Jax needs to share first. This unexpected news is going to be epic!

Everyone will know soon enough.

It seems rude, but it's the only answer I can give. I swallow a lump of guilt and panic as I read the word, "everyone." I was starting to think Emma and I could be *friend* friends, and not just AP Club friends. Is she going to give me the silent treatment after she finds out? Or is she going to yell at me? Maybe in front of Jax and Alonzo? I can't decide if I'd rather be ignored or yelled at.

Have U talked to Emma about her brother yet?

Not yet. I will today.

Asking Emma to talk to her brother about Payton is going to be uncomfortable since she'll find out soon enough that Jax is going to the prom with me. But a deal is a deal, so I text Emma.

Got a min for a call?

My phone rings immediately, which makes me drop my phone. I fumble to pick it up before it goes to voicemail.

"Hey there. Long time, no see," I say, a little out of breath.

"Hey," Emma says, and I hear a thickness in her voice.

"You okay?" I ask.

"I asked someone to prom, and he said he needs to think about it, which is the same as a no." I'm suddenly paranoid that Emma can read my thoughts. That she knows about Jax asking me.

"Everyone ends up with the right person in the end," I say like some cheesy meme with a sunset in the background. I'm glad Emma can't see me cringing.

"I suppose so," Emma says. "What's up?"

"You know Payton, right?"

"Sure. She's in Pep Club," Emma says.

"Well, she wants to go to prom with your brother."

"*My* brother?"

"Of course, *your* brother. Is there any other kind?" My sarcasm isn't helping, so I bring it down a notch. "She's hoping you'll put in a good word for her."

"He doesn't have a date yet." Emma pauses then adds, "I don't think he'll go for a junior, though."

"That's what I told Payton, but she wanted me to ask. I promised her I'd do it. Sorry. I know it's awkward." *You have no idea how awkward this really is.*

"Kinda. But no worries. I'll check."

As usual, Emma is being so nice. That could change soon. "You sure you're okay? You sound kinda sad." What am I doing? What if she tells me exactly why she's not okay and I have to lie?

"I'll be fine. Today was pretty amazing buying the necklace, wasn't it?" I can hear Emma's voice perk up. "Prom seems less important, you know?"

Emma is wiser than most of us give her credit for being. I hope Jax tells Emma soon about me being his prom date. I can't take another day feeling sick to my stomach with guilt. We end the call, and I text Payton.

> Emma's gonna talk to her brother.

I've done my part and have no control whether Pete will ask her. I guess anything is possible. After all, Jax asked me to prom.

CHAPTER 45

MISS HEATHER HALDEN

Yesterday, as students were writing about their preferred quotation, I tried to guess who would write about love, success, or hope. I would have chosen hope. Teachers wouldn't show up for work if we didn't have a healthy dose of optimism.

As I sit at my dining table this afternoon, I smile as I correctly predicted Emma would write about love. I also correctly predicted Adele's choice, which was hope. Alonzo stayed after third period a few days ago to pick up the AP Club handouts. I hope he doesn't cause a bigger issue with his parents by continuing to complete some of the activities. He wrote about hope and cited the glass ceiling some people face in leadership positions, something he'd learned in his business opportunities elective. He likened this to a glass ceiling some students face.

We can see the opportunities, but it's hard to reach them.

I'm seized by an image of Alonzo on a ladder pushing and straining against impenetrable glass and am relieved to read he had learned about grants and scholarships that could launch him toward a college degree. Alonzo wrote that he's tempted with more affordable, rapid, and lucrative opportunities, such as trade school, yet he wrote: *If we're talking about the purest form of hope, I hope I attend an Ivy League school. With a generous scholarship, of course.* He keeps thriving at school, because despite setbacks like lying to his parents and being forbidden to attend the AP Club, he still believes that he will find a way to go after his goals. I wish I had that kind of optimism.

With my teacup warming my hand, I continue reading. Guilt squeezes my stomach as the duplicity of Alonzo's request to continue with AP Club activities and my role in his deception sinks in. Do I support parents' wishes or the students'?

I've kept my home and school life separate until I shared with my friends how upset I was that my mom's friend was accused of stealing a necklace from a house she cleans. I never imagined that people from outside my neighborhood would step up to help, but Jax, Adele, and Emma have proven that barriers can be breached, and justice served.

Jax, Adele and Emma are picking up the necklace this weekend to replace the lost one. Although I have no idea how this all will turn out, with every successful step, the glass ceiling cracks just a little.

When I started the AP Club, I worried about the students' AP exam scores, how it would look to my colleagues, and how it would impact my decision to stay at my current high school. Reading about what Alonzo and his friends are hoping to achieve, their scores matter far less. I feel petty for worrying about scores and achievement when something profound is happening because these students have become friends who inspire each other to take a stand against an injustice. Tears are pooling in my eyes and I'm unable to continue reading. I dab my eyes with the palm of my hand.

I write a few comments on Alonzo's quick-write and move onto the next missive. Just as teachers hope to challenge students' thinking, their thoughts challenge us. I pause from reading student essays to consider what do I hope for? I disagree with Adele's far-too-practical view that hope is just determination. Hope requires a little bit of love and success to keep it alive. Sometimes, though, disagreeing with someone can be just as powerful as being inspired.

I've finished reading my third-period stack and need to give my eyes a rest and my brain a chance to puzzle out something. About two weeks ago, I attended a district-wide Advanced-Placement information session for parents. A woman sat next to me with her husband, and before the presentation started, she was talking loudly. I tried not to eavesdrop, but I couldn't help but hear her prattling on about a housekeeper who stole an expensive necklace. What captured my attention is that I automatically didn't like this woman with her assumptions and lack of awareness or concern that people might overhear her. I'd wager my hard-earned money that she's the same woman Alonzo described in his essay. I wish I had introduced myself; then I'd know who she was. No need to wonder. My AP Club members have this handled.

CHAPTER 46

ADELE QUESTIN

I'm standing at my locker, checking the small mirror hung on my door to make sure I don't have any bits of strawberry smoothie between my teeth, and Emma approaches.

"Has Jax talked to you?" I ask Emma when she arrives, trying to ignore the minor heart attack I'm having right now. Does Emma know about Jax and me? My arms and legs are twitchy.

Emma gives me a puzzled look. She must notice my nervousness because she asks, "Did something happen with the necklace?"

"No! The necklace is fine," I say, my voice a little too high-pitched. "It's about—"

Out of nowhere, Natalia interrupts. "How'd you convince Jax to ask *you* to prom?"

"Are you talking to me?" I ask Natalia, which is a stupid question because of course she's talking to me; she's six inches from my face.

Natalia makes an "uh" cough sound, points at me, and says to Emma, "Jax asked her to prom." Natalia's face looks like she just bit into a sour lemon slice.

"Is it true?" Emma asks me, her eyebrows high and mouth partly open. "He asked you?"

What the hell? Natalia isn't supposed to be the one to tell Emma. Jax is... or I am. Emma grabs my arm to pull me away from Natalia. Of course, people are stopping in the hallway to stare at Emma and me. I don't care as much what people think, but I'm sure Emma and Jax do.

Emma whispers to me, "Let's head to the counseling office. It's more private."

"Mrs. Annatol?" Emma says as we enter the waiting area. "We need somewhere to talk." Emma's face is bright red. I'm sure Mrs. Annatol can tell this is serious. "Is it okay if we sit here, and then could you write us a pass to class?"

"Sure. Is everything okay?" Mrs. Annatol asks.

"Yeah. We just need to talk," Emma says.

I say, "Jax told me you asked him to prom on Saturday," as we sit down on the couch.

"Why didn't you tell me Jax asked you to prom when we talked yesterday?" Emma looks like she's about to cry.

"It wasn't the right time." I stop talking, waiting for Emma to say something.

"I thought we were friends, Adele. It's always the right time to tell a friend something like this."

"Jax needed to tell you, not me. He's the one who made the decision." She sniffles and sighs. "That makes sense."

"Now that Natalia has spilled the beans... On Saturday, he left your house then came back over to mine. I thought I should tell him 'no' because you and I are friends, but I told him, 'yes.' I mean, who, in their wildest dreams, would've thought I'd be asked by a guy like Jax?" I pause, take in a loud breath, and then I grab Emma's hand. "I'm really sorry, Emma."

"I think…" Emma scoots forward on the couch and pivots toward me. "I think I had this idea that Jax was supposed to be my date. Now I realize I wasn't that into Jax. I just wanted a prom date."

"How can you be so calm?"

Emma shrugs. Unexpectedly, a smile takes shape. "At least he's not going with Natalia."

We actually giggle at a time like this. Go figure.

"So, you're not mad at me?" I must look like a sad puppy right now.

"I'm mostly embarrassed. Everyone knows. Why would I be mad at you? What if you said, 'no' and then Jax didn't take me either? What good would that have done us?"

"Good logic," I say. "Thanks for being so nice right now."

"What choice do I have?"

"What do we do about Natalia and the haters?"

Emma says, "We already stood up to the AP exam petitioners. This is just another time to stick together."

"Yeah. They'll see all of us sitting at lunch and they'll know we're okay with everything. We don't owe anyone an explanation."

"I like that," Emma says, with a sigh. "I need to figure out how to talk to Jax before lunch so it's not awkward."

CHAPTER 47

JAX LOURDE

I'm hurrying down the hallway because Emma texted me five minutes ago and asked me to meet her outside the 200 wing. "Dude!" It's Eric's voice behind me. I need to get outside to talk to Emma but ignoring my basketball-baseball buddy would make me even less popular than I am already.

"Yeah?" I say as I turn around.

"What's this I hear you asked that eyeliner girl to prom?"

Eyeliner girl? What the hell? "Adele? She's great." I tuck my hands in my jeans pockets, trying to look as casual as possible. I predicted I'd get questions. I just hadn't thought about what I'd say.

"She's a ball-breaker!" Eric says, with his face all scowly and judgy.

Again. What the hell? "She actually isn't..." What am I doing standing here justifying my choice? I hold out my palm, sort of like a surrender.

"You know what? I asked the right person. You're gonna have to take my word for it." I've never felt more certain, and I nod.

"I also heard you complained to the school board about the AP Club petition!" Eric continues. "You're turning against us. What's up with that?"

"Against *us*? Who's 'us'?"

"A bunch of us that don't like that people who aren't in AP get to take the exam."

"It's not just AP Club members." I shake my head. "You know that anyone can sign up for an exam, right?"

"No, they can't," Eric says.

"Yes, they can." I fold my arms and wait. When Eric doesn't say anything, I keep talking. "It's not like the College Board gives out a limited number of exams, Eric. The AP Club is not taking anything away from you or anyone." I see Joey—the most determined narc ever—approaching us, speed walking. If I wasn't still pissed with Joey—or Mr. Buccio—for busting Raleigh, Nick, and me, I'd laugh at how ridiculous he looks pumping his arms and squeaking his sneakers on the tiles. I whisper, "Joey's coming. We better get going." Then, I hiss, "And quit bringing up the petition. You need to get over it."

"I'm not—"

"Not so fast, guys." Joey—Mr. Buccio—is holding up his hand like he's stopping us. "Eric, get to class. Jax, come with me."

Eric says as he walks away, "We'll talk later."

"Well, this is a familiar seat," I say to Mr. Pency in a lousy attempt at humor. I didn't plan on being here again, and I didn't count on Eric being all up in my face either. So much for talking to Emma.

Mr. Pency lowers his chin and looks over his glasses. "Why did Mr. Buccio see you near the 200 wing exit this morning when you should've been in class?"

"I tried to tell Joey, I mean Mr. Buccio, that I needed to take care of something with another student."

He takes off his glasses and sets them on his desk. "With Eric? ... You know what? Don't answer that." He folds his arms across his chest. "And where's your hall pass?"

"I told Mr. Hunter I was heading to the bathroom. He lets us leave without a pass."

"But you weren't in the bathroom," Mr. Pency says.

I sit up a little straighter. "A girl asked me to prom this weekend, and I told her I needed a few days to think about it."

"Harsh," Mr. Pency says.

Did he just use the word "harsh" on me? Is he allowed to do that?

"Sorry," Mr. Pency says, "you were saying."

"I needed to tell her I asked another person to the prom. I didn't want to text her or have her find out from someone else."

"Respectful," Mr. Pency says.

"Yeah, but Mr. Buccio, as usual, was stalking me and now the girl's wondering why I didn't show up to talk to her."

Mr. Pency picks up his phone and holds up his finger, signaling for me to wait a moment. He says into the phone, "Are you available for a few minutes?" He asks the person on the other line to help with another student and hangs up. Then, he says to me, "Would you like your counselor to call this student in so you can give her the news now? We may as well take care of this." He sighs. "Neither of you will be able to focus on schoolwork."

Why is he being so nice? Calling Emma to the counseling office seems like a good option. "Sure," I say.

"Head to the counseling office and take care of your business," Mr. Pency says, muttering under his breath, "Prom, sports, extra curriculars... such a distraction from learning."

Just when I think Mr. Pency is cool, he says something like that.

Emma walks into the counseling office, saying to Mrs. Annatol, "Did I forget something?"

"There's someone here for you," Mrs. Annatol says, and Emma notices me sitting on the couch.

"Hey," she says. Her cheeks streak red, and her voice is hoarse. I hope she's okay.

"Hey," I say. "Sorry I didn't make it to the parking lot. Joey's tracker skills paid off again and he brought me to Pency's office."

Emma sits on the edge of the couch cushion like she wants to run out of here.

"Um..." Emma starts. "I talked to Adele this morning. I know you're taking her to prom."

"Yeah, about that—"

"It's okay, Jax," Emma says with her palm facing me. "Honestly. It's okay. Finding out from Natalia wasn't great... but I get it." She looks at me and shrugs.

"Natalia?"

"Yeah. She was all in Adele's face this morning, which is how I found out."

I don't know what to say, though, judging from her calm expression, I think I should say, *Thanks for being so nice.*

"You and Adele go together," she says, and she laughs. "You both are sarcastic as hell. Your personalities make sparks." Her hands expand like an explosion. She adds, "In a good way."

I hadn't thought about it like that, but what she says makes sense. Having Emma understand my choice makes Eric's comments about the "eyeliner girl" matter less.

"I guess I like sarcastic," I say, and I snort out an awkward laugh. "So. You and me. We're okay?"

"We're okay," Emma says in her hoarse voice, nodding.

"Hey, before you go. Eric just stopped me in the hall and was giving me crap about going to prom with Adele. Have you heard anything?"

"Yeah. I've heard some things. I guess when you shake up the way things are, people get nervous. What matters most is that we know the way things are. Jax, we're friends who stick together."

I'm stunned. "You're a regular Yoda, Em."

"Yoda, huh? I might be small, but I'm wise. Is that what you're saying?"

"Basically, yes."

She smiles and gets up from the couch. "See you at lunch?"

"See ya," I say. That was too easy. Is she going to think about it more and then go ballistic at lunch? I ask the main office lady for a hall pass. Mr. Pency steps out of his office. "Everything work out, Jax?"

"I think so." Emma was trying hard to be okay and doing a good job at it. I turn to leave the office, then pivot. "Thank you."

I never thought I'd thank Mr. Pency for anything. Maybe one day, I'll thank him for making me go to AP Club.

CHAPTER 48

ALONZO HERNANDEZ

My Metro bus broke down this morning. I wish I'd arrived at school before the bell rang so I could've been with Adele, who was probably surrounded by people talking about her.

She texted me on Saturday night. Said Jax asked her to prom and that she's worried about what people will say. Rare for someone as bold as her.

Of all the days to be late.

I hurry into school at the end of first period. Adele waves at me when I spot her in the crowded hallway. She's smiling, which is a good sign. I slowly jog to close the distance.

"How you doin'?" I ask, examining her face for a hint of stress.

"Actually, good," Adele says. "I was worried about Emma, but she was amazing. If I was her, I wouldn't be that nice." Adele gives me a lopsided grin. "I'd be destroyed."

"Jax stopped by the car wash on Saturday," I say, "and told me Emma asked him to prom. Then, when I saw your text later, I wondered how today was gonna be."

"So, you knew about Emma on Saturday too," Adele says.

"I guess I should've texted you about that. It wasn't for me to say."

Adele says, "I get it. No worries. It's complicated only if we make it complicated."

"Okay. We'll go with that," I say, though I'm not so sure.

Adele, Emma, and I are sitting at our usual table in the commons and Emma sees Jax heading in. She waves, then pulls her hand down quickly. She says to Adele, "I guess you should be the one waving."

My heart speeds up as I watch Adele's hand gently grab Emma's arm. Then she lifts it into a wave. "We're still friends. All of us," she says. Emma's hand is flopping back and forth. "Wave if that's your thing."

I'm relieved all three of us are laughing.

When Jax arrives at our table, he holds out his fist for a bump with me. Then, he turns to Adele and Emma. "In honor of equality... bump?" Jax hovers his fist toward each of them.

Props to Jax. I can't help but smile when he blushes as he bumps fists with Adele. I can see how they fit. Jax asking Adele to prom makes sense, though I wish Emma hadn't been caught up in all that.

Jax turns to Adele. "I'm gonna need the necklace this afternoon. Would it be okay if I stopped by after school to pick it up?"

Adele and Jax arrange a pick-up time. I want to ask Jax about his plan, but I know it's best I don't know.

CHAPTER 49

JAX LOURDE

Every minute of this afternoon passed so slowly that I felt like I was stuck in a saltwater taffy machine. I ran through possible scenarios, including skipping school and breaking into the lady's house to put the necklace back into her jewelry box instead of going with my crazier plan. What if the lady already found her necklace but hasn't fessed up to Rosie's mom? What if the housekeeper recognizes me? I can't let doubts creep in and get in the way of my original plan.

Thinking about Alonzo and how he seems less on edge since we decided to clear Rosie's mom's name helps. I keep telling myself: *We're doing the right thing. We're doing the right thing.* And my stress is making the shade about me and Adele matter less.

I'm a total noob with prom. What am I supposed to do? Are Adele and me... Are we, like, a thing now? Should we hold hands? Should I hug her goodbye? Are we going to prom as friends, so hand-holding and hugging is not an option? All these questions swimming in my mind are harshing my happy.

Adele hands me the necklace in a small leather bag. She's already in her sweatpants; she's washed her face and looks natural and amazing leaning her shoulder against the doorjamb.

"Crud," I say when I look at the bag in my hand.

"What?" Adele's whole body goes rigid and upright.

"How do we know if she lost the necklace inside the bag or not?"

Confusion crosses Adele's face and then her eyes widen. "If you leave it in the bag and she still has the original bag, she'll be suspicious."

I nod. "She'll know something is off."

"If she wore the necklace, she probably didn't put it back in the bag," Adele says. "Especially if she lost it."

"It'd be harder to lose if it's in the bag," I say, growing more certain that I'm right.

"Take the necklace," Adele says as she holds out her hand. "I'll hang onto the bag."

I drop the bag into her palm. "Adele, what're we gonna do if the lady doesn't get in touch with Rosie's mom to tell her she found the necklace?"

We're frozen and quiet.

"Let's just get past today," Adele says. "At least we'll make the lady uncomfortable. She'll have to think hard about her accusation, and she'll know she was wrong."

"Yeah," I say. "She'll suffer, even if it's just a little." It won't be enough. I know it and Adele knows it. I say goodbye and walk away certain that if our plan doesn't work, we all are going to be devastated. Especially Alonzo.

CHAPTER 50

ALONZO HERNANDEZ

I 'm on a break at the Sudsy Auto and read a group text from Adele telling us Jax has the necklace and is heading to the lady's house. I want to throw my phone across the pavement. I know how this is going to end, even if Jax gets the necklace inside the lady's house.

I imagine knocking on the lady's door and telling her the whole thing. How four high school students were crazy enough to pool a crapload of money to buy a necklace to clear someone's name. How she needs to apologize to Rosie's mom. My heart is galloping, and I hate this feeling. I imagine the lady not opening her door because she doesn't know me. I imagine her calling the police to report a stranger at her door. I imagine finding a pro bono lawyer. But what exactly would contacting a lawyer do?

Adele keeps telling me to be patient. Patience can't change a thing while we wait and wait. I pace with my phone in my hand. My patience is tapped out.

I'm lying in my bed with a pen and my spiral notebook. If there's any lasting lesson I've learned from school, it's that writing out my thoughts helps me. With my covers over my head and reading light clipped to my notebook, it's just me and my pen. Writing makes me think logically because I can cross out my angry words and replace them with something less emotional and more rational. Let's face it: emotions push us into action, but logic wins.

Hearing my brother's deep breathing in the bed across our room slows down my heart. I think about what my friends and I are doing and, in a small way, we're making things better for my brother. Even if the woman doesn't apologize, one day I'll tell my brother that I stood up for Rosie's mom and I'll tell him to do the same if the opportunity is there. I'm finally able to close my notebook and set it with my pen and reading light on the floor under my bed, along with my AP Club notes and handouts, and try to fall asleep.

CHAPTER 51

JAX LOURDE

My twenty-three-year-old cousin, Simon, pulls into the lady's driveway. He turns toward me in the passenger seat. "You sure about this?"

I run my finger over my fake mustache to make sure it's secure. I'm wearing one of my dad's suits. This last weekend, I told Dad I was trying it on to prepare for prom and asked if I could hang onto it.

"Let's do this," I say to my cousin as I open the passenger door and step out of the car.

We both stand on the porch as we wait for the house cleaner to answer the doorbell. My heart lurches when Elizabeth swings open the front door, and my cousin holds out his business card to show Elizabeth. "I'm Simon Sutherton, with Housesafe." Simon really is an Housesafe agent and we're counting on Elizabeth not knowing which insurance the lady has. For all we know, they have Progressive or something. "We're here for an inspection to assess possible vulnerabilities in this home. You might be aware that a necklace was reported stolen."

"Yes," Elizabeth says, "I'd heard." She studies me a moment, which makes my pits damp. Her eyebrows lower, shadowing her eyes. "Come in. I'll stay out of your way."

Simon asks, "Which way is the master bedroom? We understand her jewelry box is there."

"Second floor," Elizabeth says, and she's peering at me again.

I shouldn't have come. My cousin could have planted the necklace without me. I want to check my mustache to make sure it's still fully stuck to my lip, but it would draw attention to it. "I'll take the second floor, and you take the first," I say to my cousin. I turn to the house cleaner. "We'll let you know when we're finished, Elizabeth."

Elizabeth's neck stiffens, and her brows crease. "How do you know my name?"

My cousin jumps in before I blow our cover. "The homeowner told us you'd be here and gave us your name."

Her body relaxes. "Oh. Okay." Elizabeth walks toward the kitchen, and I hurry up the stairs.

I make my way down the hallway, stepping into rooms, pretending to check windows—any access points for a robber. My cousin and I need to be quick so we're out of here before the owner gets home from work or wherever she is. But we need to stay long enough to look legit.

After two bedrooms, I find what looks like a master bedroom. I wander around the bed, through a walk-in closet, and into a spacious bathroom, deciding where it's best to drop the necklace. The laundry hamper strikes me as the best option. The lady or the house cleaner would be certain to find the necklace there, doubling the chances of the necklace being found.

I've just opened and closed the master bedroom window, pretending to assess entry points, when Elizabeth steps into the room with a basket filled with folded laundry. Thirty seconds earlier and she would've caught me dropping the necklace into the laundry hamper. "Your work is never done, right?" I say, though I regret being friendly the moment I open my mouth. The more I talk to Elizabeth, the greater the chance that she'll recognize me. And if she's bringing up clean laundry, it means she may not check the hamper before she leaves. It means we might have to wait a whole week before the necklace will be found, which will be torture.

CHAPTER 52

MISS HEATHER HALDEN

Jax, Adele, Emma, and the rest of the club members are nervous as I place the exams on their desks face down. None are talking and their eyes are wide.

"Do not turn over your exams until I say the word."

"So, no flipping over the exam, then?" Jax says, which makes us all sputter out uneasy laughter.

We hear a knock on the doorjamb, and our heads swivel to see Mr. Johnson standing in the doorway.

"Hey, Mr. Johnson," Samesh says.

Mr. Johnson says, "I hear y'all are taking a mock AP exam. Just wanted to stop by to tell you good luck."

I'm standing in the middle of the room. "They don't need luck. They're prepared for this."

Mr. Johnson steps away from the door, I return to my desk, and ninety minutes feels like thirty. I tell the AP Club members, "Time's up." All nine of them groan, which is a bad sign. "I'll get you your multiple-choice results by Thursday and your essays to you by next Tuesday."

As the AP Club members leave my classroom, Mr. Johnson is waiting to come in. What the hell does he want? Has he been lurking in the hallway all this time, watching the clock, ready to pounce?

"From the look on their faces, that may not have gone well," Mr. Johnson says to me as he approaches my desk.

And what might the faces of all your AP students look like after a mock exam? I want to ask. Mark Johnson is playing on my fears; his words are hard to ignore when my heart's pounding. The students' collective groan nags me and I'm eager to dive into their multiple-choice portion to see how bad the carnage is. I can't, though, because the worst human on the planet is standing in front of my desk. Maybe not the worst. After all, he did defend us at the board meeting. I stand so he doesn't have the upper hand. "We'll see soon enough how they all did. I noticed your AP students faces were pretty pale and drawn as well. What does that say about your teaching?"

"Touché," Mark says, smiling.

Why is he smiling?

He pulls a chair in front of my desk like he's planning to stay awhile. "Mind if I sit?"

"I'm in a hurry. I have one minute." I gather the papers and shove them into my backpack. "What can I do for you, Mr. Johnson?"

He remains standing, taking my hint, which is unexpected given his awful social skills. "I'll make this quick." He clears his throat. "I've noticed a marked improvement in Jax's work in my class." He loosens his tie and opens the top button as if he's getting comfortable for a long chat. "You've had a positive impact on Jax."

A compliment? Surprising coming from him. "I'm glad to hear that. I hear he raised his grade."

"Since Jax was attending your AP Club, I allowed him to make up work." He clears his throat again and adds, "I didn't want you to think I was a total jerk."

Too late.

It's silent for a few breaths. Is he waiting for me to say he's not a jerk? He'll be waiting till he's a wrinkly, hunched ninety-year-old.

"Jax is earning an *A* minus now," Mark says.

"Thanks for letting me know. I'll have to congratulate him on Thursday." I pause. "Maybe part of the reason Jax is doing better in your class is because you gave him an opening to succeed."

Mark winces. "Possibly."

"Now if you'll excuse me, I need to get home."

Mark's face softens, and he almost looks like a nice guy. "I hope the exams turn out well."

I watch Mark leave as my body has gone from cold to hot in a span of thirty seconds. What was that? How can he transition from his initial rude comment to being... actually... kind?

As I drive home, I replay Mark's and my conversation. First with his comment at the board meeting and then in my classroom, seeming to approve of the AP Club. Has he had a change of heart? If he has a heart. No, it's cruel to think that. Of course he has a heart. He's a teacher and teachers get into this profession because we care about kids.

I step into my apartment and settle at my dining table to score the AP mock exam multiple-choice portion. I try to focus on this task but am distracted with thoughts of Mark's visit. Why is it so unsettling? And why drop by on the evening of the mock exam?

Mark Johnson represents doubts. Faculty's, students', and, if I'm being honest, my doubts that a few nights a week can build stronger scholars. My AP Club members' expressions during the mock exam were a kaleidoscope of frowns, confusion, and worry—basically disbelief and fear creased into their faces. And why did Mark Johnson want me to know he made an exception for Jax, allowing him to make up missed work or retake exams?

I wobble my head, shaking off my negativity. Enough with the doubts. There are mock exams to be scored.

As I score the multiple-choice section, I make note of all the terms and skills I need to teach and reteach in future AP Club sessions.

We have only four weeks to learn all this material... Impossible.

CHAPTER 53

ADELE QUESTIN

Just a few hours earlier, during lunch, Jax told everyone that he'd successfully planted the necklace in the laundry hamper and that it was a matter of time before Rosie's mom would hear from the lady.

Now, Jax and I walk to his car after school, heading to grab a bite to eat before AP Club. "I *hate* the lady in the house! I'm about ready to go over there and yell at her," I say to Jax. "We should go right now!"

"Adele, calm down," Jax says.

I turn to him with my eyes shooting bullets. Calm down? Calm down at a time like this? I know he's frustrated, too, but *"calm down"*?

"Okay. Okay," Jax says, holding up his palms. "It was stupid to tell you to calm down. Adele, we are not going to the lady's house. For one, someone in the neighborhood might recognize us and think we're casing the joint. And two, you're too hyped up."

As we sit in his car in the burger place parking lot, I snatch a few of his fries. In between chewing our burgers, we air our opinions.

"You're the one who started this whole 'let's do something about the necklace' thing," I say.

"Yeah, but that doesn't include yelling at strangers and making things worse."

"Yeah, but it doesn't include torture and just sitting around waiting!"

Back and forth we go. Do something now. Wait. Do something now. Wait. Finally, exhausted and frustrated, our debate ends with waiting until Monday evening because it's most likely that Elizabeth will find the necklace when she grabs the laundry out of the hamper.

Jax starts his car and turns toward our school.

"I still think we should have gone to the lady's house," I say, to get the last word, and grab the last of his fries and stuff them in my mouth.

As Jax drives us back to school, Jax tells me how he impersonated an insurance guy, and planted the necklace in the lady's house. *OMG! That's a whole new level of crazy.* I ask, "What if Elizabeth tells the lady that Housesafe Insurance guys came to the house? What'll happen if she gets suspicious and calls the cops?"

"What crime is the lady reporting?"

"I don't know. Fair question." I sigh, turning to Jax. "I'm a worrier. I can't help it."

He takes hold of my hand, squeezes it, and says, "Everything is going to be fine... I hope."

When we arrive at AP Club, Miss Halden has a bunch of College Board information projected on the screen about how exams are scored. She starts with, "You'll see it's not as bad as you think."

Jax says, "Is that supposed to cheer us up, Miss H.?"

He acts like he's joking but I can tell he's nervous to get his results back. I wonder why he hasn't mentioned taking mock exams in Mr. Johnson's class. Maybe they haven't taken one yet.

I flip over my paper and see a big, fat 55 percent staring at me.

"At least half of you didn't correctly answer the question about extended metaphor." Miss Halden hands back exam results, flipping them over on each member's desk. "Emma earned the highest score on the multiple choice, and she says she wrote a song about figurative language to help her remember." Miss Halden is smiling like this is going to be fun.

"I sing in the shower, not in public," I say, tucking my hair behind my ear. If Jax hears me singing, he might regret asking me to prom and cancel.

Jax says, "You sing in the shower?" A huge grin is spread across his face.

I waggle my finger at him. "Uh-uh. Don't go there." I'm secretly loving that he's flirting with me.

Natalia tsks and rolls her eyes at us. Jealous much? Girl, get over it. She wasn't at AP Club on Tuesday, and it was better when we didn't have to deal with her snark.

Emma stands at the front of the class and leads us in a song about metaphors and similes—the worst singing I've ever heard, to the tune of Katy Perry's "Firework."

We're all singing, "Do you ever feel... like you don't understand..." We sound like nine cats that are being forced to take baths at the same time. The best part is that I'm so focused on trying to stay on pitch and making the words match the tune that I forget about the necklace, about Natalia, and my 55 percent. I've never done this badly on an exam. *Not as bad as you think?* I disagree with Miss Halden this time.

After singing, Miss Halden asks us to highlight words in the exam we can't define. I pretend to stretch so I can glance over at Natalia's desk. Miss Halden gave her a blank exam so she could review it, since she didn't take the exam on Tuesday. It's glowing with yellow ink. I shouldn't enjoy her stupidity, but I do. I highlighted only four words. I know most of the terms; I just couldn't make sense of the questions.

After the singing nightmare, Miss Halden puts me in a group with Natalia and Stewart to share what we know and don't know. Great. Natalia as a group member. That'll be a kick.

"That was ninety minutes of your life you'll never get back," Natalia says in the snottiest tone I've ever heard. I'd slap her but I'm not the violent type.

"Even though we're all stressed," I say, "I'm glad we practiced. At least we know what we're up against." I'm trying to sound optimistic. *Glad we practiced?* We all know that's a lie. If we can't handle a fake exam, how can we handle the real exam in May? How can we handle college?

"I'm not gonna take the exam," Natalia says. "It's just not worth it. That's why I didn't come on Tuesday. Look at this," she says as she points to her pages. "I don't know half of this. What's the point?"

At least she's being honest. I'll give her that... I wave away the temptation that the exam is optional. I'm not bailing on this. "Let's get to work." I could have said this nicer but why bother?

"Whatever," Natalia says. Stewart and I look at each other and shrug.

I write our highlighted words on poster paper. The other two groups do too.

Miss Halden collects the posters and hangs them on her whiteboard. We all gasp.

CHAPTER 54

MISS HEATHER HALDEN

"Holy crap!" After the club members have left, I'm pacing at the front of my room and feeling slightly dizzy. I've really stepped in it now. The sheer quantity of terms staring back at me knocks the breath out of me.

I'm looking at a ridiculously long list of terminology my club members *don't* know. I peer up toward the posters and need to sit down. "I'm leading them to the slaughter," I say to no one. I snort deep breaths into my nose.

I tell myself I'm doing the right thing and that the students know more now than they did a month ago. I remind myself what Alonzo wrote about the necklace, his AP friends, and hope. Scores are not a complete definition of who the club members are. I hear a soft knock on my door and get up, take a moment to level out my breathing, and open the door.

"Sorry to bother you, Miss Halden. I wonder if you have a few minutes," Judy says.

"Of course. Come in." I'm relieved it's not Mark Johnson.

"I didn't want to wait till tomorrow to talk about my score on the exam."

Judy, who's enrolled in Mr. Johnson's AP Lang and Comp class, earned the lowest score. Even though I want to challenge Mark Johnson's elitism, I don't want any kid to be miserable, and Judy looks miserable.

"Could I retake the exam? I could stay after school and try again," Judy says, desperation dripping from her words.

"Aw, Judy. It was for practice. It shows you what you need to work on for the next time. It's not necessary to retake this."

"But I have to!" Her voice is raised, her fists clenched at her sides.

Her tone and body language are jarring, but I strive to keep my breath steady and voice even. A stubborn urge is building in my chest. She's not earning a grade in an after-hours club, so why does she need to retake this? Get over yourself, kid. It's a mock exam for God's sake. This is exactly what I didn't want to happen when I started this club—to have overachiever kids clamoring for more. "Judy. Why is this important to you?" I attempt to quell my anger and find compassion.

Hiccupping sobs burst out of her. Seemingly out of nowhere.

This poor kid. The mock exam must feel very real to her. I grab a box of tissue, direct her to a desk, and sit next to her. "Where is all this coming from? It's not like this counts toward your GPA."

"I've never done this bad on anything," Judy sobs. Sobs with boogers trailing toward her lips and tears streaming down her cheeks.

I pull out a few more tissues and hand them to her. I can't help but think that sometimes performing poorly is character-building. It develops resilience. Despite my beliefs, I'm sure mentioning resilience right now would make things worse. "Let's back away from the Lang exam," I say. "What AP course is going well for you?"

"AP History," Judy says with a hint of a smile.

"So, history's your passion?"

Judy nods and tears have stopped falling.

I say, "Why is this mock exam so important?"

"I need to get into an Ivy League school. I need to make my parents proud!" Judy chokes out.

Oh dear. The tears are back. Desperate for something helpful, I finally say, "Judy, performing poorly on an AP Lang *mock* exam or even the real AP exam isn't going to hold you back from achieving your goals. Causing yourself this much stress and strife? That'll hold you back." I pause to let this sink in and give Judy a moment to blow her nose.

She audibly sighs twice and stands to collect her used tissues littering the desk.

"I'm doing you a kindness by not allowing you to make up the mock exam," I say and mean it.

"But..."

"Retaking the exam will just deplete you. Focus on moving forward. Now, go home and give some thought to how you're going to ease up." I stand up to guide her toward the door. A driven kid like this is going to run herself ragged by the time the real exam rolls around. "Maybe stop by the counseling office tomorrow. Or talk to a teacher you trust. Do something to keep from burning out, okay?"

"Okay, I guess," Judy says.

"We still have close to four weeks before the AP Lang exam. We'll get there. And we'll get there together without burning ourselves out. Got it?"

I close the door, and it hits me. How many other club members are crumbling like Judy?

CHAPTER 55

ALONZO HERNANDEZ

I t's early Sunday morning and my brother is probably in the living room because I can hear cartoons on the TV. I'm lying in my bed thinking about whether I have what it takes to succeed in college and if it's all worth it. I sit up so I can breathe better. Then I think about Rosie and how I get to see her today. Our families are having a barbecue this afternoon. My stomach growls at the thought of the marinated flank steak and *elotes*.

Being near Rosie helps me forget about AP and school. We're sitting in folding chairs on the lawn, our legs are touching, and our parents are sitting on the patio, laughing about something.

Rosie points toward my mouth and says, "You have corn stuck in your teeth." She giggles, which makes me laugh. I'm kinda embarrassed, but not really. I use my barbecue skewer to pick out the corn and show Rosie my teeth again. "All clear?"

She nods and her eyes crinkle and sparkle as she peers into my face. Rosie's parents are strict. She's too young to have a boyfriend or go on dates, they say. Her parents' attitude is kind of Victorian, I'll admit. Prom will be our first time together without our parents nearby and anticipation electrifies the air around us.

"Was Jax able to plant the necklace in the lady's house?" Rosie asks.

I pause to consider whether I want to ruin our moment with talk about the freakin' necklace. I can tell Rosie senses my anger, because her leg has shifted away from me. She turns to face me. "We have to talk about this, *mi amore*."

When Rosie speaks to me in Spanish, it gets my attention. "Why? Why ruin today with the ..." I lower my voice to barely audible, "necklace?"

She swirls her hand in the air and says, "It's here anyway."

I half nod. I hate admitting she's right. "True."

"What will you do if the lady doesn't apologize to my mom?"

"I'm still deciding. I have a few ideas."

"Ideas? Want to tell me about them?"

"Not now," I say. "I have an idea about prom, though." And I tell Rosie what I've been thinking for the past week. She agrees and tells me she'll take care of the details. "Let's go talk to my uncle about the limo."

As Rosie and I walk toward my uncle who is cleaning the grill, she brushes the back of her hand on mine, and it feels like electric eels swim up and down my body.

"*Tío*, if you keep cooking up delicious steak and corn, I'm not going to be able to fit into my tux for prom!" I say in Spanish to my uncle.

He laughs and pulls me in for a hug. I tell him my Sudsy Auto schedule and we arrange for me to work at the store the following week. "I need to keep some time to study," I tell him, and then I confirm our limo plans.

"You want to study together?" Rosie asks as we both stand near my uncle. "I could quiz you on you-know-what terms and you can help me with precalc."

"Sure." She means AP terms but knows not to discuss AP in front of my family. My friends took a mock exam, and I didn't. Even though I'm bitter about my circumstances, I'm still hopeful that I'll be able to convince Papá to let me take the real exam.

It's nighttime and I should be asleep, but I wrestle with my emotions—mostly anger and sadness—about the lady and the necklace. Instead of falling asleep, I tuck my covers over my head with my pen and notebook and get started.

CHAPTER 56

JAX LOURDE

After the club session on Thursday, Adele seemed sad about her score, so I pulled her in for a hug and it felt good to be in this together. I've noticed that whenever Adele and I touch, I don't see fireworks like in the movies. I just feel so amazingly relaxed, like I'm floating on a huge pile of pillows. It's nice.

It was weird on Friday, because Mr. Johnson was totally grilling me on how I did and how the rest of the AP Club members did on the mock exam. I was embarrassed to tell him I got 65 percent. He wanted to know how the students that weren't in AP did. Why did he need to know?

I'm in an AP class *and* am spending extra time in the evening, so my score should've been way higher than Adele's. It's not high enough. I earned basically what amounts to a *D*, which is the same as her. This is why I'm sitting at my desk in my bedroom on a Sunday afternoon studying AP Lang terms loving and hating the Katy Perry earworm about figurative language that Emma taught us. I'm gonna remember the definitions of metaphor, simile, and allusion forever. We're gonna learn another song on Tuesday, which'll get stuck in my head too. A small laugh bursts out of me as I imagine what we must've looked and sounded like last Thursday.

My phone buzzes, and it's a text from Eric asking me if I'm showing up at the park for a pickup game of basketball. I need to get rid of some stress and the best place to do that is on the court.

See you in 10 mins.

When I arrive at the park, I see five of my teammates warming up at one of the baskets, practicing free throws. Raleigh is here, which I hadn't expected. I think about leaving but realize my days of avoiding my former friend need to come to an end. Enough. Just play the game, I tell myself.

"Lourde. You're on my team," Raleigh says as he waves me over, which shocks the hell outta me. As I'm heading to the court, he passes the ball to me and, from where I'm standing, I sink a three-pointer.

"Not as rusty as I thought," I say, laughing a little at the surprise of it. I pass the ball back to Raleigh and we begin our game. The ball feels good as I dribble and toss, just playing and not worrying about who wins. The mock exam should be like this. It doesn't matter what our score is. *Just practice and show what you can do.* My shoulders relax and we all enjoy playing basketball for about thirty minutes.

I lob the ball to Eric. "Thanks for inviting me, man."

"I invited you because we need to talk," he says as he dribbles next to me.

"Talk?"

"About you talking to the board and shutting down the petition." He throws the ball to Raleigh.

Then Raleigh passes the ball to me, but I miss catching it. It rolls off the court, and Raleigh runs to catch it.

"We had every right to tell the board about the AP Club," I say.

"Whatever, man."

"The petition was stupid, and you know it," I say. What a douche.

Raleigh steps next to me and says to Eric, "I didn't sign it either because I thought it was senseless."

My head whips towards Raleigh. "You didn't? ... Didn't sign?"

Eric sneers and says to Raleigh, "So, you were against us too?" His legs are wide, and his arms are folded, like he's standing his ground or something.

"Eric, there's no for or against here." Raleigh presses his hand toward Eric. "We're just having a conversation right now. You all act like there's a limit on who gets to score a five on the AP exam."

"I said the same thing!" I'm stunned by how in sync Raleigh and I are. I didn't think this was possible. Ever again.

Raleigh says to Eric, "Do you think that by taking away something from someone else that you'll get more for yourself?" The basketball is tucked under one arm and Raleigh looks so calm. Kind too.

I notice that by now the other three basketball players are circling around us and, interestingly, they're standing closer to Raleigh and me than to Eric.

Eric's arms have loosened as if he might agree with me and Raleigh.

"Eric," Raleigh says, "are you going to let this go or not?"

"I don't know," Eric says as he picks up his sweatshirt from the ground. "Maybe." Eric heads toward his car.

"Thanks, man," I say to Raleigh.

"No need to thank me," Raleigh says. "When Eric asked me to sign the petition, I acted like I didn't have a pen. Then, he asked me again and I told him I'd do it later. Then, last week, when I heard you didn't sign it either and you presented to the school board, I decided to say something instead of avoiding it."

It hits me that the thing with the necklace is the same. I'm doing something instead of avoiding it and doing it because my AP Club friends are right there with me. I want to ask Raleigh if today means we can be friends again. To tell him I miss our pickup games and hanging out. But I don't.

"I hope Eric lets it go," Raleigh says, and he walks away.

CHAPTER 57

ADELE QUESTIN

"Hang on a second," I say into the phone to Jax. I race from the kitchen up to my room, sit on my bed, and lean against my headboard. "Hey there." I'm out of breath and can tell my voice is louder than it should be.

"What's up? You said in your text you needed to talk," Jax says.

"Nothing big. Just frustrated Rosie's mom hasn't heard from the lady in the house about finding her necklace." My chest is squeezing. This must be what it feels like to need heart medicine like Dad takes. I stand to look in the oval mirror hanging on my wall, and my face is beet red. I pace the floor with my phone on speaker. "Isn't there more we can do?"

"I honestly don't know." Jax sighs. "We just need to wait and see."

I'm still pacing, thinking I *have to* go to that lady's house tonight. If Jax won't come with me, I'll go alone.

"You still there?" Jax says.

"I'm here... and I'm *pissed!*"

"Me too."

"Okay then, let's do something. Let's go to the lady's house. Now."

"Could we please park where we did before?" I say to Jax as he pulls up near the lady's house.

"What's your plan?"

"If I tell you, it'll jinx it. You okay with waiting for me while I go up to the house?"

"Let's hope the lady doesn't have a shotgun."

"Not funny," I say, and I hear my voice quaver. "If I don't come back in around ten minutes or you hear gunshots, come rescue me. Got it?" I'm joking but the possibility makes my hands shake as I attempt to open the car door.

"Got it."

I ring the lady's doorbell and wait for at least one minute. I ring the lady's doorbell again and, as I'm waiting, I survey the porch. I see a video camera above the door. "I know you're home! I know you're in there!" I'm looking straight into the camera and pointing toward the lens. I look like a total loon, but I don't care.

I'm still yelling when a tall man with brown hair and brown eyes opens the door a few inches. "If you don't leave, I'll call the police."

"Oh..." I say as my eyelids lower, "you do that. I'm sure they'd love to hear about the—" then I raise my voice, "—*not-stolen necklace*!" I have no idea whether the police would be interested in my information, but it sounds convincing to me. I hear the click of heels on their marble entryway floor and hope it's the lady coming to talk to me. I hear a lady say in a sappy voice, "What's this?" She stands behind the man who's probably her husband.

I pull my shoulders back to look upright and normal. The blonde, very thin lady opens the door wider, and says, "What's this about a necklace?" My gaze lands on an ugly, huge necklace—different from the David Yurman one. This one looks like a yoke an ox would wear to plough a field. It's over the top. I didn't like her before, but I hate her even more now.

"Hi," I say, and I wave, which feels kind of ridiculous. "I'm a high school student and a friend told me you accused his neighbor of stealing a necklace. I know my friend, and he's *honest*. If he says your house cleaner didn't steal your necklace, then she didn't steal it!"

The probably-husband says, "Honey. Is she talking about the necklace you reported stolen to our insurance company?"

The lady says to her probably-husband through gritted, gleaming white teeth, "We'll talk about this later, dear."

Of course, she claimed the necklace on her insurance policy. I watched a documentary with my mom about insurance fraud, so I know a little about that. Now that the necklace is returned and I assume she found it by now, I wonder if she called her insurance company to let them know she doesn't need them to give her money for it.

"What proof did you have?"

"What?" the lady says.

"Wouldn't your insurance company need proof your necklace was stolen?"

"You don't know what you're talking about. You need to leave," the lady says, taking hold of the door.

"Actually, I think I do know what I'm talking about," I say, though I have no idea what I'm talking about. Then, I lower my voice to try to sound calm and in control. "I can leave—"

"Are you the one that sent my wife a letter?" the probably-husband interjects.

So, he is her husband. "What letter?"

The lady sneers at me. "Don't act like you don't know."

"No. I really don't know. What letter?"

The lady clip-clops away while her husband stands mute at the door. She comes back with a folded piece of lined notebook paper and turns it around so I can see it.

It's Alonzo's handwriting! "When... um... When did you receive that?"

"Yesterday?" the husband says. "It's very well written. Persuasive." The lady scowls at her husband for saying this. I can't help but smile.

Alonzo's a good writer, but was it enough to convince the lady to call Rosie's mom and apologize? I'm tired of waiting for this biotch to apologize. I know what might speed up her apology. I look toward the husband and say, "You know about social media, right?"

"Of course, I do," the man says.

"I'll leave but then I'll go to the sidewalk at the end of your driveway," I say pointing toward the road. "The *public* sidewalk. Then, I'll record myself explaining that an innocent person lost her housecleaning job over an accusation with no proof."

"You wouldn't dare. That's libel!" the lady says.

"Would it be libel? Libel is printed and slander is spoken," I say. "You know what? I'll just ask my mom... She's a lawyer."

The husband turns to talk to the lady. "Now, honey. You know the letter made some good points and you said you'd think about it." The husband turns back to me and says, "There's no need to post anything. We'll take care of it."

CHAPTER 58

JAX LOURDE

Exactly ten minutes have passed, and I open my car door to head up the driveway to check on Adele. Then I see her racing out onto the sidewalk like Sha'Carri Richardson. What's her expression? Terror? No. Happiness, maybe?

Adele climbs into the passenger seat laughing and panting. Is she okay? I open my Hydro Flask. "Here. Take a few sips of water. Catch your breath." She glugs, takes a breath, and then glugs some more. We're still parked. I want to make sure she's fine before I start driving.

She turns to me, and her gorgeous blue eyes twinkle like she has a secret. "That was so amazing! You're not going to believe it."

"Just tell me what happened!" Now I'm out of breath too.

Adele describes their conversation, her social media threat, and what the couple said. No apology, yet. No remorse. I don't want to be a total buzzkill for Adele, but her rant at the couple changed nothing.

"Alonzo gave them a letter. It arrived yesterday," she says.

"A letter? No way! How'd he write it without ratting me out? Without saying we planted a necklace?" Alonzo's got some *cojones* writing a letter and delivering it. Risky move for all of us. Though, who am I to talk when I pretended to be an insurance agent?

"Maybe the same way I did. I just said the previous house cleaner didn't steal the necklace, and they have no proof. I just played on her conscience—"

"If she has one," I say, and this makes Adele laugh. "They said they'd take care of it?"

"Yeah," Adele says. "Maybe to stall me posting something on social media tonight. I'm pretty sure they need to talk to each other. Make a decision."

"From what you've described, sounds like the husband is more reasonable. Nicer."

"I thought that too," Adele says.

Both of our phones ping and we open a text from Alonzo.

> UR not going to believe this.

> Rosie just said the lady called her mom to say sorry. Said she'll pay wage for past month! I'll tell U more in AM.

Adele and I are laughing and screaming in my car. I'm drumming my hands on my car roof, and we're high-fiving. Tears are pouring down Adele's cheeks.

We settle, and Adele is wiping her tears with her sleeve. She texts Alonzo, saying she's excited to hear more in the morning.

"Alonzo wrote the lady a letter, huh?" *Brilliant move, bro.*

Adele nods.

"I wonder what was more convincing for that couple: an angry teenager or a quiet, persuasive letter."

Adele's cheeks are red, her voice is soft. "The quiet letter." She looks out her passenger window, then turns to me and smiles. "Who cares? We all did it. All four of us."

After I drop off Adele, I wish I could go to Raleigh's house and tell him about the necklace and what we did for Alonzo's neighbor. Raleigh would have loved hearing this happy ending.

CHAPTER 59

ALONZO HERNANDEZ

Rosie, her mom, her Grandma Maria, and my mama are standing in the middle of our living room. Both our moms are crying and hugging. Rosie's dad is at work and my dad has one hand on Mama's shoulder. I'm trying not to cry in front of Rosie, but I want to because I'm so happy, relieved, and frustrated. Frustrated that we had to defend her mom in the first place. Frustrated that we had to wait so long for an apology. Frustrated that I had to write a letter weighing on the lady's conscience instead of her apologizing on her own. Watching my mama, papá, brother, Rosie's mom, Rosie's grandma, and Rosie... it's like the stress we've felt for the past few weeks is being washed away, one wave after another.

I did this. Words pushed the lady into doing what is right. I can't wait to tell Miss Halden about my letter.

After Rosie's family leaves, I say to Papá, "I need to talk to you about something." Mama hears me say this. There's something in her expression that makes me wonder if she knows that I had something to do with the apology and that I've been continuing to study AP Lang and Comp. She leads my brother to bed, so Papá and I have privacy.

"I need to confess something. Actually, two things," I say. Papá's face drops into a frown. Maybe I shouldn't have led with the word *confess*, especially after being caught in a lie about AP Club.

Our joyful celebration has come to a halt, at a dead end. But I hope I can build a road through this. I taste salt and swallow my fear. "I need to tell you about AP, my friends, and what we did." I switch to Spanish to show respect and hope that the angry expression Papá is wearing will fade.

I swallow again. I explain that I've continued lying to him and Mama, because I've kept up my studies of AP despite not being at the club physically. I explain that I am signed up to take the AP exam in May. I explain that three friends and I replaced the missing necklace. I describe my letter to the lady, and that writing it made my future as clear as the infinite night sky exploding with stars. I point out the window upward and, for a fleeting moment, believe my confession to my papá is convincing him. Then, I look into his cold stare.

Papá shakes his head, raises his voice, and says in Spanish, "You're not taking the AP exam! You're not going to college. You are working in my store."

Trying to reason with him is like talking to a wall. For a moment, I'm tempted to just give in. To agree to work in his store. Then, I imagine my brother, down the hallway, straining to overhear Papá's and my debate. "I want to be a lawyer. I want to defend people like Rosie's mom. And sticking up for her showed me what I want to study in college."

Then, I see Papá's jaw relax just a little and his fists unclench. Maybe my words removed a few bricks from the wall I was talking to a moment ago. But then he says, "You need to go to bed. We'll discuss more later."

So, that's it for now? No resolution. And when is *"later"*? Where're the props for what my friends and I have accomplished? There's no, "Thank you." No, "You did a good job." No, "Way to stand up for what is right."

I quietly climb under my covers, trying not to wake my little brother. Then, I hear my brother whisper, "I'm proud of you."

The following morning, Jax, Adele, Emma, and I meet in front of my locker to celebrate. When I tell them about my letter, Adele says, "Did you keep a copy? I'd love to read it."

My face flames hot. "Sure. It's right here," and I pull it out of my backpack and hand Adele the spiral notebook.

"Okay if I read it out loud?" Adele asks.

I look at Emma and Jax, and they nod like they want to hear too. "How about if I do?" I say. "It's messy. My rough draft." I clear my throat and then it's like the four of us are inside a sealed bubble where no movement or sound can distract us.

"Dear homeowners: A few weeks ago, you fired a person who's important to me. I've tried unsuccessfully to ignore my sadness and discouragement with the injustice of your accusation. I'm writing to you because I can't ignore this any longer. You accused this honest person of stealing a necklace with no proof to back up your claim. I know this person well and she would never put up a fight, even over an egregious lapse in justice."

"I like your use of egregious," Adele says.

"Shhh," Emma says to Adele, holding her finger to her lips.

I continue, "Your former house cleaner doesn't know I'm contacting you. You need to know your action created a far-reaching reaction—one you may never feel in the comfort of your home. Of course, financially, your former house cleaner's family took a hit. What hit hardest, though, was the broken social contract established in our community (and this includes you, if you're thinking we're separate). As you know, our justice system is based on being innocent until proven guilty. You did not afford this right to my beloved neighbor. I can't help but wonder what your investigative evidence proved. If you investigated at all." I look up at Emma, Jax and Adele and their faces are intense and focused.

"This is my initial plea that you apologize to your previous house cleaner and pay her for wages lost this month. I sincerely hope to hear from my neighbor that you've made the necessary phone call."

"Ooo. Polite but firm," Jax says. "That's good!"

"I purposely used the phrase 'initial' to hint I wasn't going away," I say. "That'd I'd keep bugging them."

"A gentle threat," Adele says, and then steps beside me and looks over my shoulder. "Did you sign it with your name?"

"Nope. I signed it with 'a member of our community.' I even underlined 'our.'"

"The pen is mightier than the sword!" Jax says, pointing his finger toward the ceiling in a theatrical gesture.

We laugh at Jax's corny quotation and head to class happier than we've felt for a long, long time.

What I didn't tell my friends is that I won't be able to take the AP Lang and Comp exam in May. At least, not until I can convince my papá to let me. If I can convince him.

CHAPTER 60

MISS HEATHER HALDEN

For the past four days, I've worried about this evening's AP Club session, with the terms and vocab looming on the poster paper reminding us of what the students don't know. To my surprise, the students' energy is buoyant.

I return the mock AP essay they wrote last Tuesday, and their scores buoy them even more.

"Redemption!" Jax yells as he raises his essay with both hands above his head like a trophy.

"I got a five out of six," Adele says. She high-fives Jax.

Judy isn't here. I wonder if she'll be back on Thursday. Either she's easing up on her relentless schedule or giving up. I hope it's easing up. No sign of Natalia either and I push away my panic over dwindling club members.

Club members race through flashcards with terms and vocabulary. They'd decided to divide into teams and time themselves for friendly competition. I can't help but smile at their energy.

"Ha!" Jax yells. "Twenty-three words right!"

"We were close. Twenty-two's not bad," Emma says to Jax's group. "If Alonzo were here, we'd beat you guys."

I see their confidence and my confidence grows too. We end the session on a high note.

Adele is packing her vocab list into her binder. I step over to her desk, gesture with a stack of flash cards, and ask, "Do you think if I gave these to you that you and Alonzo might study them together?"

Adele takes the stack from my hand. "We might."

After club members have gone, my high note slides down an imaginary trombone to a low note when I read an email from Mr. Pency telling me that Judy's parents called to complain that I wouldn't allow their daughter to retake the mock exam.

Just great. Now I need to take time tomorrow to talk to Mr. Pency and deal with Judy's parents' complaint. For now, though, I won't allow one student and her parents to taint my AP Club joy.

My heels are stinging because I'm walking down the hallway—more like stomping—toward Mr. Pency's office the following morning. If I looked in a mirror right now, I would see steam coming out of my nostrils and ears.

"What's the harm in having Judy retake the mock exam?" Mr. Pency says once I'm sitting in his office.

"The intention was for the mock exam to show me and the students their successes and gaps. Judy now knows her gaps and can study from there. She gains nothing from retaking the exam except possibly ulcers and a nervous breakdown."

"That's quite dramatic, Miss Halden," Mr. Pency says.

Of course I'm dramatic. "I'm being dramatic to prove a point that she is under tremendous stress. She's stated as much."

"No more stress than other students here," Mr. Pency says.

"This isn't just about Judy. It's also about my time and stress. I'm already adding hours to my week with the AP Club and don't need to add more with an unnecessary retake."

Mr. Pency says, "The parents don't see it as unnecessary."

"I fail to see the advantage."

"Please allow Judy to retake the exam."

I detect a strain in his voice. "Mr. Pency, are you directing me to do this?"

"No. No, of course it's your choice. It would be better if you allow Judy to retake it," he says as his eyes blink rapidly.

"So, basically, you're directing me."

"It would just be better."

I set my hands on the arms of my chair. "I need to think about this." Then, I stand to leave. I pause at his door. "I'll circle back with you by tomorrow."

I march toward my classroom fuming. My first-period students will be showing up in ten minutes, and I need a calm, friendly Miss Halden face, not a frustrated, defeated face.

I close my classroom door, keep it locked for a few minutes, and plop down in my desk chair. My chest is heaving, and I vacillate between just giving in—allowing Judy to retake the stupid exam—and not bending to the will of perfectionism. This is not what I intended when I started the club in February. I wanted it to be about the climb, not the top of the mountain.

I unlock my door, and, with a warm welcome—albeit a fake warmth—greet my first-period students waiting outside.

I make it through the day without allowing my frustration to seep into my lessons and call it a victory. Then, I wallow in self-pity as I walk toward Mr. Pency's office after school.

"Mr. Pency, with all due respect, I've thought about it, and I will not allow Judy to retake the mock exam. I'd like to tell her myself and send an email to her parents, if you don't mind."

He leans forward, his mouth flat and brows furrowed. "I heard from Judy's mom again, after you and I spoke this morning. She said one of Judy's friends saw a post on social media last night. Judy posted that she wanted to kill herself. That she felt like a complete failure."

Oh, God. I recall Judy's free-write from her therapist's point of view. Her mental health is at stake.

Mr. Pency continues, "Mrs. Annatol is in contact with the family to set up a safety plan for Judy. We think it's best for her to take a break from the AP Club."

"I feel terrible."

"Don't blame yourself, Miss Halden. There are likely multiple factors in Judy's current crisis."

He's right. My intentions were good when I urged Judy to ease up on her schedule, though my guilt over my stubbornness nags at my conscience. If only I had allowed her to make up the mock exam, she would have felt less desperate. Perhaps. But this is a slippery slope. We can't snowplow the way for every teenager. It's impossible. If it hadn't been a mock exam that pushed Judy too far, it would have been something else. A math test? A relationship breakup? It's hard to predict.

Still wallowing in self-pity and concern for Judy, I walk down the hall toward my classroom. My eyes are stinging, and I blink to withhold tears.

I'd at least like to make it to the privacy of my classroom. I glance toward movement and see Mark Johnson coming out of his classroom into the hallway.

I blink hard. Why him? Why now?

"Heather, is everything all right?" Mark asks.

Remarkably, his tone is sympathetic, and he called me by my first name, which he's never done before. My tears start to trickle. I swipe my cheeks and turn away, embarrassed.

"Hey. What's going on? Come in." He leads me through his door. I've never been inside his classroom. I scan the walls of students' posters and celebrations of scholarly achievement. I hate to admit it, but it's impressive... and pleasant. He sets a box of tissues on the desk where I'm seated. This act of kindness releases more tears.

"You're usually stoic," Mark says. "Something awful must've happened for you to cry."

I shouldn't trust him. Mark might bask in my misery. I sniffle. Maybe I can trust him. After all, he's a teacher. We're in this together. "It's one of your students. Her parents complained." I leave out Judy's post for now.

Mark's mouth flattens sternly. "Let me guess. Judy's mom. She's pushed back on just about every graded assignment that was less than an *A*... including complaining to Mr. Pency on a few occasions."

So, we're allies now? The thought is surprisingly comforting. "It's worse than that. Judy posted on social media that she wants to kill herself. Over an exam. Some of these kids are so fragile. It's a frightening responsibility."

"Welcome to the frightening responsibility club," Mark says. "Of course, kids are in crisis elsewhere, but it goes with AP territory."

"So, basically, pushing for greater academic achievement has a dark side."

Mark shrugs. "Pretty much."

It's stone quiet in here and now that I've stopped crying, it's awkward sitting here alone with Mark. I don't know what else to say and want to retreat to my own classroom. "I better get going. I'm sure you have a lot to do."

He nods. "So do you." I'm almost out the door and he says, "My first year teaching AP..."

I turn around to listen. He continues. "I panicked when my students took their first mock exam and saw their dismal results. To add to my panic, a kid attempted—not just threatened—suicide after the results."

I can't believe he would admit to having alarming student results. I can't believe a kid would be suicidal over a practice exam. Then again, I *can* believe it. I've placed tremendous importance on my AP Club members' results. So much so that their results could determine whether I stay at or transfer out of this high school.

"One more thing," Mark says, breaking into my thoughts. "I'm truly sorry about the AP Lang students who started that petition."

My back tightens, and the goodwill I was feeling toward Mark Johnson fades.

"Mr. Pency told me a couple of my AP students started a petition opposing your AP Club members taking the AP Lang and Comp exam. That's why I came to the board meeting."

My hands are on my hips. I look away and back to Mark. "Thank you for saying that some of your students earn twos." As much as I don't want to thank Mark, he deserves it.

"No need to worry, Heather. Jax and Raleigh have put a stop to it for good." Marks says with his palms outstretched. "Then, I followed up with the two students that started it."

"That's not the point!"

"What is the point, then?"

"The point is"—I blink as I consider what to say next—"is that there are not limited exams or Frederick Douglass books or National Merit accolades. Students should have access."

I spin to face the door and leave without another word. I hear Mark saying something. I'm sure he said, "I agree."

CHAPTER 61

ADELE QUESTIN

We're sitting at the dinner table, and my mom has just asked me for the money left over from my prom dress. I thought she'd forgotten about the cash since she seldom asks me for change after I go to a movie or to the Chilly Swirl.

"I—I spent it," I say, hoping she drops the subject.

"You spent it? All four hundred dollars?"

I nod, though not convincingly, because Mom says, "Adele Jean Questin, you're lying to me." Her eyebrows are high on her forehead, which means she's going to question me like I'm on the witness stand.

"Don't be mad," I say, leaning forward. "There's a logical explanation."

"Oh, I hope there is."

I explain to mom about the necklace, and she listens without interrupting, which is rare.

"Huh." Mom pauses like she's putting together facts. "Maria mentioned to me that her daughter was accused of stealing a necklace and that the homeowner recently called her daughter to apologize—"

"Wait. Did you just say Maria? Our Maria is... Rosie's grandma?"

"Who's Rosie?"

"Rosie is Alonzo's neighbor, and it was Rosie's mom who was accused."

Mom's face brightens. "You had something to do with the homeowner apologizing?"

"Not just me. Four of us did it." I clutch my mom's arm. "But you can't tell Maria because they can't know we did this. We want them to think the lady at the house just found her necklace." My eyes well up with tears. "I helped Maria too?" *Wow. Full circle.*

Mom sets her hand on my cheek. "You helped more people than you know, honey." She leans in to kiss my forehead. "I'm so proud of you." She sits back in her chair. "But you should've told the truth from the beginning. You've breached my trust, so for the next few months, I expect you to give me a receipt and the change. Understood?"

"Yeah," I say. "You're right." It's best not to argue with Mom.

"The tent, awning thingy my mom is renting for us should hold sixteen people sitting in chairs, so of course we'll have enough room for your date," I say to Emma while we're eating lunch. "Your date is your brother's friend, Greg?"

Emma nods.

"And his last name is Knight?"

Emma looks confused. "Yeah. So what?"

"It's like Jane Austen's *Emma*. You're going with the family friend, Mr. Knightley! Except it's Knight."

Emma nods and claps.

"You're such a cheerleader," I say. Six months ago, who would've guessed I'd be joking with a cheerleader about being a cheerleader?

Emma smiles and says, "How did I not think of the parallel before? Funny."

Alonzo is saying names and counting on his fingers, then says, "You'll have plenty of room. So far, there are six of you, so you could fit another ten people."

"I can't believe prom is just three weeks away," Jax says. Every time Jax brings up prom, I try to act all calm on the outside, but I'm terrified on the inside.

"And we have spring break next week," Emma says.

I nod and then look toward Alonzo. His expression looks like he's up to something. "What are you thinking right now?"

Alonzo takes out his wallet and pulls out two prom tickets for our school. I snatch the tickets out of his hand. "Why do you have these tickets?"

Alonzo smiles. "Why do you think?"

"Does this mean you're going to both proms?" Now I'm clapping.

Emma swats my forearm, laughing at me. "Who's the cheerleader now?"

I can't help but laugh. Me? Acting like a cheerleader? That's funny.

"Last weekend," Alonzo says, "Rosie and I decided to get a refund for her prom tickets and buy them for here instead. I couldn't miss our prom. Not after everything we've gone through together. Rosie wanted to be here too. We're bringing the best burritos in LA for our picnic."

Jax rubs his hands together. "Ooo. I love burritos!"

My mouth is still wide open. I finally say, "I'm in shock!... That's amazing!"

Alonzo nods.

"You sneaky sneak! You've known since last weekend and didn't tell us?" Do I love that he surprised us? Or am I upset that he didn't tell me a week ago? I slug him on his arm.

"Ow!" Alonzo says.

I cock my head. "That means I finally get to meet the mysterious Rosie." And I'm not one bit jealous. Alonzo is still my friend. After AP Club and the necklace, nothing will change that. I reach for Jax's hand and lace my fingers through his.

"Rosie gets to meet *us*," Jax says.

CHAPTER 62

MISS HEATHER HALDEN

Over spring break, I caught up on resting, reading essays, and hiking a couple of times with a friend. It was a relief to get out from under piles of student papers and to take a break from thinking about Judy. Yesterday, our first day back from break, Mrs. Annatol assured me Judy would be fine, but I would have felt more certain if I could hear Judy say she's okay.

Today, of course, Judy isn't at our club session. After the club members are settled, I say, "We have two more sessions before your exam." I try to ignore the blender in my stomach. I notice Natalia's not here tonight. Her attendance has been inconsistent since we started in February. And Alonzo's absence leaves the biggest gap.

I continue. "Does anyone feel like the closer to the AP exam we get, the faster time accelerates?"

"Yeah," Adele says. "It's like Sonic the Hedgehog."

I nod. "Do you all want to come in for both sessions or take Thursday off?"

In chorus, all seven club members say, "Come in!"

"You have prom this weekend and you won't be too distracted to study? You don't want to rest up?"

"We can handle it, Miss Halden," Adele says.

I don't always need to take care of these capable people. They'll decide what they can and can't handle. We discuss what's most urgent and land on a Socratic Seminar, reading a late-nineteenth-century essay about why society shifted from Romanticism.

"They talk funny and are hard to understand," Emma says, scrunching her mouth and nose.

"Ye olde English, me thinks, is confusing," Jax says with a smirk.

Jax's corny humor gives us a break from the intensity and pressure of limited time. My eyes sting with sentiment as I make eye contact with each of these hardworking, likable people, and listen to them refer to the text to support their observations and commentary. Though, the discussion's not the same without Alonzo.

All ten students were registered for the exam a while ago, so it's available if Alonzo wants it. I've been tempted to encourage him to take it. After all, the exam is during the school day. Yet, it means interfering with his parents' wishes. I've been tempted to contact his parents to explain the importance of the exam, but will I make things worse? If I feel this conflicted, how must Alonzo feel?

CHAPTER 63

ALONZO HERNANDEZ

"Could we sit down to talk, please?" I ask Papá in Spanish, making sure my language is formal to show respect. I pour us both a glass of water and hope my stomach calms down. It's been churning all day since I asked Papá last night if we could talk about my future. I think he made me wait until today on purpose. To make me sweat.

"Right now, my friends are at our second-to-last AP club session." I pause to check my papá's expression to see if it's okay to continue. I can't read his face but at least he doesn't look as angry as he was a few nights ago. His hands are folded on the kitchen table as he waits for me to continue. "I was able to get all *A*'s in my classes, be at the club two nights a week, and work at least twenty hours." My papá folds his arms. Not a good sign. I take a sip of water. "You've always taught us not to quit." My voice cracks. "I feel like I'm quitting."

"You didn't quit," Papá says in Spanish. "I told you not to go. It's different."

I try a different tactic. "You were able to open your business because you were a good investor. I was named one of ten National Merit Scholar candidates at our school." I look straight into his eyes. "Working hard at school is like an investment. I'm a *scholar*, Papá."

"So? The auto store needs *scholars* too!"

I hesitate, trying to think of something to say that won't add fuel to Papá's frustration. Then we hear, "He doesn't love cars like you do."

Papá and I turn to see Bennie standing in the kitchen doorway. "Papá, who works on cars with you? Who asks questions about pistons and ignition and alternators?" Bennie shrugs his shoulders as if he's waiting for an answer. I don't dare say anything. Finally, Bennie says, "I do. I love cars. I want to work in your auto store." Bennie swallows, then adds, "Alonzo doesn't." He looks to me, like he's asking for approval. I nod once, and I can feel my eyes sparkling with love for my loyal and brave brother. My gaze shifts from my brother to Papá. I'm afraid to see his expression.

Papá's hands are flat on the kitchen table. At least his arms aren't crossed anymore. "What are you saying, Bennie?"

"Alonzo has his nose in his books. I have my nose under the hood of a car," Bennie says. His statement is poetic and true. Does he realize how eloquent he is?

Papá turns to me and sighs. "A scholar, huh?"

He's challenging me and it's best to keep my response simple. "Yes." I sit up straight in my kitchen chair.

"You want to be like your friends?" he says, his eyebrows rising like a challenge.

"No, Papá," I say, and place my hand over his. Surprisingly, he doesn't pull away. "Jax's parents are divorced, Emma's mom is dead, and Adele is lonely and doesn't have a brother like I do." I look over at my thirteen-year-old brother and smile. "I just want to be me and be in this family. *And* attend the AP Club..." I may as well ask for it all. "And take the exam."

"You *lied* to me." Papá's voice has an unyielding edge to it. "Lied to Mama. I forbid you to go to the club on Thursday." Dad looks at Bennie and then me. "You *may* take the AP exam, though. Let's see how that goes." He pats his hands on the table, like he's adding punctuation to his statement, then leaves the kitchen without another word.

CHAPTER 64

JAX LOURDE

Our last AP club session is not the same without Alonzo. We're competing in a rematch of the flashcard terms and I'm fidgeting with my basketball under my desk between my knees. Moving my hands helps me focus.

Prom is one day away, and I'm amazed I'm not nervous. Not at all. Adele is easy to be around. I laugh at the surprise of this. Who would imagine Adele being easy to be around?

We'll be surrounded by our AP club friends. It'll be like our lunch table, only in fancier clothes.

I'm more nervous about the AP Lang exam the following week.

My mom and Adele's mom set up the large awning tent thing, chairs, and two folding tables. Mom brought a few extra chairs in case we want to invite any last-minute picnickers. Folded fleece blankets are tucked over the backs of three chairs in case anyone is cold. Mom thought of a lot of stuff, like water bottles in a cooler; candles to keep bugs away; and clippy, weighted thingies to keep tablecloths from blowing off. And, of course, solar-powered twinkle lights, which she unwound from a tree in our yard—just as determined as the four of us not to spend extra money.

Alonzo and Rosie arrive with a pan of burritos. Rosie seems shy but she'll probably be more talkative once we sit down. Adele and I brought prawns and cocktail sauce. Emma and Greg walk up the path toward us with a tossed salad and two kinds of dressing. Pete and Payton arrive with macarons, whatever those are.

Another car parks a hundred yards from our picnic area as we're setting out the food. A guy and girl get out of a shiny SUV and the guy is carrying a grocery bag. I turn to get a better look at this couple and the guy waves at Pete. I swear it looks like Raleigh.

Who invited... Why is he...? Confusion is flooding my thoughts and I'm walking toward Raleigh and his date, Abby, who was our basketball manager. Raleigh offers his hand for a shake. I take his hand and place my other hand on his shoulder.

"You're probably wondering why I'm here," Raleigh says.

"Wondering, but happy too." I feel a nervous smile twitching.

"I've been carpooling with Pete. He told me what you all did for Alonzo's neighbor." Raleigh pauses, lets go of my hand, and is looking at me with what I'd like to think is respect. "Pete and I were saving money on gas to help out."

"I heard, but I didn't know you were in on it." I'm trying to act all casual like it's every day that my former best friend and I talk like this. "We really appreciated the money," I say and can feel my voice shaking a little.

Raleigh just says, "Definitely." He sets a bag of tortilla chips and two kinds of salsa on the table. Adele tears open the bag, takes a chip, and dips it into the pico de gallo.

"We have extra seats. Do you want to join us?" I say.

"Of course they're joining us," Alonzo says.

Emma says as she giggles, "Jax. A few of us knew Raleigh was coming. We wanted it to be a surprise."

"It's a surprise." I turn to Raleigh. "A good surprise."

Raleigh and Abby sit near Emma and Greg, and Adele and I sit near Alonzo and Rosie. Our conversations are like an accordion. Sometimes the whole group discusses one topic and other times there are separate conversations. Sometimes, we speak in Spanish and Alonzo and Rosie beam.

"This is way better than a restaurant," Raleigh says to the whole group. "It's quiet enough for us to hear each other."

"And we don't have to wait for a waiter to take our order and bring us our food," Emma says as she swats at the air. "I could do without the wasps, though."

"The wasps are part of the experience," Raleigh says as he waves over his plate to keep a wasp from landing on his burrito.

Pete brings up the basketball championship game, and Raleigh and I just groan and ask to change the subject.

Raleigh says, "I've heard several juniors say they want to join the AP Club next year."

"I hope I can convince my dad to let me join," Alonzo says.

Adele says, "Miss Halden said she'll be our advisor again."

"Our AP Lang exam is next Thursday," I say. "Is everyone ready for it?"

"As ready as I can be," Adele says. She places her hand on Alonzo's shoulder and sighs. "It won't be the same without you."

Alonzo smiles and announces, "I talked to my dad, and he agreed to let me take the exam." We chorus a loud cheer, and Rosie's eyebrows raise.

I say to Rosie, "We're a rowdy bunch. Sorry we startled you."

She says, "No worries. I'm happy for Alonzo. You're rowdy, amazing friends." She glances at Alonzo. "I thought he might have been exaggerating about you all, but he's not."

It's weird to have Raleigh here... as if we hadn't been feuding with or ignoring each other for the last three months. Our necklace plan repaired an injustice, and it might have repaired Raleigh's and my broken friendship too.

Mom and Mrs. Questin return to clean up for us, so we don't have to in our formal clothes. The girls change out of their sports shoes or Birks and the guys change out of their Crocs into their fancier shoes for photos. Mom guides us in front of what looks like an ancient tree and starts taking pictures of couples and the whole group.

Mom makes us pose for more pictures as a group, as couples, all the boys, all the girls, goofy, and serious.

I say, "Mom! Our cheeks are sore from smiling. No more."

"Just one more picture?" She loops her arm through Raleigh's arm and mine and walks us toward a basketball court on the other side of the park.

She holds up her phone and takes one of me and Raleigh with our arms around each other's shoulders. Just like the one on the basketball page in last year's yearbook, only better.

CHAPTER 65

MISS HEATHER HALDEN

When I signed up to be a prom chaperone, I didn't expect Mark Johnson to be here too. After crying in his classroom, I've been avoiding him at school, embarrassed that I said too much and cried too much.

"Look who's assigned to coat check," Mark says when I arrive for my shift.

An awkward silence fills the cramped space. We're squished into a small bookroom with a table outside the door.

I appreciate the distraction of arrivals and avoid eye contact with Mark. Gussied up students arrive, and Mark and I find a rhythm with him taking coats and purses from students and me handing out claim tickets.

"We make a good team," Mark finally says, probably trying to be friendly.

We are not destined to be friends according to my calculations and I sense he feels the cold shoulder I'm giving him.

"Look," he says, "we got off to a bad start earlier this year when I was upset your students were reading Frederick Douglass. I didn't—"

"Upset is an understatement," I interrupt.

"Okay. I had a coronary."

"More accurate." Against my will, I smile.

"Marching up to your door with the book in hand? I overreacted." He pauses. "And I'm embarrassed."

"Miss H.!"

I turn to see Jax, several AP Club students, and their dates crowded at the coat check window.

"Look at you all dressed up and somewhere to go," I say while tears collect in my eyelids. Jax and Adele as prom dates make sense; they're perfect for each other.

"Are you crying, Miss H.?" Alonzo says.

"Maybe a little," I say, and I swipe at a stray tear.

Mark says, "She's been doing that a lot lately," and he laughs to prove he's joking.

"Ha, ha. Not funny," I say to Mark, and then turn to the students. "I'm just so happy you're here. So proud of you all."

"Miss H.," Alonzo says, "I'm taking the AP exam after all. My dad's letting me take it."

"You deserve this," I say to Alonzo, and I feel a jolt of adrenaline with this news. Of course, I want to hear the whole story, but he's with his friends and a date. I hold out my hand. "I'm Miss Halden."

Alonzo's date accepts my handshake and says, "I'm Rosie. I've heard a lot about you."

I clasp my free hand over our handshake. "You're Rosie from Alonzo's essay!"

She smiles. "Nice to meet you."

Then I say to all the students, "Now, go have fun."

When the students step away from the window, Mark says, "I'm sorry for the coronary."

I weigh my options. I can accept his apology and stop avoiding and resenting him. Or I can continue to justifiably give him the cold shoulder. Finally, I say, "Don't be sorry. You did those kids a favor. If you hadn't been so obnoxious, I might never have started the club in the first place."

Mark's eyes go wide, and his jaw drops. Then, he laughs with such gusto that he's slapping his knee. I can't help but laugh too.

After an hour, the attendees' arrivals ebb to a trickle, and two chaperones give Mark and me a break. We're standing together on the perimeter of the dance floor watching couples dancing to an up-tempo song I don't recognize. Alonzo, Rosie, and Emma dance like they belong in a music video and Adele's spasms pass for dancing, but Jax doesn't seem to mind, grinning like a lovestruck paramour. Jax stops Adele from dancing, taking hold of her hands, and leans in to kiss her. I turn away from their not-so-private moment and smile at the thought of tough Adele losing her edge to an unlikely guy like Jax. It's a perfect wrap-up to an eventful school year.

Next to me, Mark rocks back and forth from heel to toe. I wasn't a huge fan of my senior prom, and this awkward standing on the sidelines isn't much better. I pretend to be intently watching students but am aware Mark is sneaking glances at me. Then, twangy guitar notes fill the air.

"Would you like to dance?" Mark asks, with one side of his mouth lifting.

I hesitate. "Maybe."

A full smile lifts the corners of his mouth, and he leans closer to my ear. "I requested this for you." He gazes at me, and his expression is hopeful instead of smirking and amused. Shania Twain belts out "Man, I Feel Like a Woman," Mark holds his arms out for me to join, and I clasp his hand and set my other hand on his shoulder. We two-step our way around the floor, and I hear what sounds like Jax saying, "You go, Miss H!" I think I hear Adele yelp, "Yeehaw!"

Mark's lips are near my neck. "I'm jealous none of my students are cheering me on."

I smile at him. "Maybe next year."

Epilogue

Alonzo Hernandez

Rosie and I sit in her backyard on a perfect July evening. A breeze catches her hair, billowing a coil of curls across her cheek.

"My mom said her friend was working at a huge event at the lady's house."

"The necklace lady's house?"

Rosie nods, saying, "Yep. The necklace lady. This friend overheard the lady saying that she was puzzled with how she ended up with two of the same David Yurman necklaces." Rosie raises one eyebrow. "I guess the lady said that the dry cleaners found her necklace in the pocket of her husband's tux, which had been at the cleaners for over a month. They put the necklace in a plastic bag on the hanger. According to my mom's friend, the lady just shrugged and changed the subject as if it was nothing."

"I'd say it was six hundred and thirty dollars' worth of something." I sigh. "At least the mystery of the necklace is solved, though I can't say I feel much better."

Rosie takes hold of my hand. She sits up, facing me. "Alonzo, it's a sign. A sign that you should convince your papá to let you attend the AP Club next year instead of lying again."

I nod, saying, "If the necklace is resolved, my future needs to be resolved."

The following day, at the Sudsy Auto, my phone buzzes in my back pocket. I throw the chamois into a bucket, wipe my forehead with my T-shirt sleeve, and open my phone. The mid-July sun makes it hard to read my screen, so I step under a carport. I read Adele's text, telling me AP Lang scores are posted online. I stare at the text, my heart pounding, trying to decide if I want to look now or later. Deciding on now, I log into the College Board scores site and hold my breath while I wait for the results to load.

I peer at my screen, my arms raise above my head, and with one hand holding my phone, I shout, "Yes!"

My phone vibrates with another text from Adele asking me if I can join Jax, Emma, Judy, and her at Chilly Swirl at four o'clock to celebrate our scores. I text Adele to tell her I'm off at three, and I can make it.

Before we left for the summer, Miss Halden asked the club members to write an email to her, after we received our scores, with a brief reflection on what we thought of our results.

"What'd you write to Miss Halden?" Jax asks, making eye contact with all four of us at an outdoor table at Chilly Swirl.

Judy sets her spoon in her frozen yogurt cup and says, "I told Miss Halden that my score of a 3 was better than I thought it would be." She glances around the table. "I'm glad I had the courage to take the exam. My therapist told me to talk to my anxiety like I'm talking to a person." She puffs out a laugh. "Probably sounds ridiculous. Anyway, I told my anxiety that it would regret not taking the exam and to please be quiet while I take the test."

"Telling my anxiety to be quiet," Adele says to Judy. "I like that."

"You boss everyone else, why not your anxiety?" I say, smiling.

Adele swats me on the shoulder. "Not funny."

Jax laughs. "It's a little bit funny." He points with his cone. "You know, all this time I've been focusing on college, but I got a 3 on the exam."

"A 3 is great, Jax," Emma says.

Jax shrugs. "I'm not so sure about college anymore."

Adele says, "You know I'll give you the silent treatment if you don't, at least, apply to colleges in the fall."

"I think I want to be a police officer. I liked solving the necklace situation," Jax says.

Adele smiles at Jax. "If you're a cop, I'll keep you company during stakeouts." Adele turns to me. "Tell 'em what you got."

I feel my cheeks burn. "I—I got a 5, and it's exactly what I need to convince Papá that college is in my future." I can't hide my smile any longer.

"Dude! You did it," Jax says to me. "I knew you'd get a 5."

"I decided to tell everyone that I got a 4," Emma says. "I'm no longer hiding like Cyrano in the shadows. I've also decided that I'm gonna be a cheerleader next year. And, of course, I'll join AP Club again."

Adele takes hold of Jax's hand. "What I like about dating Jax, is that he's confident enough to not mind that I got a 5. We will both be at AP Club next year. I'll make sure of it."

"Maybe," Jax says, one side of his mouth lifting.

We all are quiet for a moment, and from the Chilly Swirl, I can hear a hint of waves crashing onto the coastline. I think back to the day I talked with Jax in the commons about Rosie's mom being falsely accused of stealing and how a riptide of fury threatened to pull me under. Jax's friendship and sureness buoyed me and showed me that trusting someone offering me a lifeline is the best way to keep from drowning in stress and anger. Taking hold of Jax's lifeline—Emma's and Adele's too—proved that we shouldn't have to stay afloat on our own.

ACKNOWLEDGEMENTS

Thank you, reader. If you enjoyed this novel, you could play a role in its success by submitting a review on Amazon. Search for *The Uncommon AP Club*, click on the book cover image, scroll down that page, and you'll find: Review this product. Click on "Write a customer review." For author updates, follow me—fedorewriter—on Facebook and Instagram, and check out monthly blogs at fedorewriter.com.

Also, if you're interested in social media's impact on teenagers and the benefits of farm life, you might enjoy *Pigs and Flakes*, available on Amazon.

The multi-stepped process of publishing a book wouldn't be possible without the support of many people. My Pacific Northwest Writers group members, Danielle Ste. Just, Amy Sommers, and Judy Taylor provided monthly feedback for at least three years and have played an important role in my success as an author. My sister, Karen Winter, has listened to me read every chapter out loud, asked helpful questions, and laughed at the right places along the way. In addition, beta readers Gretha Brakel, Kelsey Tretheway, and Josie LeJeune provided insightful critiques. My editor Sara DeGonia, with Reedsy, gave me an editorial assessment that shifted parts of this story for the better and she provided copy edits for a polished final product. Lastly, I'm grateful to Dana Sweeney for formatting this manuscript and giving me periodic advice.